FORGOTTEN ISLAND

BY

ARTHUR O. FRIEL

AUTHOR OF "TIGER RIVER," "RENEGADE," "THE
MOUNTAINS OF MYSTERY," ETC., ETC.

WALTER J. BLACK, INC.

2 PARK AVENUE, NEW YORK, N. Y.

FOREWORD

Once upon a torrid afternoon, while I was lounging beside a stone on a high hill of Barths and gazing seaward, some inner mentor prompted me to glance aside. Only a few feet away, on a rocky bypath hitherto empty, stood a barefoot, wide-hatted little lady in faded blue, with a braid of shining blonde hair. Mutually surprised, we stared. Then we laughed, and after that we talked a while, and by and by we went our ways. And from that chance encounter was born the story character of Céleste.

Her father, too, grizzled old Pierre, has his prototype in real life on that stony isle. And his feeling toward France, Guadeloupe, and America is representative of the opinion of most of his fellow islanders. Time and again the very words accredited to him in this narrative were spoken to me by others.

The pirate Montbars, though but a shadow hovering in the misty background of the present novel, was a terrible reality to the Spaniards of his day. As a youth of eighteen he went to the Caribbean with his uncle, a French naval officer, in 1663. Spaniards killed the uncle. Thereupon young Montbars turned buccaneer, with the fixed purpose of avenging that death on every Spaniard unlucky enough to fall into his power. This intention he carried out with such ferocity that he became known as The Exterminator. Between forays the French isle of St. Barthélemy (now, locally, Barths) was a favorite rendezvous for him and others of his unholy brotherhood; and, though his own fate is veiled in mystery, there are those who declare that somewhere on that starved isle his loot lies buried to this day.

Hence this tale.

THE AUTHOR

CONTENTS

CONTENTS

FORGOTTEN ISLAND

FORGOTTEN ISLAND

CHAPTER I

AT MIDNIGHT

Dark on the moonlit sea, the island slept.

Softly seething up on its silvery sands, gently splashing along its rugged rocks, creamy little waves laved it in lulling caress. Over its humped hills and down its crooked hollows steadily flowed a soothing northeast breeze, sweet with the pure breath of a thousand leagues of open ocean. Across its puckered face now swept the radiance of a tropic half-moon, now roved the slumberous shadows of drifting clouds. All around it, cuddling and cradling it between her pulsing breasts, the languorous Caribbean lay adream.

Other babes, too, lay on the broad bosom of the sea mother; many others, scattered in a long arc from shoulder to shoulder; and most of them, strong featured with volcanic peaks and vigorous with forests and waterways, were far more handsome than this shriveled dwarf. Not all of these were yet asleep. Here and there among them still glinted lights not cast by the moon; the twinkling lamps of towns wherein men drank and gambled and women wantoned. But those were the lustier brethren of the brood, whose life ran strong. On the starveling body of little St. Barths, inhabited by a

starveling people, no glimmer showed. Black and forbidding, this forgotten isle slumbered scowlingly, as
if brooding on the bygone years when it had been the
rendezvous of pirate and privateer; when its beaches
had roared with carousals of men and crash of guns,
and when bonfire and tavern window had flamed from
dark to dawn.

Those had been the days when Barths, for all its
wizened face and humpbacked frame, could turn an
arrogant eye on its more shapely brothers. Then its
harbor, famous among sea rovers for its shelter and
careenage, had bristled with masts; its warehouses had
been gorged with loot; its homes had been palaces of
stone, its men brave blades, its women witching, its
children gay—though often fatherless. Now that harbor
held only a couple of roachy sloops; its storehouses
were gone, its taverns crumbled to ruin, its forts sunk
to mere rock heaps, its mansions cracked and sagging;
its handful of men existed only by petty shopkeeping,
and its women as they could. Out among the hills, the
country folk grappled grimly with starvation, wresting
scant sustenance from the wrinkled steeps. Along the
curving bays the fishers seined for their daily food,
often to find that the roaming schools had passed
them by. Gone were the boisterous sea dogs, the seductive sirens, the portly squires and dames of yesteryear;
lost and forgotten amid the rank weeds and tumbled
headstones of neglected cemeteries. Barths had had its
day.

Yet now, while all the isle lay sunk in silence, an acho
of that long lost life was stealing toward it across the

moon-kissed waves. Stealthily it came, and spectrally a craft at sight of which any watching habitant—had any been abroad at this hour—might have felt the creep of a chill along his spine. A bare-poled schooner, lean and ghostly in the sheen of moon and stars, crept in from the western sea. Now it was visible, though phantasmal, against the half-lit waters. Now it was gone, engulfed by the shadow of some wide cloud. At the next spread of light it was there again, moving on a fixed course.

Without lamps, without sails, it advanced against wave and wind.

Unseen by any eye of man, unchallenged by even a barking dog, the ghost ship closed in on the isle. A long gunshot outside the harbor it passed, bearing in slant-wise upon the indented coast to the sou'east. A crazy craft this must be, to ignore the anchorage and drive on toward the grim headlands beyond; a senseless vessel steered, perhaps, by sightless dead men. To the peering moon, which had seen more than one corpse-crewed boat sail these mysterious sea lanes to final crashing doom, the decks of this schooner might well seem manned only by cadavers; for the figure hunched at the wheel, the one lying forward on the short sprit, and the half-dozen sprawling on the planking all were motionless. Yet the weird craft held to her course as if guided by keen eyes and sure judgment. The harbor faded behind; coves crawled past abeam; and still she bore on. And now, with those hollow-voiced coves catching and returning every sound borne astern by the breeze, was revealed the secret of her power to defy the opposing wind. From their stony throats echoed the burbling of a water-muffled engine.

On and on, crawling past a snaggy point of rock. Then, all at once, the dead sprang to life. The man resting along the bowsprit stood erect, waving an imperative arm to port. The helmsman revolved his wheel. Three of the recumbent forms sat up, glanced about, and, by shove or shake, aroused their mates. As the schooner swung inward her deck became peopled by men standing and scanning the gaunt-sloped valley opening before them. A brief command from the steersman, and the fellow at the bow trotted to a companionway and vanished below. A moment later the beat of the motor ceased.

The ship drifted beachward under her own momentum. None of the erstwhile sleepers spoke. All peered up the jumbled slope rising half seen, half guessed, from a white beach: a chaotic vista of stark rocks, scattered trees, blots and streaks of black shadows, mounting to a rugged skyline of hills. In their poise was a hint of stealth, in their gaze an intense eagerness, fitting well with their mysterious mode of arrival and their silence of tongue. When, at length, one of them broke into speech, the rest jumped as if startled by a gunshot.

"Hey, you!" a burly man snapped at the steersman. "This isn't the place! What's the matter with you? You said you knew this coast!"

"Monsieur, I am knowing dis cyoast!" retorted the wheelman. "Dis being de very place, sir! Dis being L'Anse Gouverneur!"

His voice and his heavily mustached face, sallowly

sunburned, were those of a white man; his accent and words those of a Frenchman who had learned his English from the negroes of the isle of St. Thomas. Identical were the skin and diction of the bowman, who now rose from the companionway.

"Oui, yas!" he seconded. "Dis being Governor Bay, sir."

"Aw, where d'you get that stuff?" growled the bulky man. "You can't put that over on me! I've been here before!"

"From de sea, sir?" countered the pilot. "You cyoming here 'foretime from de sea?"

"No. From over the hills. But———"

"Ah! Over de hills! De place be looking dif'rent when you seeing from de water. But it be de same place. I cyan't be losing 'self here, sir. 'Foretime I living long time on Barths."

"Hrrrup!" rumbled the faultfinder, his harsh voice echoing back from shore as he dubiously scanned the desolate scene anew. Then spoke another man: a long, lean individual, soft toned, yet clear voiced.

"Pipe down a little, Thirsty. You're making more noise than you realize."

"Aw, forget it!" was the sulky retort. "There's nobody living at this cove, I told you. Smallpox wiped 'em all out last year. Nobody would move into the old shacks after that."

"Smallpox!" exclaimed another, short and stocky. "You never told us that part of it———"

"No, but I made all you birds get vaccinated, didn't I?" The corpulent commander grinned, his big teeth flashing in the moonlight. "Trust your Uncle Thirsty Thurston, m' lads! Now, you Louis! Put over the dinghy and take me up to where I can see the houses. I'm going to see 'em myself before we unload. Comprenny?"

The pilot shrugged. Then, with a sharp glance at the approaching beach, he sprang forward to drop anchor. The drifting schooner dragged, swung, stopped, and rested a biscuit-toss from the sands.

Over the side the crew lowered a cockle-shell rowboat and a runty ladder. Into the former lithely dropped Louis the bowman, and down the latter clambered Thurston. So quiet was the surface of the bay that the tiny dinghy pitched hardly at all; but so awkward was Thurston's descent into it that he nearly tumbled overboard. He swore loudly at the sea, the boat, and the boatman who supported and guided him to the bow seat. Louis, without reply, notched an oar astern and sculled deftly away.

Deep laden, the diminutive ferry plowed shoreward, Thurston's crouching shape looking squatty and toadlike against the moon sheen and sand shine. It beached, and its men debarked as they had boarded: Louis with agile surety, the other with lurch and stagger. Through the susurrus of the wavelets sounded another ill-tempered growl. Then the pair plodded across the strand and merged into the dusk of the short, broad-headed trees.

From the tallest man left aboard sounded a brief laugh.

"Three sheets in the wind," he said, nodding toward

the vanished Thurston. "Been hittin' the bottle again. If I couldn't handle a load better than he does I'd lay off the stuff."

"You said it, Jack," agreed one. "And I'll say he's getting altogether too grouchy and bossy."

"Oh, he'll be all right when he sobers up," predicted another. "And what do we care? It's only for a few days. We can stand him that long."

The others said nothing. They watched and listened toward shore.

Some time passed. At length one of the shorter men sat down on a big metal cylinder abaft the foremast, felt in a pocket, brought forth a packet of cigarettes; felt again, and requested:

"Match, Larry."

The lean one turned, extending a matchbox; then drew it quickly back.

"Get off the tank before you light up," he drawled. "You're as bad as Thirsty. How many times do you have to be told that tank leaks?"

"Oh, let it blow up," grumbled the sitter. But he arose, sniffing the air and scanning the deck. From the planking came a faint smell of gasoline.

"Craziest arrangement I ever saw," he added. "The bonehead that put the engine into this old hooker must have thought the tank was a sprinkler."

"It is," grinned the other. "Get off it."

Moving to a safe distance, the smoker ignited his cigarette and flipped away the match. It fell on the deck, still flaming. With a muttered "Sacré!" the helmsman swiftly stepped on it.

"Aha," nodded Larry. "Thought you'd do that, Van. Those paper matches don't always go out. And speaking of boneheads——"

"Oh, shut up!" snarled the culprit. "You talk too much."

Larry grinned again and turned his face once more toward the island.

After a time the blank sand again showed life. From the shadows emerged the baggy-trousered shape of Louis, which shuffled to the dinghy. Several minutes later appeared the stout form of Thurston. Stopping on the margin, he sent a hoarse hail across the water.

"All right! Get up the stuff!"

With that he sat heavily down and wiped his face. The dinghy shoved off and left him there.

"Huh!" sneered Van. "Look at the king of the cannibal islands! He loafs while we slaves work."

Nobody answered. Sudden briskness seized the ship. Coats were doffed. The silent steersman and two of the passengers disappeared down the aft companionway, the other three grouping at the top. Lights shone up from the cabin. A box rose, to be seized by waiting hands and carried to the ladder dangling overside. Another followed, and another; wood boxes, pasteboard cartons, bundles of varying size and shape, dunnage bags, folded cots, kerosene tins, and, last, tools: picks, shovels, crowbars, and an ax. All went into a pile at the ladder head, where Louis, arriving in the dinghy, tied up. At length the helmsman, sweat-soaked, reappeared from below, to pad his barefoot way to the ladder and pass down cargo to his waiting compatriot.

Loaded to capacity, the cockle-shell departed, Louis sculling. No passenger traveled with him; he had no space for one. For the moment the men on deck were content to rest and grow cool in the gentle breeze, though all looked with suppressed eagerness to the land. As they watched, one snickered:

"Something's bit your cannibal king, Van. Look at him. Sat on a scorpion, I bet."

The loafer on the beach had jumped up. His arms jerked in queer motions. He took several quick steps, head forward, searching the sand.

A chorus of chuckles swept the group. Then it grew quiet, watching the odd actions ashore. Thurston made a rush for the dinghy, now grounding. Across the murmurous water came a quick, jerky mutter of words, indistinguishable but instinct with panic. Louis began hastily pitching his cargo aground.

"Hey! What's the matter?" yelled Van.

No answer came for a minute. Thurston stood glooming at the schooner. Louis finished unloading and pushed out.

"Send a flashlight!" then came curt reply. "Lost something."

The group grew rigid. Thurston resumed questing the sand in a scared way.

"Lost what?" snapped from Jack. "D'you mean you've lost—*it*?"

Thurston gave no sign of having heard. Casting about like a hound off the scent, he worked toward the

17

spot where he and Louis had first gone into the rubble to seek houses. There he stopped.

Heads turned. Eye sought eye. As Louis came alongside Jack demanded:

"What's wrong over there, Louis?"

"He losing piece paper, sir," panted the native. "He wanting 'lectric lamp. He maybe drop de paper on de hill."

Again the eyes, some narrow, some wide, darted together.

Unspeaking, the easy-moving Larry picked up his coat, from a pocket of which protruded a powerful electric torch; let himself down the ladder, and sat. After him came Van and Jack. The rest remained on deck, for the tiny ferry was already overcrowded.

Thurston, returning, met his companions at the water's edge. His worried expression confirmed Jack's guess. He had lost *it*.

"Who's got the flash?" he asked huskily, all the former assertiveness gone from his tone.

"I," replied Larry. "But are you sure it's gone? Looked all through your clothes?"

"Yes. It must have dropped out somehow while I was climbing up above—rough going up there. I can't understand how— But it's up there somewhere! It's got to be!"

"It had better be," retorted Van, a hard note in his voice.

"Huh? Say, what d'you mean by that, Van Horn?"

"I mean it looks fishy! Now that you've got us

18

down here you lose your trick map before we're ashore. Fast work, all right. What's the game?"

Thurston stared. His face darkened, his jaw muscles bulged, his fists shut. Then came the voice of Larry, cool, yet compelling.

"That'll do for you, Van. You're out of order. Thirsty, never mind him. Now where did you have that paper last? Aboard ship or where?"

Thurston, still glaring, swallowed. Van Horn, with a mutter, turned away. Jack, thumbs in belt, watched and listened with outward nonchalance.

"In Saint Thomas," at length replied Thurston. "Haven't looked at it since we sailed from there. Thought I'd look it over again now, while I was resting. It was gone. But it's just dropped—Let's have that flash——"

"Wait. Where did you carry it?"

"Here." Thurston opened his thin blue coat, exposing the left armpit. "Secret pocket, rubber-lined and buttoned——"

"Hm! That's it, eh? I wondered why you wore that coat all the time. Do you know the outer seam under that arm is ripped?"

"The devil! No!"

"It is. It was that way when we left Saint Thomas. I noticed it when you climbed aboard the schooner."

Thurston was shucking the coat as if it were afire. Now he turned it up to the moon, exposing the ripped seam; thrust a finger through, felt about. Larry switched on the electric ray. In the brilliant new light

19

both examined the garment inside and out. At length Thurston glumly announced:

"It's cut. The rubber lining's slit, too. Somebody used a razor."

"Uh-huh. And what were you doing, to let them get away with it?"

"I—I—well—I was drinking some, you know, and —I took a little nap in my chair—down at Pegleg Benny's speakeasy, it was——"

His voice trailed off.

"That's the answer." Larry snapped off the light. "You let the booze loosen your tongue and tie up your brains, and somebody got next to you. But if you remember the figures and the bearings we don't need the map. *Do you?*"

A short silence, while Thurston struggled mentally.

"No, I don't," he admitted then. "But, by the jumping Judas, I'll get that map back! It was that Portugee that got it! I know it! And I'll go get the dirty sneak and choke it out of him! All hands back on board!"

His eyes glittered, and his voice was fierce with command.

Then up spoke the silent listener, still standing with hands lazily hooked over his waistband. His face was dour, but his tone calm.

"Go get him. Break his neck. But, speakin' for Jack MacLeod, I say you go alone. The rest of us stick here, make camp, get organized. You get your map and come back hotfoot. Then we'll dig and skip."

A pause. Then said Larry:

"Sounds sensible. What do you say, Van?"

"Suits me," curtly concurred Van Horn.

"All right, then. Thirsty, get aboard and tell Bill and Dan. Run the rest of the stuff ashore and then pull out. Step on it."

Thurston grunted and boarded the dinghy. Louis oared him across. For the next quarter-hour the work of transfer proceeded fast. Then it ended.

Five men stood on the sand, backed by their jumbled equipment, fronted by the softly laughing sea. Three men stood on the schooner: two French West Indians hoisting anchor, one burly American harrying them for greater speed. No farewells were spoken. As the heavy hook bumped home, Louis dropped below decks. The engine once more purred. The bow swung, and the sea-farer glided out to the open ocean, curving westward. Past the northern headland she slid, shortening to nothing. Before the five men lay only the moon-lit waters.

Beyond the promontory Louis stopped the motor and returned to the deck. Jean, the helmsman, lashed his wheel and came forward. A few minutes of work at boom and halyard, and the bare masts were trans-figured with great white wings. Under the push of the erstwhile opposing breeze the ship lay over and leaped ahead with new-found lightness and speed. Fast and faster she fled from the dark, dry, dour Barths with whom she had held clandestine communication at mid-night.

Forward, Louis curled up on the deck and slumbered. Aft, Jean again hunched, heavy eyed, over his wheel. Between them Thurston slouched on the clumsily contrived gas tank, scowling at the deck, brooding savagely on his ill luck. After a while he drew from a hip pocket a capacious flask.

Two hours passed. Back on the sands of Governor Bay five men lay somnolent, awaiting dawn before exploring their unknown environs. Out on the yacht the man who had brought them there had slipped down to rest with his back against the metal cylinder. His eyes still were partly open, but his gaze was blank, his brain stupid, his body sodden. At length he fumbled at a pocket and, by concentrated effort, succeeded in finding and lipping a cigarette. Another protracted attempt brought out a card of paper matches. Several times he struck; then a match ignited. An instant later the whole pack flared into flame. With a startled oath he dropped it. It fell under the tank.

Up on the highlands of Colombier, westernmost extremity of Barths Isle, a prowling dog cocked eyes and ears seaward. Across his sight had flickered a faint, swift light, and from the distance had come a tiny sound like the pop of a gun. Far out on the waters he now saw a fire. For a few seconds it blazed fiercely; then it sank and settled to a steadily glowing spot of red. At last it weakened, died out. Nothing remained save the great plane of moon-misty ocean stretching into the mysterious darkness where sea and sky were one.

Long before the last ember had expired, the lone watcher had turned indifferently away and resumed his prowl. Within the little huts of farmer and fisher, and down on the sands of L'Anse Gouverneur, all eyes remained blind, all ears deaf. The breeze played on among the hills, the clouds drifted serenely across the stars, the wavelets kept up their laughing sport on strand and stone.

Dark on the moonlit sea, the island slept.

CHAPTER II

BOÎTE DU MORT

L'Anse Gouverneur rested in a horseshoe of hills. To right and left climbed steep, stony slopes, swinging together at the rear to form a knobby but continuous ridge. Within this cordon of heights lay the deep waters of the bay, the gleaming bow of seaside sand, a dry gulf, and a tilted table-land. Scattered upon this mid-slope stood four stumpy, shingle-sided houses, each flanked by a stone-walled corral once tenanted by hardy goats, which, like their hard-living owners, had gleaned existence from soil whereon creatures less tough would have starved. Now the whole barren bowl was inhabited only by sun-loving lizards and five sun-dodging men.

These men, like many a wild rover in the bygone days of the buccaneers, had stolen in from the mysterious sea by night. Now they lived in the house of a dead man; a house to which, though doors and windows stood wide to the air currents, still clung a faint odor of sulphur, aftermath of recent fumigation. Though all natives of the isle still shunned the vale desolated by pestilence, the newcomers dwelt there without fear and with comparative comfort.

24

Food, tinned or glassed or dried, stood ranged on rough shelves about their one-room shelter. Water, warm but clear, lay in a rock cistern behind the house; rain water, deluged from the sky in the wet season and automatically stored by the catchbasin whose unknown builders had vanished. Beds, in the form of army cots, lined the walls. A couple of rickety chairs, a cracked stool, and recently emptied boxes formed seats, and a plank table served many purposes. For cooking, a rock fireplace was available at the back door. For bathing, there were the rolling waters of the bay.

Six times since the landing of these midnight mariners the sun had risen, and five times it had set. Now it was once more sliding down the westward field of blue; but light and heat still were intense. Shadows of weathered house and shapeless stone and stunted tree lay black and sharp against the brown-burned earth. Cracks and crevices in brutish boulders and knife-edged lava were clear to the half-observant gaze of the man lounging on the shaded doorstep. And to him and all his companions, despite the steady fanning of the trade wind, the grilling heat was incessantly palpable. Fresh from northern winter, none of them was yet inured to the blazing bake of the Tropic of Cancer. None, however, gave thought to the hot present. Their minds dwelt on the perplexing future.

Tall Jack MacLeod, lolling shirtless on the sill and sucking a dead pipe, bent his black brows moodily as his brown eyes roved repeatedly to the empty sea. His wide, thin-lipped mouth drooped, and a long hand slowly passed through his disordered hair. Behind him, within the house, three of his mates sat in equal silence, glancing now and then at the fourth, who deliberately sketched something at the table.

Bill Mallory, square-set and ruddy, also puffed at a pipe; and his curly black hair was rumpled as if he, too, had been rubbing his head in thought. Now both his elbows were planted solidly on his broad knees, and his whole attitude bespoke cheerful patience. A merry-faced fellow was Mallory; and even in his present abstraction his blue eyes twinkled at times, and once he glanced at the toiler as if about to voice some jest. But he withheld it. Like the rest, he waited.

Carl Van Horn, on the contrary, looked sulky. His eyes, like Mallory's, were blue; but in them lurked a look hard and cold, and on his broad face rested a surly expression. His hair, muddy blond, lay flattened to his skull, parted precisely in the middle and slicked down by sweaty palms. His stubby lips caressed no pipe. His knob-knuckled hands hung between his thighs, unmoving. Fixedly sour, he slouched on the edge of his cot and scowled at the floor.

Dan Devlin leaned against the wall, prematurely bald head glistening, shaded spectacles misty from his own damp heat. His gaze, habitually sharp, seemed boring through the wall opposite; his long jaw chewed nervously on a quid of gum, and his thick fingers drummed silently but continuously on his khaki-clad legs. His tilted chair rocked slightly, and at times his feet twitched. In frame and stature he was similar to Van Horn. In restless activity he was the antithesis of both the immobile Van and the patient Mallory.

26

Alone of them all, the loose-jointed Lawrence Spearman showed no sign of worry. Slowly he drew his lines, lifting his deep gray eyes at times to look casually outside. Under his clipped dark mustache dangled an unlighted cigarette, pasted lightly to a corner of his good-humored mouth. Calm of feature, easy of posture, he seemed merely amusing himself with amateurish artistry. At length he laid down the pencil, lit his cigarette, and languidly stretched.

"Got it?" swiftly asked Devlin.

"No-o-o," came drawling reply.

Faces fell.

"I've got the general idea," Spearman went on, exhaling smoke, "but I don't know where to put the important details, and I don't remember the directions and distances. I never was much good at memorizing figures and compass bearings, unless they were easy; and those things on Thirsty's map were all sort of funny —odd numbers and half points, and all that. So this is the best I can do."

It was the seemingly phlegmatic Van Horn who was quickest to reach the table and first to snatch the paper. He pounced on it with both hands and held it close to his chest, while his eyes glued themselves to the strange characters recorded by Spearman. Mallory and Devlin, peering from either side, voiced their remonstrance.

"Say, give us a look!" prompted Mallory.

"Loosen up, tightwad!" seconded Devlin. "Trying to hold out on us?"

Van Horn, without complying, backed doorward—

27

to find himself suddenly traveling at double time. Mac-Leod had risen and stretched a long arm, closing a fist on the approaching shirt collar. Pulled off balance, Van fell backward out of the doorway and sat hard on the ground. Forthwith four men laughed.

"Thanks for fetchin' it to me," chuckled MacLeod, picking up the dropped sketch. "Your way of approach was a wee bit odd, but your speed was marvelous. Now let's see what's on the paper the nice boy brought to Jack."

For a few seconds Van Horn sat speechless, glowering at the derisive faces at the door. Then he threw himself to his feet. Hoarse, stuttering with fury, he answered MacLeod's raillery with menace.

"MacLeod—you damn big stiff—you ever put a hand on me again—I'll lay you cold! Cold! Get me? You—you——"

His voice choked with venom. Laughter ceased. Devlin, Mallory, and Spearman looked soberly, MacLeod curiously, into the blazing blue eyes. As the full deadliness of the threat sank into him, MacLeod stiffened, jaw hardening and lids narrowing. For a minute the place was very still.

"Oh, come out of it, Van," then urged Mallory. "Can't you take a joke?"

"You heard me! It goes for all of you!"

Devlin snorted. Mallory sniffed. MacLeod replied coldly:

" 'Twas a bit rough, maybe. I apologize. Didn't think 'twould hurt you."

His tone was formal, his face bleak, his eyes watchful. Van Horn continued to glare. Then his gaze wavered; and abruptly he turned away.

The observers relaxed. MacLeod turned to the house wall and slid the upper edge of the paper under a shingle. Around it the four grouped. Van Horn sulked alone; then, drawn by interest stronger than his subsiding anger, joined the others, who made room for him. His sudden outburst was tacitly ignored.

Standing thus reunited in the shade, all studied this draft:

"That," drawled Spearman, "comes pretty close to being the whole layout. All that's missing is a few little letters and figures."

"And without them," said Devlin, "it's beautiful but dumb."

"Precisely," grinned the artist. "It's helped to pass

the time, and that's about all. We'll have to wait for the rest of it until Thirsty blows in."

"About time he did," muttered MacLeod, glancing at the empty bay.

"Oh, he'll be back soon," predicted Mallory. "Maybe the engine went bad, or he's doing a few days in jail for beating up the Portugee. That's a good piece of drawing, Larry; the outline's perfect."

"It ought to be. All I had to do was look at the scenery," deprecated Spearman. "It's that stuff in the middle that gets away from me."

All eyed the central characters anew; then turned to scan the scattered trees and myriad boulders cluttering the floor of the Boîte du Mort.

"Not a thing in sight that fits this plan," complained Devlin.

"I know it. But do you see anything wrong with the sketch?"

"It's just the same, as I remember it," declared Mallory. "Except, of course, that it lacks the instructions. And Thirsty's chart didn't have these words in the lower corner, either."

"It did originally, Bill, but he cut them off, so that if anything should happen to it there'd be no clue to the location of the place. Which, in view of the fact that the map's been stolen since then, was a canny move. As for the words, Barthélemy is the old French name of this bunch of rocks. The maps call it Saint Bartholomew now. But———"

"Wait a minute!" ejaculated Devlin. "Maybe we're on the wrong island, after all. There was a pirate named

Barthélemy. That might be his signature, and the Dead Man's Box might be buried on some other——"

"No," interrupted Spearman. "That fellow was Portuguese. Bartholomew Portuguese, they called him. And he got wrecked on the Isle of Pines, away over south of Cuba, and dropped out of the picture. This chart was made out by a Frenchman. And this island was the regular hangout of that French devil, Montbars the Exterminator. And Thirsty himself came down here last year, you know, and snooped around until he found this particular cove; and the outline tallied perfectly. This is it."

"But he didn't locate anything but the cove." MacLeod's voice, though declarative, held also a note of interrogation.

"No. He couldn't, for two reasons. The smallpox was in here then. And the gendarmes over at the harbor were nosey and kept shadowing him. So he had to play safe. Besides, he wasn't equipped for digging up the stuff or getting away with it. He had to come back to the States and get things organized."

"Get our money organized, you mean," sneered Van Horn. "He didn't chip in. We're the suckers that put up the cash."

"He put up every cent he had!" contradicted MacLeod, impatiently. "It wasn't much, or he wouldn't have needed us. But 'twas all he had. And you jumped at the chance to get in on the loot. And, what's more, you put up less cash than anybody else. Now quit your belly-achin'!"

Van Horn shot a rancorous look at him, but held his

tongue. Mallory quickly turned the conversation back to the chart.

"Where did he get that map in the first place, Larry?" he asked.

"All he ever told me," Lawrence shrugged, "was that he bought it from 'a dago out of luck'. Where, when, or how, I don't know."

"That's what he told us, too. Well, what do you make of these doodads?" The questioner stretched a hairy forefinger to the odd inscription. "One's a tree; this one at the lower left. And the fer-de-lance—what's that?"

"Fer-de-lance means lance-head. Down this way it's also the name of a bad snake. But here it's a sharp stone standing on end. And this thing at the upper left is another rock, lying down. And the thing diagonally opposite may be a boulder with several splits or slanting strata. The fourth corner must be a crooked tree, probably dead. And this thing at the edge of the sand might be a big rock with a black streak in it. Anyway, it looks like the starting point for a gang landing on the beach—the first thing for them to look for—because, you notice, the dotted line starts from there. On Thirsty's map there are figures and compass notations along each line. If we only had them——"

"Say, I don't believe we need them!" Devlin broke in. "If we can find that rock with the black streak——"

He halted as abruptly as he had began, looking a little blank. Spearman and MacLeod both grinned.

"Sure," agreed the latter, "If we can find it. And when we do find it, where do we go from there?"

"The stuff's been buried nearly three centuries," added Spearman. "The trees died and fell long ago. And the rocks must have weathered; probably split apart, changed shape, fallen over. Or maybe they're buried or moved by the rain. Tons of dirt have washed down these slopes when the rains were doing their annual stunt. Stones would get undercut and roll down-hill, and so on. Even with Thirsty's chart we'd have a hunt. Without it——" He shrugged.

A glum silence followed. Devlin rubbed his jaw, Mallory scratched an ear, MacLeod gloomed at the map, Van Horn scowled across the multitude of stones litter-ing the lumpy slopes. Spearman plucked his sketch from the wall.

"So that's that, my merry men," he concluded. "All my vast knowledge is now at your disposal, and if you feel like going out yonder and juggling the rocks around until you hit the right one, go to it."

"Too hot," sighed Mallory. "And Thirsty will prob-ably blow in tonight, anyway."

"Full of liquor," muttered Van Horn.

A pause. Then said Devlin: "Don't make my throat any drier than it is. Man, how I'd like a good cold drink!"

"Well, this is a French island," suggested Spearman.

"Fat lot of good it does us poor maroons," mourned Mallory. "I'm with you, Dan. I want a long, fizzy highball—full of ice."

MacLeod's gaze moved quizzically across their faces.

"Drink hearty, lads!" he mocked. "What I want, now, is a live, lithe lady—full of fire."

"Well, this is a French island," repeated Lawrence.

The brown eyes swung to him, smiling; then rambled along the summits of the enclosing hills.

"Right you are, Larry," he responded. "I'll bear that in mind."

"But I've heard," his tormentor added, "that the country folks here are of old Norman and Breton stock, and the girls are very devout and decorous."

"Umph," grunted MacLeod.

Devlin and Mallory chuckled and lounged back inside. MacLeod still contemplated the harsh heights. Van Horn, slowly scrutinizing the whole desolate scene, spoke in an undertone.

"Boîte du Mort. Dead Man's Box. How many dead men in it? How many more coming? How many more?"

Spearman, leaning against the wall, gave a long, speculative look. MacLeod eyed him cornerwise. Soon he moved away, to disappear around a corner.

"Queer jigger," thought the listeners. But in later days they were to wonder whether that queer jigger had not possessed some crude gift of clairvoyance.

Chapter III

OVER THE HILLS

High on a bouldery acclivity forming the closed end of the Boîte du Mort, Spearman and MacLeod sat in the breezy shade of a tall outcrop of stone. Before them lay the whole slanting expanse of the Box, its myriad details sharply etched by the morning sun. Away down near the shore moved three little figures methodically inspecting rocks. To right and left of the observers a twisting goat-track of a path wormed along the steep sides of other hills. Behind them rose stones, stones, stones: some ghostly, gray, erect, saw-edged; others bulky, dark, strangely stratified, lying at queer angles, eroded into fantastic shapes; the fleshless bones of starved Barths, protruding through a withered skin.

MacLeod puffed slowly at his pipe, gazing seaward. Spearman pored over a two-foot United States Naval chart. At length he folded the stiff sheet and slipped it into a pocket of his loose khaki coat.

"No good?" lazily queried MacLeod.

"Nothing that'll help. The whole island is about two inches long and runs in two different directions; doubled over as if it had a belly-ache. And Dead Man's Box is so small that it hardly shows. Fact is, I'm not sure I even found it. There are a whole flock of coves."

"Gouverneur's not charted?"

"Not by name. This whole southern section is marked 'Grande Saline Bay,' and there are three different coves in it. The coast here runs northeasterly from a promontory marked 'Negre Point.' On the other side it runs northwest."

"Uh-huh. Negre Point, eh? Negre means Nigger, maybe? Coincidence! I was just thinkin' about a tiger-lily lassie I used to know in New Orleans. Octoroon, she was, mostly French. And hot stuff? Oh man!"

"I didn't know you were color blind, Jack," observed Lawrence, eyes atwinkle.

"Oh, I've got no use for the black ones, but when they're sort of pale golden they're—ah—exotic, that's the word. And there's somethin' in what Kiplin' says. You know:

" 'Now I aren't no 'and with the ladies,
    For, takin' 'em all along,
    You never can say till you've tried 'em,
    And then you are like to be wrong.
    There's times when you'll think that you mightn't,
    There's times when you'll know that you might;
    But the things you will learn from the Yellow
        an' Brown
    They'll 'elp you a lot with the White!' "

He chuckled and slid a look at his companion, adding: "I take my fun where I find it. And I'm bettin' you do the same, you elongated codfish, only you're not as open about it as I am."

"Sure I do," smiled Lawrence. "I have a lot of fun, in my own way. But my way is a bit different from yours. I like to keep women at a distance. Distance, you know, lends enchantment to the view."

"Ow, yawss," mocked Jack. "You mean you love 'em and leave 'em—same as I do."

"Nope. I leave 'em before I love 'em."

"Huh! Tell me another."

Lawrence laughed, making no rejoinder. His eyes rested on the virile features of the cynic beside him, then roved to the scene beyond. A debonair scapegrace was MacLeod, well liked by most men, too well liked by many women. Spearman, on the other hand, was liked by all men but regarded with affection by few women. The difference arose, perhaps, from their own mental attitudes; the one was essentially polygynous, the other monogynous. Otherwise they were much alike. Among the half-dozen men composing the expedition, they had instinctively paired.

Between Devlin and Mallory, too, existed a natural congeniality. Spearman, regarding them now from his eyrie, observed that their brown helmets remained near each other, while the whitish straw headgear of Van Horn moved always aloof. It was ever thus. While the others gravitated together spontaneously, by two or by four, Van Horn found no chum. True, he now was the odd member of the five; but the situation had been the same when the five were six. In fact, between him and the aggressive but none-the-less companionable Thurston had existed an antagonism bordering on enmity.

"Jack," the watcher said thoughtfully, "just what do you make of Van Horn, anyway?"

MacLeod withheld answer a moment, lids narrowing. Then he yawned.

"Piker Dutch," he replied casually.

"Meaning what? My Dutch education was neglected."

"Well, son, a Dutchman's usually foxy and thrifty. If he's got brains he's likely to be a whale in business. A Dutch piker's got the same instincts minus the brains, and he's just narrow and suspicious and tight; a mean little nickel squeezer and a dirty loser, who usually ends up by steppin' on his own foot. Van himself has got a rotten temper, as you've been noticin', and no savin' grace of humor. Take yesterday, now, when I sat him down so quick and graceful. It didn't hurt him physically. 'Twas when we all laughed that he blew up. Well, there you are. He can't take a kiddin'."

Spearman nodded.

"Too bad," he said. "He doesn't fit. Any fellow who can't give and take is out of place in this gang."

"He'll have to learn to stand the gaff. If he does it'll do him a lot of good. Otherwise he's even more out of luck than when he——"

He caught his tongue. Spearman, studying him sidewise, demanded:

"Than when he what? Come clean, Jack."

Gray and brown eyes held each other. Then MacLeod shrugged.

"Well, Larry, since it's you that's askin', I'll say this much: Just before we sailed from New York I heard that a young gentleman closely resemblin' Van Horn was missin' from a bank in Philadelphia; and so was considerable cash. The said gentleman, workin', as assistant cashier, had been borrowin' said cash to play the stock market, and made a mess of said play. The bank examiners dropped in unexpectedly. Now go on with the story."

Spearman sat silent for a long minute.

"Did Thirsty know that?" he then wondered.

"I don't know, old dear. I said nothin' and asked nothin'. And I'd say nothin' now, if I didn't feel that you'd say exactly the same. But Thirsty wouldn't care where any of us got our money. Why should he? This is no Sunday-school picnic."

"No. Hardly that," smiled the lanky man. "In a way, I suppose we're all a bunch of thieves, or will be if we find our treasure and make off with it. Legally we ought to hand it over to the French officials here. But I can't picture any of us doing it."

"Not much! Pirate gold is for pirates like us, not chair-warmin' frogs. Any snail-eater that tries to gyp this swashbucklin' crew out of its loot will sure dangle from the yardarm. We're tough, I'll tell the cock-eyed world."

Spearman laughed, once more contemplating the trio below.

"As pirates we're a fine bunch of misfits," he chuckled. "You're the only one who looks the part——"

"For your deft compliment I thank you," interjected the smoker.

"——And the rest of us are lubbers. Average men, like a million others——"

"But adventurers all," again interrupted MacLeod. "And so's every other man, if you ask me. Maybe he never gets the chance to go adventurin', because he's got relations to feed, or, worse luck, a wife. But once let him get loose from his chains, and then watch his smoke! Oh, baby! Take Devlin, for instance."

He puffed again.

"Well, go on," prompted the listener. "I never knew any of you chaps until Thirsty brought us together, so your lurid pasts are news to me."

"Well, would you size up Devlin as a school teacher?"

"School teacher!" echoed Spearman, incredulously.

"Ex, or emeritus. Very much ex. So much so that he'd be shocked and grieved if he knew anybody suspected it. But once upon a time, Larry me lad, Dan was a proper, repressed, bespectacled teacher in a certain boys' school—never mind where. And he had one wife, which same was a temperamental hellion. And suddenly said hellion eloped with a minister, said minister leavin' behind him a wife and several children, not to mention concubines in his congregation. 'Twas the juiciest scandal in many a long moon in those parts. And Dan let go all holds, went to New York, and became one of the wildest plungers on Wall Street and one of the dizziest sports on old Broadway. That was the most thrillin' kind of hazard he could think of, and he sure reveled in same. Makin' money was nothin' to him; he blew it as fast as he made it, or faster. 'Twas the adventure that he wanted. And 'twas adventure that brought him here with us. He'll take a chance on anything but women; he's off them for life. But he'll gamble his head off on any other game. And he's the best two-handed drinker I ever put under a table, which is sayin' plenty. Pretty good for a pedagogue, eh wot, old chappie?"

"Excellent," laughed Spearman. "By the way, where did you get that comic English of yours? I've met a few Englishmen myself, but none of them talked like that."

"Oh, I've knocked around. 'Twas in Shanghai, I think, that I met the bloomin' blightah of a silly-awss British remittance man who used that accent. Or maybe 'twas in Canada or Mexico. He was a rare bird, anyhow."

Spearman drew a cigarette from his shirt, lit it, blew smoke.

"You've drifted a bit," he suggested.

"Too much. So much that I can't stay put. 'Drifted' in the right word. I'm a drifter, a no-good derelict washin' around the world, goin' whatever way the winds carry me. Why? No brains, that's why. If I had a head on me like yours, now, I might be what you are —the biggest backer of this expedition, with plenty more money in the bank—instead of a piker that bought in on this gamble with poker money."

The lean man frowned slightly at the reference to his financial status, then eyed the self-styled ne'er-do-well quizzically.

"We're all on the same footing," he asserted. "The sum each of us put into the pool doesn't matter. As for drifting, I've washed around a bit myself, particularly in these Indies. Tried developing cotton on Nevis, and limes on Dominica, and several other things. I had some luck and pulled out before it went bad. Otherwise I'd be on the beach right now. But what were you saying about poker money?"

MacLeod grinned again.

"My passage to this island of delight, old inquisitor, was paid by some misguided mortals in N'York who thought they knew the manly art of poker. First, I got acquainted with Thirsty in a night club, and after sundry fluent drinks he uncorked his tale about this Boîte du Mort and invited me to buy in. Bein' intrigued by the yarn but practically null and void of the price of admission, I hied me thence and found me some hot-sport gamblers who felt ripe for a killin'. And the killin' took place, but not the way they figured it. The stranger in their midst cleaned them, and then galloped away by taxi and shoved his profits under Thirsty's nose, plaintively askin': 'Do I qualify?' And Thirsty, after countin' said profits, vociferated that I was admitted to the holy brotherhood, consistin' at that time of him and Bill and Dan. Then afterwards he hooked you, and the handsome contribution you made started us all floatin' south."

They smoked in silence a minute, smiling reminiscently. Then Spearman probed farther.

"You're leaving out Van Horn," he reminded. "He was in when I joined."

Jack's nose wrinkled slightly.

"He sneaked his way into the game by way of Bill Mallory. Bill's one of the world's incorrigible optimists, always lookin' on the bright side and willin' to believe everybody's a square shooter. That's what broke him. He was in real estate on Long Island, made a barrel of money, but trusted his partners too far. They cleaned him. But his heart's just as big as ever. Van Horn got wind of this treasure hunt some way and came to Bill, beggin' to be let in. He pulled the bewhiskered sob stuff about aged parents and a mortgage on the old homestead, and all that rot; and Bill fell for it and got Thirsty to take him on. Afterwards Thirsty wanted to give the Dutchman back his money and let him out. But Van threatened to blow the whole works to the French consul and thereby sink the expedition. So there was nothin' to do but bring him along."

Spearman slowly exhaled a thin blue stream, absently tapped off an ash, and gazed meditatively at a near rock.

"I see," he said. "Well, that's interesting. By the way, you've been a newspaper man, haven't you?"

MacLeod's face tightened.

"What makes you think so?" he countered.

"Some of your expressions. And the fact that you evidently know how to get information and keep it to yourself till you feel like using it. And your whole general attitude. I've known a few drifting reporters before now."

"Oh. Well, I'm not denyin' that I've written a few words here and there to feed my face when nothin' else offered. But it's a lousy life to stick to, if you ask me; so I've never stuck. It kills every illusion you ever had, if any. And when a fellow's got no illusions left, he's through livin'. I'm still hangin' on to one or two,

43

includin' pirate gold in this Dead Man's Box. And, speakin' of that, what d'you suppose has happened to Thirsty?"

His companion looked out again at the open sea. Far off glinted the sail of a sloop heading for the tall volcanic cone of St. Kitts, forty misty miles to the south. Nowhere else was visible any vessel; and the presence of that one tiny spot of white only emphasized the emptiness of the immensity surrounding it.

"Well, the chances are that Bill's guess was right," he ventured. "Thirsty found his Portugee and mauled him so badly that the police jugged him. I don't know what else to think. There's been no rough weather, and those sailors know these seas too well to run onto a reef."

"Uh-huh. Well, if he's in the cooler he'll have to serve his time; he was flat broke when he blew out, so he couldn't pay a fine. And while we're waitin' for him I suppose we ought to be sniffin' around for the stuff that brought us here. Oh-yo-hum!"

Jack yawned, stretched, and lazily arose. Spearman grinned and stood up with equal languor.

"I suppose so," he assented. "But before we go down let's climb a little higher and see what's over the top. Somebody might be living on the other side of these hills."

"Righto! Let's go! Climbin' a hill just to see what was on the other side was always my weakness. It's never worth lookin' at when you see it, but it keeps a man movin'."

Settling their helmets over their eyes, they sauntered

out into the sun. A minute later they were lifting themselves among protruding blocks, working deliberately, avoiding the fanged cacti lurking on shelf and in crevice to wound unwary hands, toiling toward the summit of the hill. At length they surmounted the crest, to find themselves on a flattened, windy space of bare earth. Below fell a long valley, backed by a range of precipitous mountains. On the floor of that hollow were a score of houses, scattered at varying distances from a long lagoon.

"Apparently I guessed right," commented Lawrence. "Somebody's living down yonder; several somebodies. And now I know why this section is called Saline. That lagoon is a salt pond."

The still water toward which he pointed was divided into several rectangles by walls, each evidently marking the property of one of the countrymen domiciled near by; and along its rim ran a wide gray-white band of dry salt. Here and there in the barren fields, delimited by fences of stone, munched goats; and on the strong northeast breeze came the shrill bleating of a kid, followed by the deeper blat of its dam. At the nearest house a couple of children played in the shade with a small white dog. At another, beyond, a woman moved slowly toward the tiny black square forming a doorway.

"There's a woman, Jack," added the speaker.

"Too old to be interestin'," replied MacLeod, squinting through the sun-slant. "About a hundred, I bet. She moves as if her joints were ossified. You can have her. You like 'em at a distance."

They turned their eyes elsewhere, scanning the

45

country. At the farther end rose other abrupt hills, apparently blocking all exit and making the valley a cul-de-sac. Near that end, however, showed short sections of yellow roadway. Evidently there was some way of ingress to this settlement from the north and west, where lay the harbor and the dilapidated town of Gustavia. Spearman nodded in satisfaction.

"We're safe enough from snoopers, as far as that place is concerned," he judged. "The road runs away to the northward; and nobody's going to climb this stiff drop. Well, let's trot along home."

They ambled back to the rim of the Box. There they slowed, looking to right and left.

"While we're up here, why not take a look at what's on both sides of us?" suggested Lawrence. "Remember that path we found a little below here, running off to east and west? It's only an old goat track, but it must go somewhere. Suppose you go one way, and I the other, and see if there are any other houses tucked away around here."

"Just what I was thinkin'," agreed MacLeod. "Which side do you want?"

"It's all one to me. Take your pick."

Jack looked east, then west; and, characteristically, left his course to chance. From a pocket he drew a dime, which he spun aloft.

"Heads right, tails left." He caught the descending coin. "Heads it is."

He turned westward, tossing over his shoulder a parting jest.

"If you find any good-lookin' girl that you don't

know what to do with, deacon, send out an S O S and I'll gallop over."

"I will, if I don't know what to do," promised Lawrence.

And with that they strode away toward the extremities of the flat, soon to dip down the declivities beyond and thus lose sight of each other.

MacLeod, descending a gradient at first gentle and bare, presently found himself confronted by harder going. A sharper slope led him down to a rubble of stones, a tangle of dry brush, and a chevaux-de-frise of cacti. Angling seaward to avoid this, he picked a zigzag course, ending at a straight drop of naked rock. Below fell a series of natural terraces. From one to another he let himself down, halting at the fourth. Along this ran the cross path leading from wall to wall of the Box: a narrow groove, old, worn deep by goat hoofs and rains, but showing no sign of recent use. It led toward a small notch between two of the bumps of the ridge: a notch where grew green masses of brush and trees, stunted, but much more dense than at any place along the Boîte du Mort. Toward this the rambler swung with lazy interest.

Spearman, on the other hand, met easier footing on his downward way, though thickets of ugly thorns and patches of cactus forced him also to pursue a meandering course. On reaching the path, however, he found the route ahead more tortuous and hazardous than that followed by Jack. It shot up stiff slants, ran along the edge of bone-breaking outcrops, snaked around brutish boulders and back again, led under

47

leaning rocks which looked ready to fall at a touch. It, too, worked toward and into a fold between heights; but this was a wider depression, flanked by taller crests, than that luring MacLeod. When at length the investigator reached the top of the pass and caught glimpses of the farther heights through the masking thickets, he paused to regain breath and fan himself with his helmet. And when he resumed his way it was with only a perfunctory speculation as to what awaited his attention. The view beyond, he thought, was only the bold promontory and the creamy beach composing the outer end of the valley of Saline.

A few rods more of laborious progress, and he halted. The brush had ended as if mowed away by a great scythe. Beside him towered a huge slab of rock, shooting upward as straight and smooth and sharp as the prow of a steamer. Before and below him lay a short, blunt, bluff-coasted point, shouldering outward into Saline Bay. Across the water stood a height shaped like an elephant's head, its slanting trunk vanishing under the waves. There, undoubtedly, was the coastal entrance to the salt pond. But his gaze did not travel beyond the foreground of the scene. Down there, in the middle of a wide stone-walled field, stood a house.

Door and window were open, and within the window was visible a white head, seemingly motionless. Near by browsed several goats.

"The devil!" he muttered. "We have neighbors, and too near!"

As his voice sounded, a dry leaf crackled beyond

the lofty stone at his side. He glanced toward the noise, then turned his eyes back to the house. Only a scurrying lizard, he thought. Yet within a few seconds he began to listen keenly, sensing the proximity of a personality more vivid than the soulless entity of any tiny saurian; something just around the angle of that petrified ship's bow. A moment later he heard a faint, dry rubbing sound. Suddenly into the path before him fell a broad straw hat.

Swiftly he stepped forward, rounding the angle in two strides. There he stopped as abruptly as he had moved. On a low, flat boulder, leaning tensely forward and staring up at him, sat a girl.

For a moment neither moved nor spoke. The man, amazed, saw in one quick survey a head of shining blond hair, simply parted and braided into a heavy plait hanging over one shoulder; curving brows, straight nose, lightly tanned cheeks, parted lips; a wide neckerchief, a drab home-made dress, an apron, and, peeping from under the hem of the skirt, sunbrowned little bare feet. The hat, lying at his toes, had been the cause of the slight rasping noise, rubbing along the rock beside her as she sought to peer, then slipping off to betray her.

Gray eyes and blue met again, and this time the gray ones smiled. A hand rose in careless salute to his helmet. In quick response, the upturned face softened with a look of relief and an answering smile.

"Bon jour, ma'm'selle," he greeted.

"Bon jour, monsieur," she demurely replied.

At about the same moment, Jack MacLeod emerged

49

from the brush in the westward notch and looked about an odd pocket in the hills. At one side rose a semicircle of sheer stone, enclosing level grass ground as in a broken cup. The remaining arc of enclosure was formed by trees on rolling slopes. Within stood a dingy house, a weatherbeaten cistern, and the inevitable corral for goats. The house seemed untenanted, the end nearest the intruder showing only a window shuttered against the sun. But on a line strung between two gnarled trees swayed a patched shirt, an apron, and a faded one-piece dress.

He walked on, rounded a corner of the house, and slowed. This was the front of the dwelling. On the low doorsill sat a woman.

Lolling forward, with chin cupped in one hand, she gazed absently at the ground. She wore only an old-fashioned chemise of the type still common among the islands, long and loose as a nightgown. Now that garment was drawn to the knees, and against the white cloth her shapely bare arms and legs contrasted like pale gold on snow. An aureate woman, this, with silky skin of topaz tint. Heavy black hair, unbound, lay in a wide mane down her back. At each slow breath a voluptuous bust swelled the low bosom of the thin robe as if about to billow over the rim.

This much MacLeod observed before his presence was discovered. Then, with a slight start, the woman lifted her head and turned her face to him. Dark, long-lashed eyes, with more than a hint of slumberous passion in their depths, scanned him with surprise, but with no indication of alarm. Sensuous lips, faintly smiling at some day-dream still lingering in her mind, retained their curve. Unperturbed, she looked with swiftly growing interest at the tall, devil-may-care fellow who had so strangely materialized from no-where. And the stranger, reciprocating her attentive gaze, smiled in mounting approval.

Despite her golden skin, she was indubitably white: a Caribbean white, yellowed by sun. The heavy black brows and the straight, strong nose bespoke a Castilian ancestry, the wide cheekbones and the oval chin a French heritage, which, together, formed a Latin blend irresistibly intriguing to a wanderer susceptible to "tiger-lily lassies."

Now her smile widened still more, disclosing firm white teeth. Leaning back against the door frame and insouciantly crossing her ankles, she half sat, half re-clined, watching him and awaiting his greeting.

"Hullo, kid," he grinned, forgetful of the fact that he was on French soil. But the reply came in kind.

"Hah-lo, Jack," she responded in broad English. "Where you coming from, eh?"

CHAPTER IV

THE GIRL OF THE HEADLAND

Spearman, standing with thumbs hooked carelessly into side pockets, smiled down at a girl who now declined to return his gaze. Poised in shy dignity, she looked out at the bay, obviously waiting for him to go. Only the recurrent blush in her cheeks and the furtive effort to draw her small feet entirely out of sight betrayed inner embarrassment.

For a minute or two longer he looked at her, noting anew the clear blue eyes, the firm little nose, the resolute chin countervailing the softness of the lips; marveling, too, at the wealth of fine, fair hair gathered into the great braid. Having been among the Antilles before, he knew that the vast majority of their people were black, varied by gradations of brown and yellow; that even the comparatively few clean-blooded whites were usually dark of hair and eye, and that resident blondes were virtually non-existent. To find here a fair-haired and blue-eyed native seemed like discovering a snowflake. It was not, however, mere wonder that held his attention. Nor, despite the fact that he had discovered a good-looking girl and did not know just what to do about it, did he think it necessary to summon Jack MacLeod.

The silence grew a bit strained; and to the girl the continued regard of the stranger became intolerable. Stooping, she snatched up the fallen hat and swirled it into place on her head. Enormously broad, it blocked the standing man's view of all above her waist. He laughed, moved down the trail a few feet, and sank on another stone, where he could once more watch her face.

"Do you live down here?" he asked, nodding toward the house.

She looked quickly at him, but made no reply until he repeated the question in French.

"Oui, monsieur," she then answered.

He turned, viewing again the lonely scene.

"It is a solitary place," he suggested. "Far from other people."

"Not too far, monsieur," she differed, defensively. "We have friends just over the hill." Her eyes moved to the long ridge forming the seaward wall of Saline.

"Ah, yes, the people of the salt pond," he led her on.

"Oui. And there were others in this next valley until——"

She stopped short, regarding him with sudden alarm. Then:

"Monsieur! You did not go to the houses down there?"

One hand lifted, waving back toward the Boîte du Mort.

"Er—they seemed to be closed," he evaded. "Why do you ask? Is anything wrong there?"

"Oh, oui, very wrong, monsieur! All the people there

died of a pestilence! You must not go there, or you will catch it!"

"Merci," he acknowledged, unsmiling. "I shall remember it. But why are you up here, so near that bad valley?"

"Because this little goat strayed up here and was caught in the rocks, monsieur." She looked down at something behind the stone. Peering, he perceived for the first time an angular little head, beady dark eyes fixedly watching him, and a tan-colored body lying down.

"I see." He smiled at her serious face. "He is a bad baby. You must spank him and teach him to stay at home."

Another quick glance was followed by a burst of merry laughter, trailing off like a dying chime of silver bells. Watching his wholesome grin and twinkling eyes, she continued to smile after her mirth had ceased. They sat in silence a moment. Then her gaze dropped, she began drawing upon her hands a pair of cloth sheaths at which he squinted curiously.

"Mittens?" he puzzled. "Are your hands cold?"

"Cold? But no, monsieur. How foolish! They are to keep off the sun. One must not have the hands black like the negroes."

"Ah! Certainly not." He eyed again the huge hat, the broad kerchief, and the high-necked, long-sleeved, long-skirted dress—the typical sun armor of all white country girls of the islands. "Of course. Well, now, you never go into that valley of the pestilence?"

A headshake and a flash of repulsion answered.

"And do you never go elsewhere?"

"Ah, oui. I go to Saline, monsieur. There is a path along the shore." She pointed toward the curving beach rimming the sea. "And from there I sometimes go to the church at Gustavia, but not often. It is a long way. And my father cannot be left long alone."

A shadow crossed her expressive face, and she straightened up on her stone to look at the humble home below. Within the shadow the white head still was visible. But, after a second or two of watching, she stood up, rising with an odd stiffness totally unlike her previous graceful motions.

"I must go, monsieur," she said, with a return of her shy manner. Then, speaking to the kid: "Allons, Babette!"

The little creature behind the stone refused to move. The girl stooped, gathered it up in her arms, and straightened with lithe ease. But as she stepped down the path she winced and halted.

"You are lame?" quizzed the investigator.

"A—a little thorn in my foot, monsieur," she stammered, blushing again. "But it does not matter. Good day."

"Oho!" He nodded comprehension. That, then, was the reason for her presence on the rock, and for her remaining there so long; she had been trying to remove the painful impediment when he came, and had since retained her position in the hope that he would go. "Well, let me see that bad thorn. I will take it out."

"Oh no no no! It is nothing— I must go——"

He arose, blocking her path, spreading his arms wide. With a touch of sternness he commanded:

"Sit down! Don't be silly. How are you to carry that animal down there when you can hardly walk? I can take out the thorn in no time. Sit down!"

At his mandatory tone she lifted her head sharply, a combative spark flickering in her eyes. But then, before the steady force of his regard, she looked down again, first at her burden, next at the rock, and finally at her hurt foot. Her cheeks now were rose-red with confused embarrassment. Very unused to attentions from strange men, obviously, was this lone maiden of the Saline headland.

Without further words he put a hand on her shoulder, pressing her down toward the waiting stone. Half unwillingly she sank to the rough seat. Forthwith he plucked from her embrace the kid, which bleated in alarm, then lay quiet on the earth where he laid it. When he turned to her again he found one foot timidly awaiting him, the other being hidden under the long skirt, which draped itself in modest folds around the visible ankle. As he reached for the injured foot it drew quickly back from him.

"See here! No more nonsense!" he scolded. "I am a doctor. Now give me the foot!"

And he seized the hurt member with firm grip, turning the sole to the light. The fair brows lifted in pleased surprise, and the foot yielded obediently. This man was a doctor! That made things different, of course.

Inwardly laughing at himself, "Doctor" Spearman

examined the pierced sole. The thorn was long, driven slantwise into the ball of the heel, broken off under the skin. After inspecting the wound a moment he drew out a fat pocket knife, the case of which held not only blades but several tiny tools; and from this he opened a lancet and a thin pair of tweezers. Looking up at her, he noted approvingly that she did not flinch from the sight of the steel.

"I may hurt you a little bit," he warned. "But it won't last long. By the way, what is your name? I always like to know who my patients are."

"Céleste Blanchard."

"Céleste? That's a pretty name. I suppose they gave it to you because your eyes are blue as the sky, yes?" He began work, gently slitting the skin sheathing the thorn. "Now my name is not so sweet. It is Lawrence Spearman. Can you pronounce that?"

"Ah, oui, monsieur: Laurent Spimman. Oh!"

"Hurt you? It's nearly done." He turned the tool, grasping the tweezers. "Now hold steady. Yes, Lawrence Spearman. And it means——" He probed for the butt of the thorn, now exposed in the cut. "My last name means L'Homme-de-Lance. And they gave it to me because I am so long and thin, like a spear, and my head comes to a point at the top. That's why I have no brains. My head was so sharp there was no place for the Lord to put them. If you don't believe it, take off my hat and look."

"Ha ha ha ha ha!" Her clear laugh rang again. "Doctor Man-of-the-Spear, you are so funny— Oh oh!" A little cry of pain cut short her merriment, and for an instant her hands fluttered in the air.

"C'est fini," he announced, exhibiting the black thorn in the grip of the pincers, then flicking it away among the rocks. "So now you are well."

He arose, shutting his little surgical kit. She set her foot gingerly on the ground, pressed it down with tentative firmness, then smiled gratefully.

"Merci, merci, docteur! It does not hurt at all. And —and could you now cure Babette?"

"Hm! Let's see. I am not a doctor of goats, but——"

He squatted and felt the forelegs of the little animal, lacerated and swollen from the grip of the entrapping rocks. Babette protested shrilly, drawing from one of the goats below an indignant response. The examination continued, however, until he was satisfied that no bones were broken.

"Babette will stay at home a few days," he announced, "and then she will be ready to wander off again. There is nothing to do but let her rest. Now I'll carry her home for you. Let's go."

Picking up the temporarily crippled runaway, he began sauntering down the rough track. She watched him a few seconds, then, smiling, followed.

Slipping at times as pebbles rolled under his shoes, but holding his balance, he carefully descended the zigzag pitches to the open land below. At the bottom he looked again at the white head in the window, then turned to her.

"What is the trouble with your father?" he asked.

"It is the heart, monsieur. He has lifted too many heavy stones. Now he can do nothing but sit in the house. If he should even fall down it would be the end. But— Oh, doctor, perhaps you— Could you cure him?"

Eager hope flooded her face. Soberly he shook his head.

"I fear not, Céleste. The heart is a very delicate organ, you know, and when it grows old and weak it cannot be made strong again. But I shall be glad to look at your father. That can do no harm."

She brightened again, as if that slight attention to the invalid might be of value. Perhaps, indeed, this stranger was too modest, and could do more than he claimed. The thought shone plainly in the look she gave him as they walked onward, now side by side.

In the shadow of the house he lowered Babette to the ground, removed his helmet, and wiped his brow. Céleste swept his hair with a swift glance.

"You have told me a big story, monsieur!" she reproved. "Your head is not at all pointed!"

They laughed together. Then she addressed the old man within the window, whose dark eyes peered steadily from beneath bushy gray brows at the stranger: a weatherbeaten, heavily mustached, square-jawed farmer whose expression seemed permanently somber.

"Mon père, this is a doctor. He says he will look at you."

The brows drew together, and the downward droop of the mustache became more pronounced. A cheerless voice replied in tones of dismissal:

"There is no money here, monsieur."

"Money?" drawled Lawrence, level eyed. "Who spoke of money? I am not asking for any."

"No? Then you are different from that swine of a government doctor at the town, who will not move from his bottle unless he hears the jingle of francs. What are you? An Englishman?"

"American."

"No! Truly? From the American hospital at S'n Thomas, perhaps?" The forbidding look vanished. "A good island, S'n Thomas, since the Americans took it. Many of our people have moved there. Do you know the Lechards, and the Carbets, and the Thibaudeau family who left here last year?"

Lawrence shook his head.

"I am from the States."

"Oh."

A pause, while the invalid probed the uncommunicative countenance of the visitor. The latter moved to the door, strolled into the poor but scrupulously neat room beyond, and approached its ailing master. With an assumption of professional sang-froid, he slid his fingers inside the farmer's well-washed shirt—once blue, now nearly white—and felt for the heart.

The place grew very still. Motionless, the Frenchman sat watching the face above him, which remained expressionless. Céleste, hovering near, looked questioningly into the gray eyes fixed absently on something beyond her. Presently Lawrence lowered his head and pressed an ear over the left ribs. Even to his amateurish touch and hearing the irregularity and straining effort of the

60

weakened organ became palpable. As he straightened, however, he gave no sign of his depressing conclusions.

"That is not so bad," he declared. "There is an irregularity, and you must avoid sudden movements and be careful of your digestion. But I see no reason why you should not live a long time. When I come here again I shall bring some tablets which may help you."

The swift joy in the young face, the faint light of encouragement in the older ones, were ample reward for his cheerful verdict. Father and daughter smiled at each other, and the invalid sat more at ease. Casually the visitor went on:

"I shall call again tomorrow, perhaps. I am to be on this island for several days. And now I had better be going back to my work. Good day."

"Work, monsieur?" quizzed the invalid. "What sort of work?"

"Investigation. I have come here to—ah—to examine the trees and bushes of your island and see what medical use can be made of them. In the morning I walk about, and in the afternoon I stay indoors and classify what I have found."

"Ah, oui." The Frenchman nodded, his curiosity appeased. "Well, good fortune to you, doctor. And many thanks. You are very kind to examine a sick man for nothing."

"Forget it. And now, bon jour. Céleste, take good care of your father, and yourself, and Babette, until we meet again."

With a grin, he sauntered outside. Beyond the door,

61

however, he turned. Soft footfalls had followed him, and now a soft voice asked:

"You will not forget to return, doctor?"

She stood on the threshold, her face now on a level with his own. Her hat had been laid aside, and once more the fair hair shone. A gust of wind, swooping around the corner, playfully pressed her homely dress snugly against her, outlining high, virginal breasts, the curving sweep of waist and hips, the shapely contour of slender arms and legs. Then it passed, and the severe garment hung all-concealing, as before.

"I shall come back, never fear," he promised, looking deep into the frank eyes. "By-by, Céleste. Call me Laurent."

"Good day—Laurent," she dimpled.

He swung away, traveling over the hard-baked open, climbing the increasing grade, lifting himself with shortened stride up the steeper pitches above. At length he reached the angular rock beside which he had discovered her; and there he paused to look down. In the black portal still lingered a girlish figure, and at the window a snow-capped head peered upward.

Off came his helmet in a parting flourish. Out sprang a hand at the doorway, waving vigorous response. Then he turned and entered the brush, and the little home was gone.

CHAPTER V

LOLITA

MacLeod pushed back his helmet and looked quizzically at the sensuous woman who had just called him by name. Through her long lashes she watched him steadily in return, the siren smile lingering on her lips.

"Where do I come from?" he echoed. "From the seas! I'm a pirate."

"Ho! So? Mon Dieu, I am scare, me!" Her face lengthened in mock terror. "You taking me away to your ship, yes?"

"Maybe," he grinned, idly advancing. "And then again, maybe not."

"No? An' why not?" Her head tilted, and she regarded him cornerwise, impudently. "Maybe I be pirate too."

"Maybe you are, at that—a love pirate, say," he cheerfully assented. Pausing before the door, he glanced into the crudely furnished room beyond her, finding nobody there. She laughed, low and throatily, albeit with a puzzled note.

"Love pirate?" she repeated, apparently unfamiliar with the phrase. "What is love pirate, Jack? Me, I know nothing about love."

63

"No-o-o?" he drawled derisively. "I was thinkin' maybe you did. Say, how d'you know my name is Jack?"

"Oh, I know you coming from the sea." One smooth shoulder shrugged languidly. "You not a man of Barth. An' all men from the sea have the name Jack, n'est-ce-pas?"

"Oh." He chuckled. "And what's your own name, little one?"

"Me, I am Lolita."

"Lolita. That's Spanish. And what's the rest of it?"

"LaFlamme. An' that's French. You know what it's meaning in English?"

"M-m, no, but it sounds like a hot one. The Flame, I'll bet."

Her lazy laugh told him that he had guessed aright. And, as if to prove the cognomen no misnomer, the screening lashes of Lolita the Flame lifted like a momentarily raised curtain, disclosing in the brown orbs a leaping fire, hot and wild as the upshooting flames around which the bygone buccaneers had reveled on the beaches at night. For an instant only it burned. Then it subsided, and, like descending shadows, the dusk-fringed lids drooped. Once more she laughed.

MacLeod, standing nonchalant, watched with his usual air of careless indifference. When he spoke again his tone was that of casual banter.

"Yes, I bet you're a devastatin' conflagration when you break out, and maybe a spontaneous combustion besides. Is that why your man keeps you hid away up here in the rocks, where nothin' will catch?"

"What man, monsieur?" Her eyes narrowed.

He tipped his head toward the patched shirt hanging on the line. Her glance darted toward that telltale garment, and a fleeting scowl crossed her forehead. But then she shrugged and turned back to him, unperturbed.

"Oh, my brother," she said.

"Oh, your brother?" he mimicked.

"Oui! My brother!" She straightened in a flash of temper. "Why you mocking me? You parrot! Parrot—not pirate! What your name, an' why you coming here?"

Flame blazed again under her Spanish brows, a flame of scorching anger, sudden as the outbreak of a smouldering volcano; and her right hand darted within the doorway, behind her, as if snatching at some weapon concealed there. That hand did not come forth again, remaining hidden beyond the jamb. Unmoved, the intruder laughed down at her.

"Well, now, maybe my name's Montbars," he jested. "And maybe I'm here to help myself to whatever I like. Ever hear of a chap named Montbars?"

The response surprised him. At the utterance of that name a strange look crept into the incensed face below; a look of amazement and bewildered terror. The flare of fury faded; the taut lips loosened, the drawn lids opened wide, the black pupils dilated. Limply she sank back against the doorpost, staring once more at the strongly marked features of the self-styled pirate, at the damp black hair on his forehead, the brown irises under his sable lashes, the powerful shoulders and the long body. Of a sudden her head turned aside, and for a few seconds she seemed to search for something at the left. Jack, glancing sidewise, saw only the prosaic clothes on the line, the two trees supporting it, and the circumvallating stone.

"Montbar'!" she whispered. "Par Dieu!"

Then her gaze returned to him, soon to contract into a scrutiny sharp and alert. Presently she laughed again; but the mirth sounded a little forced.

"Montbar'? Ha ha ha! Montbar' is dead, oh, long time. Why you telling Lolita such a big lie? You scare me a minute, Jack. 'Foretime that Montbar' kill one of my fam'ly—oh, so cruel! But you—you not Montbar', Jack, an' you not killing poor little Lolita."

Her voice gained confidence as she talked, and, at the end, the light of coquetry glinted once again through the ebon lashes. MacLeod, at first puzzled by her odd agitation, now nodded understandingly. Montbars the Exterminator, deadly enemy of all Spaniards, had vented his hatred on some Castilian ancestor of this woman, as on many another unfortunate; and the memory of his ferocity had come down through generations, to spring alive again in vivid imagination at sound of his dread name. But her momentary shock of fear now was past. So the joke might as well be carried on.

"No, I'm not killin' girls today," he assured her. "I'm not even eatin' 'em any more. The last one I had for dinner left a bad taste in my mouth."

"So-o-o?" The gurgling laugh sounded again. "Maybe she was too cold, eh?"

"No, I wouldn't say that. Badly stewed, and too

66

tough. So, lately, I just throw 'em to the sharks, unless I happen to like 'em. In that case I let 'em pay ransom."

"Ah, oui? An' what is the ransom, eh?"

"Well, that depends. Depends on what I happen to want at the time."

"Ah, so! An' what, mon capitaine," she purred, "what you happen to want jus' now, from Lolita LaFlamme?"

"Well, I'm not sure yet." He grinned at her, then looked deliberately about the open space. "But I guess the first thing I'd like is a look at Lolita's—ah—brother."

"Oh," she drawled. "So? You thinking maybe he hide, watch, listen? Go look, find him if you can. You have a long walk. He working in the town, not coming home till the week end. Only Sat'day an' Sunday he is here."

"Yes? Well, that's too bad. And so you have to stay here all alone, with nobody to cheer you up? Yes, that's certainly too bad. But what I was thinkin' was, maybe I'd ask him if he had a drink."

"Oh. An' why you not asking Lolita to have a drink?" She leaned forward again. "Maybe, mon ami, we can find a drink. Jus' us two, eh? Come, we look an' see."

With a supple movement she arose, tilting her head toward the shadows within, enticing him with sidelong glance, then stepping lithely inward. Insouciant as ever, he sauntered indoors, surveying the crude interior as he entered. Table, rickety chairs, tiny hearth, high bed in an alcove—these he saw during the first two lazy paces.

67

Then, prompted by a belated thought, he cast a glance at the floor beside the doorway, where Lolita's hand had rested when her anger erupted. His lips twitched, but he voiced no remark. There at the junction of jamb and sill, forgotten now, lay a long, thin-bladed knife.

"Thought so," he told himself. "When pretty kitty jumps into your lap at first sight, 'ware claws!"

For all that, he gave no indication of wariness of his complaisant hostess. He watched her walk to a shelf and take down a bottle, reach to another and select a pair of small cups, and glide back to him. But he was far less attentive to her choice of those inanimate objects than to the broad shawl of her unbound hair, the sinuous ease of her movements, the tout ensemble of wanton beauty wantonly displayed. And as she returned he spread his arms wide to either side, stretching himself, but smiling down as if half minded to swing them around her. Again a daring light grew in her eyes, and she came on as if about to walk straight into the impending embrace. Then, just out of reach, she stepped aside, laughing at him.

Indifferently he let the arms drop, making no attempt to touch her. Thereat she looked a bit displeased.

"Maybe you not liking this drink, Jack," she twitted, setting the bottle on the table. "If it too strong, I got goat milk."

"Cognac," he read from the label. "Oh, I guess I can stand it if you can. Let it gurgle."

She poured. Tossing his hat aside, he drew up chairs, side by side, and dropped loosely into one of them;

68

hooked a finger into a cup handle, and waited. She sank into the other seat, eyed him sidewise once more, and toyed with her own drink. Still he waited. At length, with a half-scornful laugh at his apparent caution, she lifted her cup and, in two swallows, emptied it. Then she coughed.

"You'll never be a pirate," he bantered. "A real pirate drinks like this."

The fiery dose flowed down his throat in one silent intake. Then he held out the cup for more.

"Mon Dieu!" she breathed, staring at his unwinking eyes. "How you do it?"

"It's a gift. My father was a Scotchman."

"Oh." Her tone was somewhat flat, as if the point of the joke escaped her. "Scoshman, eh? But then— Ah, now I know for sure you lie to Lolita, bad man! You not being a Montbar'! A Montbar', he mus' have French father! Ha! So! An' why you saying you are Montbar'? What you knowing about Montbar'? Now you tell Lolita!"

"Oh, very well. Promise you won't tell anybody?"

"No no, I never tell, Jack, I never tell nobody, no, not even my brother. Tell me!"

"All right. I came to Barths——"

He paused, looking at his empty cup, then at the bottle. She acted instantly on the hint. Again he took the brimming draught at one swallow.

"You guessed it," he went on. "I came to Barths to drink cognac with a pretty girl."

"Oh pouf!" she snapped, piqued, yet pleased. "You

jus' making talk! You said you coming here to take—
to take——"

"Whatever I like," he nodded. "That's just what I
was sayin'. And I like you. Maybe if I keep on likin'
you I'll take you. Just like that."

Extending finger and thumb, he lazily pinched them
together.

For a moment, studying his owlish face, she seemed
nonplussed. Then she laughed out—not the low, mellow
mirth of the doorway, but a high, wild peal of heartfelt
amusement which swayed her from side to side.

"Ha ha ha ha ha! Oh ha ha ha ha ha! But you are
funny pirate, you—you Scoshman! An' how long it
taking you to know how much you like me, eh, Sieur
Montbar'?"

"Give me time, kid, give me time. Have another little
drink on the house."

"No no!" Her shoulders twitched distastefully. "No
more! Too hot. But where you coming from, Jack?
S'n Kitts, no? S'n Thomas, maybe, yes? You American?"

"Right. I'm American."

"Ah, so. An' how the gendarmes at the town treating
you, eh?" Her gaze had become intent once more, noting that his lips tightened slightly at the question. "Or
maybe you not staying in town, not seeing gendarmes.
No?"

"Well, no. I'm not exactly advertisin' the fact that
I'm here. I wonder, now, if you can keep your mouth
shut. Or do you blab all you know?"

"No, no, not Lolita, not me." Something of his own
deliberation crept into her voice, and with it a confi-

dential undernote of comprehension. "I not living in town either, Jack, I not liking the gendarmes too. You see? Me, I like much better this place, where no sneaky gendarme sticking in his nose all time, wanting money, wanting drink, wanting—me! I pick my place an' my company, you see? An' I like you for company, Jack. I like you very, ve-e-ery much! So you trus' Lolita. Where you living, Jack?"

MacLeod passed a hand across his forehead, dropped it to his unbuttoned collar, drew the shirt further open at the neck. The cognac was working fast. Or was it the nearness of Lolita the Flame that heated his blood? Imperceptibly she had drawn very close to him, her eyes caressing, her voice cajoling.

"An' you tell Lolita why you coming to Barth, Jack, an' maybe—maybe I help you find what you come for, eh? Maybe Lolita know something, Capitaine Montbar'! An' maybe we find something together, yes? But you mus' tell Lolita first——"

A hand was on his shoulder now, and a yielding body clung closer and closer.

"Sound's interestin'," he plagued. "But maybe you're just tryin' to kid me along. Yes, I guess that's right. I've heard girls talk before. And I'd better be goin'."

He set the cup back on the table and made a feint to rise. Instantly he found himself a prisoner.

Warm arms darted around his neck, and the lithe body of the flame woman became a down-dragging weight holding him to his chair. Luring eyes burned into his own, and vibrant tones refused release.

"No no no! You not going! I not letting you go!"

Her arms tightened. "You think I only talk, talk, mean nothing? I show you! I show you I am good pirate— I prove how I like you—I— Oh, mon Dieu, you crushing me! But I don' care—I don' care——"

CHAPTER VI

A SONG OF TWILIGHT

In the shade of a short but broad-headed tree on the margin of the scythe of sea sand, Spearman and Mallory and Devlin sprawled in varying postures of relaxation. A little apart, yet well within the same shadow, Van Horn sat humped forward, aimlessly digging little holes with a forefinger. All were hatless, coatless, shoeless, sockless, and wet haired. Discarded clothing lay on rocks or hung on brush, and from low branches dangled damp towels, drying in the heat of the sinking sun.

"Tell folks up home," drawled Spearman, knocking an ash off his cigarette, "that we had a swim in an ocean warm as tea this fine winter day, and they'd envy us. And yet I'd like this water better if somebody would drag an iceberg through it."

"Well said," yawned Devlin. "There's no exhilaration in this stuff. A minute after you come out of it you're hot again."

"Well, it's better than none at all," Mallory pointed out. "And it felt pretty good to me when I soused into it after combing hot rocks all day. Supposing we were away up inland somewhere and couldn't get to it——"

"Supposing we were in hell!" broke in Van Horn. "We might as well be."

"Oh, shut up!" snapped Devlin. "Ever say anything cheerful in your life?"

"Blah!" grunted Van, jabbing his finger viciously into the sand.

"Always kicking, always belly-aching, always belching sour wind!" rasped Devlin, scowling at him. "You must have been born with a pickle in your mouth and raised on lemons. Every time you open your head you drool vinegar——"

"Cut that, Dan!" interposed Spearman, as Van Horn stiffened. "Who's spilling vinegar now?"

"Oh, the devil, I'm sick and tired of listening to——"

"Snap out of it, Dan!" urged Mallory. "What's the use?"

Devlin, thus outnumbered, shut his mouth tight and rolled over, turning his back on Van Horn. The latter glowered at him, but held his peace. Spearman drew another whiff from his cigarette, thoughtfully contemplating them both. In the past few days an increasing antagonism toward the "Dutchman" had been manifest in Devlin's attitude. If it should keep on growing. . . .

"Listen, you fellows," ventured Lawrence, in his usual quiet tone. "I've been down this way before, and I've seen and heard a good deal about the effects of this tropical sun on fellows not acclimated to it. The chap who lets it get on his nerves is heading for trouble. And it gets to some men fast. It never seems to bother me much, maybe because I'm built to stand it. my nerves being sort of loose all the time instead of pulled taut. But some chaps can't stand it any time at all; they get snappy and jumpy and fly off the handle at nothing,

74

and if they don't take a grip on themselves they're liable to go all to pieces in short order. Sometimes they go completely cuckoo. There's one island down the line here, maybe about a hundred and fifty miles south, where folks said there were at least half a dozen men— white men—out in the mountains howling at the moon, running like wild beasts, naked as the day they were born. They'd let the sun get them.

"Well, now here we are, and we're due to stay a while, and we've favored ourselves all we can, and from now on we've got to get out in the sun every day until we've looked at every rock in this Box, or until we locate what we're after. And it's up to us to get along with one another as well as we can. We're all in the same boat, and there's no sense in crabbing at things or at each other. This job's not a take-it-or-leave-it proposition; we've already taken it and we can't leave it. And the fellow that lets it get on his nerves is hurting himself more than anybody else. Let's keep that in mind, and not jump down each other's throats."

"Good dope!" heartily approved Mallory. The other two made no response. Van Horn moodily continued his useless occupation, while Devlin scowled along the ground, one hand drumming its finger tips on a pebble.

"As I was saying a while ago," resumed Spearman, "we'd better take an inventory of the grub soon and figure out just how long it's likely to last. It's pretty evident that something's happened to Thirsty. And from now on every man jack is to roll out at the crack of dawn and get on the job right after breakfast. Working systematically, we can comb a good bit of ground by noon. Then knock off, take a good swim, eat hearty, and get a siesta until about three; then work a couple of hours more, bathe again, and call it a day. Does that sound right?"

"Sounds like sense to me," acknowledged Devlin. "Lay down the law to that loose-footed MacLeod, too, if he ever comes back, and let him know he has to work the same hours as the rest of it. This stunt of rambling off somewhere and staying A W O L doesn't go."

Van Horn grunted quick assent. For once, he and Devlin were in accord.

"Oh, he'll tote his end of the log," predicted Mallory. "And, for all we know, he may have learned something worth knowing by playing hookey."

"Hump! Yes," grinned Devlin. "Perhaps he found that fiery flirt he was yearning for."

"Well, that would be worth finding, wouldn't it?" chuckled Mallory. "I wouldn't mind discovering something like that myself."

"You, too?" smiled Spearman.

"Yep, me too. I'm no holy hermit or sour-mugged woman hater. And this hot climate is no place for a minister's son anyway. How about it, Van?"

The broad visage of the man sitting aloof had broadened still more, and into his brooding blue eyes had crept the first twinkle seen there in many an hour. He said nothing, but the topic plainly appealed to him.

"Larry, you and I are the only respectable members of this congregation," opined Devlin. "And if the devil should blow in here with a quart of Scotch, now, I'd hand him my innocent young soul on a silver platter.

Man, but I'm dry! And to think we're on a French island where wines and cognac are probably dirt cheap, and an American dollar's worth twenty-five francs, and all we have to do is walk to the harbor and buy a case——"

"And give ourselves away to the authorities," interjected Spearman.

"Ay, that's the rub." Devlin rolled over again, then sat up jerkily and reached for his canvas shoes. "No use thinking of it. Come on, fellow jackasses. Let's go back to the stable and put on the dry old feed bag."

Clapping on his helmet and snatching up his other clothes, he tramped away. Moving more deliberately, the others followed, threading their way among the stones and brush patches to a waterworn groove worming up the slope, and filing along this in wordless weariness.

It had been a discouraging day, fatiguing and fruitless. No streaked boulder beside the sand, nor any fragments of such a stone, had been found. Neither had any other significant detail shown itself. The sole result of hours of painstaking inspection was the elimination of a transverse band of ground, now marked by bordering pegs, from the realm of rocks to be examined in the days to come. As they clambered toward their cheerless hovel, the innumerable blocks protruding from the surrounding hills seemed to grin at them like monstrous, misshapen teeth in malignant jaws.

Devlin, taking the last upward step which brought him across the threshold of the hot house, suddenly stopped. A moment he stood there motionless, peering

77

through his darkened lenses at the comparatively dim interior. Then he dropped his bundle of cloth, solemnly removed his glasses, and looked again. As the others approached he wheeled, teeth agleam, hand upraised.

"Gentlemen, hush!" he exclaimed. "Our wandering boy has returned and lies in childhood's innocent slumber—dead drunk!"

"Huh—what?" panted Mallory. "Put on your glasses again, Dan."

"Use your own eyes, Bill, and behold the evidence! Here on the table is a quart—or what was a quart. If it's empty, I'll butcher this sodden wreck as he lies. If it's full, it's mine! I found it first."

With a rush they crowded in after him, to squint at the bottle standing on the table and at Jack MacLeod sprawling on his cot. Then came MacLeod's voice, drowsy but steady.

"Dan, you're a cock-eyed liar and a scurrilous defamer of your benefactor. I deny the allegations and defy the allegator. I am restin' from my travels and labors as a missionary, and I brought back that bottle as an act of charity to all you besotted heathen. Smell, it, taste it, and let its blessin's flow. And then get down on your knees and do me reverence."

Devlin grabbed the bottle, glimpsed its label, shook it, and voiced a yelp of joy as he pulled the loose cork.

"Cognac! And half full! Glory to the saints!"

And the mouth of the long-necked container vanished within his own.

"Saints," chuckled MacLeod, "had nothin' to do with it."

The bottle gurgled three times before Devlin paused for breath. Then Mallory's hand closed over it, and reluctantly he let it go. Two swallows sufficed for the second drinker, but they were decidedly generous. Van Horn seized it next, and held it so long that both MacLeod and Devlin barked:

"Hey, loosen up! Larry's next. Hand it over!"

Spearman took one good swallow, coughed, and grinned. Then his expression sobered, and he looked speculatively at MacLeod.

"Good stuff," he approved. "But where'd you get it? Not at the town, I hope."

"Nope." Jack yawned, stretched, turned over. "Hand me a cigarette, somebody. Thanks, Bill." Puff-puff. "Well, now, 'twas like this: This man Spearman, the handsome hyena with the india-rubber backbone, sent me scoutin' west on a tour of reconnaissance, with strict orders to find him a woman, and the worse the better. And he went east lookin' for the same thing. And, by the way, what did you find, Larry?"

"Not a thing," calmly lied Spearman.

"Too bad, too bad. Well, I went jumpin' down precipices and meetin' man-eatin' lizards and all kinds of tropical demons, but I subjugated 'em all without turnin' a hair. I'm like Sir Galahad; my strength is as the strength of ten because my heart is pure. And after incredible feats of valor I reached the Garden of Eden, and I walked in, and the serpent was gone—though his shirt was hangin' on a line—and there was Eve, alone and lonesome. And she saw I was a pious pilgrim, and desired to know my sect. Quit snickerin', Dan; I said

79

sect, not sex. And I told her I belonged to the Society of Friends. So then we held a Quaker meetin' and let the spirit move.

"And after the service we partook of a toothsome repast, and after that I returned to you dissolute wretches, bringin' with me the holy spirit which now has entered into you. But first I made arrangements for further supplies of said spirit, along with sacramental wines and other things sold in the market place for silver shekels. You see, the serpent in the case—Eve says he's her brother, but I fear she was deceivin' me—this serpent works at the town and can fetch up a basket as well as not, as long as the shekels are forthcomin'. I left with her certain moneys to cover the expense of the first shipment, and Deacon Spearman will take up a contribution among you before my next service. Is it well, brethren? Or would you rather remain dry farmers?"

" 'Tis well, and then some!" asserted Devlin, chortling happily.

"Seconded," chimed Mallory. "And any time you feel like introducing me to Eve——"

"You're introduced already, ancient mariner; and the rest of you lads too. That is to say, I didn't give away any real names—not even my own—but I told her I was Old Man Montbars' little boy, and that I had some pals almost as pious as I am, and she was properly impressed. Oh no, I didn't tell her what we're here for. But she's wise—or pretends to be. She hinted that she knew somethin', but if she really did she wouldn't let go of it. But maybe later on, when my preachin' has had more effect— Well, that's guessin'. Anyway, I've a feelin' that she's well worth cultivatin'. And if you, Brother Mallory, feel like exhortin' the little ewe-lamb just discovered by your pastor, she's not far away. Just walk straight up to the path along the side of the hill yonder, and go west till you come into a clearin'. Turn to the left. And watch your step!"

He chuckled and inhaled more smoke. Mallory, ruddier than ever from the fast spreading heat of the brandy, smiled broadly and teetered on his toes, glancing sidewise at Van Horn; then, observing the intent interest with which the latter was regarding the discoverer of "Eve," laughed aloud. Devlin picked up the bottle again, held it to the light, and joyously imbibed another long swallow.

"Well, if you're not jealous, Jack——" Mallory intimated.

"Not a bit, Bill. Jealousy's a vain vice that I dropped years ago. There's no woman worth gettin' jealous about. For your guidance I'll add that the serpent's at home only Saturdays and Sundays, and——"

"What about that serpent?" interrupted Spearman. "He goes to town, you say, and probably he's not dumb. And the woman herself——"

"Safe enough, both of 'em, deacon. She's on the outs with the town people, for some reason or other; and she let me know that she's got her 'brother' pretty well trained. She'll handle him. What's the matter, Dan? Fleas in your socks, or what?"

Devlin, hands on hips, face wreathed in smiles, was jigging softly around the table, bowing now and then to the empty bottle. As the others beheld his paganistic obeisances they burst into a roar of laughter. Van Horn, with veins now beginning to stand out on his temples, howled even louder than the rest, ending on a hiccoughing note which evoked another outbreak.

"It's paying my devotions I am, you Presbyterian!" shouted Dan, quickening his movements to a thudding prance. "Devotions to the holy spirit that was and the holy ghost that is—for there's nothing left now but a smell, worse luck. Whoop-la!"

Leaping into the air, he thumped his heels together; lost balance, and fell with a resounding crash. Whereat MacLeod rolled bellowing off his cot, and the other three dropped into seats and shrieked in unison.

Sitting up, Dan stared reproachfully at the floor which had hit him so hard; then grasped the upset bottle, whirled it above his glistening pate, and sang:

"Five dry men in the Dead Man's Box!"

To which four voices from throats no longer dry responded:

"Yo ho ho, and a bottle of rum!
And what the devil do we care for the rocks?
Yo ho ho, and a bottle of rum!"

MacLeod threw his booming bass into the second refrain, and the house vibrated with the whisky tenors and baritones of his comrades. Devlin, waving the bottle now as a baton, signaled imperiously for an encore. It came with a zest. When it was done, Mallory suggested:

"Now how about a psalm in honor of the brave missionary? That rambling rake MacLeod, son of a gambolier! Let her go!"

And she went with a whole-heated vigor:

"Son of a son of a son of a son
Of a son of a gambolier!
Son of a son of a son of a son
Of a son of a gambolier!
Like every honest fellow
I drink my whisky clear.
I'm a rambling rake of poverty,
A son of a gambolier!"

"And there's more truth than poetry in that, if you'd like to know it," added MacLeod, with a touch of somberness, at the end. "My old man gambled away all he had before I was twenty-one, and I've been a ramblin' rake of poverty ever since, takin' life as I found it; makin' a stake and gamblin' it away on a long chance; bettin' on a woman or a horse to run straight, and gettin' trimmed every shot. And so it goes. Oh, well, what of it? Come on, let's have another song."

The sun went down. Swift twilight thickened into dusk. Still nobody troubled to light a lamp or to prepare supper. The brandy was slowly dying out of them now, but still they sang with undiminished vigor; sang in the enjoyment of passing harmony, of temporary relief from monotony, of fellowship in a foreign land, far from their kind. Marooned on a rock-heap they might be, and facing uncertainty and disappointment, perhaps

83

failure, perhaps disaster and despair. But gambling on tomorrow, they reveled tonight; and the full-throated voices rolling along the walls of the Boîte du Mort now held no note of despondency.

Strong and clear, the deep tones of the recently somnolent MacLeod trolled:

" *'Twas in twenty-eight, on a winter's night,*
  And we ran the vessel ashore
  On the Caribbee Isles, where the vampire smiles
  And the man-eatin' sirens roar.
  And we sat on the edge of a sandy ledge
  And shot at the whistlin' bee;
  And the cinnamon bats wore waterproof hats
  As they dipped in the shiny sea!"

And a lilting chorus rollicked in unison:

"Then blow, ye winds, heigh-o!
A-roving I will go!
I'll stay no more a slave on shore,
So let the music play!
I'm off for the morning train!
I'll cross the raging main!
I'm off to my love with a boxing-glove,
Ten thousand miles away!"

CHAPTER VII

THE FORGOTTEN ISLE

Noon. A straggling file of dispirited men clambering wearily up the squirmy track. Behind them, a broadened band of rubble bordered by the line of demarcating pegs. Before them, only a meal dumped from cans and swallowed with little relish, a drink of tepid water, and an unrefreshing drowse in their oven-like barrack.

As they climbed, they said nothing at all; and the glances they cast ahead were perfunctory and myopic. Only one of the five pairs of eyes ranged beyond the immediate foreground: those of Spearman, who, walking last in the meandering column, lifted his reflective gaze occasionally to the height terminating the Box, then let it rove to the eastern pass through which led the path to the blunt headland of Saline.

Into the house they trooped, to toss hats on cots, run fingers through hair stiffened by sea salt, hold brief debate as to the menu, and pick sundry tins from the shelves. Spearman brought a pail of fresh water from the cistern. Then all ate.

Few remarks were interchanged during the meal, and those few were brief and impersonal. At its conclusion, however, when Lawrence stropped his razor and lathered his cheeks, the small talk broke forth.

"It's no use, Larry. I wouldn't let you kiss me anyway," grinned Mallory.

"Don't flatter yourself, Bill," reproved Devlin. "He's going up the straight and narrow path to investigate Jack's ewe-lamb. There's been a sly look in his bleary optics all morning."

"Uh-huh. I thought there was somethin' behind this scheme of turnin' us all out to work at sun-up," contributed MacLeod. "He's been wearin' us out, so he'd have a clear field."

Spearman made no retort until his task was completed. Then, as he wiped his face, he drawled:

"Thanks for the suggestion. I was wondering what to do while you youngsters took your afternoon bye-bye——"

"Listen to him!" jeered Devlin. "Wondering whether you could put it over on us, you mean. We're wise!"

"Well, of course, if you fellows insist on driving me out into the sun I'll have to go," rejoined Lawrence, buttoning his collar. "Any messages you want delivered?"

"Make a date for me," promptly requested Mallory.

"Give her my love," added MacLeod.

"And bring back another quart," instructed Devlin.

Van Horn, smoking a fat-bowled pipe, offered no suggestions.

As if merely carrying on the joke, Spearman combed his hair, donned his coat, set his helmet on his head with exaggerated care, and went through the motions of pinning a nonexistent rose on his lapel; then, twirling an imaginary cane, sauntered to the door and passed out.

"Well, what d'you know!" ejaculated Mallory. "He's really going! Hey, Larry! Wait a minute! I'll come along and give you my moral support."

"You will not," Spearman's voice drifted back. "You'd only cramp my style."

He ambled away, working straight up the hill toward the cross-path. As he walked, one coat pocket gave forth a subdued clink of hard pellets against glass; digestive tablets in a small vial abstracted from his slim medicine case.

These were the pills which, yesterday, in his rôle of physician, he had promised to bring today to old Blanchard; useless for strengthening or stimulating the heart, but possible palliatives if an attack of indigestion should force the diaphragm up toward the weakened organ.

Climbing somewhat wearily—for he had done his full share of leg work in the hours just past—he mounted the hillside route by which a man might travel either west or east; toward an easy down-grade to the house of Lolita, or by a hard traverse to that of Céleste. There he paused, looking with some curiosity toward the brush-masked notch at the west, to which he had hitherto paid no attention. But he took no step in that direction. Instead, he covertly peered back at the house which he had just left. There, at the door, he espied Van Horn watching. With a silent laugh he turned away and proceeded—not eastward, but up the difficult face of the hill, where he and MacLeod had gone yesterday. Up he worked, and up, until he was on the top. And there, without another glance behind, he tramped toward the valley of the salt pond until he knew he was lost to sight.

Down below, Van Horn grunted through his pipe stem, then went inside and lay down. In answer to a question he vouchsafed:

"Went clear to the top and kept on going."

"Uh-huh," lazily replied MacLeod. "He's goin' to sit down in the breeze on the shady side of some rock and do some more dopin' on the general situation. Habit he has, gettin' off by himself and thinkin'."

"Rotten bad habit, at this time of day," opined Devlin, utterly relaxed on his cot.

Then fell sleepy silence.

Meanwhile Spearman had right-faced and, behind the sky line, was moving toward the pass. He came into the upshooting path again at a point where it was screened by brush; followed its toilsome quirks over the divide, and stopped to breathe and rest beside the tall rock where he had found Céleste and Babette. Now nothing was there, save an iridescent lizard which cocked a wary eye and then slithered away. The house below, too, looked lifeless.

As he watched, however, something white appeared in the dark doorway; something rectangular, which quickly blew aside in an eddy of the trade wind and became a waving banner, seemingly signaling to him in welcome; an apron, flying from the waist of a blue-clad form now visible in the opening. Had he been better acquainted with the customs and costumes of this out-of-the-way isle, he would have known this to be an indispensable part of the attire of every country girl, whether in the house or in the fields. More, he would have understood that the white apron, as distinguished from the darker colors, was dress for special occasions, and that the girl yonder had donned it in honor of the American doctor. As it was, he gave no thought whatever to the humble ornament. With a casual wave of the helmet, he resumed his way.

No answering gesture came from the girl. If she saw him, modesty forbade acknowledgment of the fact that she had been looking for him. She stood there a second longer, then withdrew.

So he reached the door and knocked before receiving a greeting. Then heels—leather heels, instead of the bare ones of yesterday—beat quick cadence on the worn floor, and he awoke to the fact that Céleste was "dressed up." Shod and stockinged, gowned in fresh blue gingham, with an ancient brooch near the throat, she appeared before him, smiling a little, blushing more than a little, and making a graceful old-fashioned curtsy as he doffed his hat. Her hair hung in its simple braid, as before, and her frank eyes knew no artifice; but otherwise she seemed a new girl.

"Bon jour, docteur," she greeted him. "You are welcome."

"My name is Laurent," he smilingly corrected, entering. "Ah, how are you, Monsieur Blanchard?"

"No better, and no worse," crustily replied the old man, sitting somewhat self-consciously beside the table. He, too, was wearing newer garments: cotton shirt, and trousers of unpatched blue jean. His hair and mustache showed careful combing. His feet, however, still were

89

bare. Either he had refused to don shoes or, more likely, owned none.

"You are late," he added. "We thought you had forgotten."

"Oh, no. Here are the tablets I promised you." Lawrence drew them from his pocket. "You are not to take them, though, unless you feel distress after eating. Then take two, with a drink of hot water. Do you understand?"

"Ah, oui. Merci bien, monsieur!" acknowledged Blanchard, accepting the bottle with alacrity. He became still more cheerful when his visitor produced a pipe and a pouch and proffered tobacco. His daughter, unobtrusively observant, brought him a stained clay pipe which he filled eagerly. Then she sank into a chair and sat with hands folded.

"I was busy this morning," casually explained Lawrence, taking a convenient seat, "and the time slipped away fast. How is the foot, Céleste?"

"Oh, it is very well, doc—Laurent. It hurts only when I turn on it."

"It hurts? Then perhaps I should examine it," he teased.

"Oh no no no!" Both her feet slipped far back under the long skirt, and her color deepened again. "It does not hurt—not the littlest bit! You—you are finding many valuable leaves, doctor?"

"Not many," he admitted, laughing at her transparent attempt to change the topic. "Perhaps I came at the wrong time. Everything seems dried up."

"That is so," agreed the father. "You should have

come months ago, after the rains. In the dry time this island is accursed. Never a drop of water, when in the other islands wonderful showers fall to feed the plants and the people. This place is fit only for the devil, monsieur. It is forgotten by God!"

"Father!" reproved Céleste. "Le Bon Dieu forgets nothing."

"Bah! Then why does He leave us in the hands of those black dogs of Guadeloupe? Why does He not bring back the Swedes, or bring to us the Americans, who rule so well at S'n Thomas? Why——"

Suddenly he started, his plaint halting short, his gaze growing keen as he contemplated the American. With equal abruptness he recommenced:

"Monsieur! Are you here only to gather leaves? Is it that your country means to make this an American island? Is it that you really come here to observe and make report to your government?"

Spearman, drawing deliberately at his pipe, looked from father to daughter and back again. Céleste, wide-eyed, was leaning forward, watching him wonderingly. Her parent's tone was excitedly hopeful. For the moment he was half tempted to accept this new honor as tranquilly as he had adopted his present empiristic status. But then he shook his head.

"No," he disclaimed. "I am here only for my own purpose. What were you saying about the Swedes?"

Blanchard puffed rapidly, still probing his caller's calm countenance. After a time he sighed.

"It is a pity," he said. "You Americans could make of this a place fit for white men. And the benefit would not be all on one side, monsieur. Our harbor at Gustavia is very good, though small. And in spite of the dryness much could be done with our ground. The Swedes, now, who owned this island for a hundred years, they made things grow. They were good people. They were white people."

He glanced at his fair-haired girl. Spearman's eyes widened slightly, perceiving an explanation which had hitherto eluded him. The silky blonde hair of Céleste, the blue eyes, the glowing skin, all so different from those of her brunette father, must be a heritage from a mother of Swedish descent.

"But then, it is now almost fifty years ago, the French took back the island," continued Blanchard. "And since then, what have we had? Oppression, misery, starvation! Oui, monsieur, death from lack of food, thanks to the swine of Guadeloupe! We old ones perish. Our young ones must go to other islands to live. S'n Barths is dead, dead, and we are forgotten by God."

Spearman looked at the girl.

"Mon père!" admonished Céleste again. "You should not say such a thing. There are two good fathers of the church on this island, so we cannot be forgotten by Him."

"Ugh! And who are they, girl? Dutchmen! Good fathers, oui—the only clean powers in our land—but Dutchmen. Our own country, our la belle France—pah! —does not send us a single priest, and so the Dutch must come to us from charity, in the teeth of the dogs who rule us!"

"Nevertheless they are here, and so we are not forgotten," sternly maintained the girl. "And, father, you should not excite yourself."

Blanchard scowled and resumed his fast puffing, but evidently realized the worth of her warning; for he made no retort. The two men smoked in silence for a little time, while the elder grew calmer. Then said Spearman:

"I don't exactly understand all you say. Has this been a French island only fifty years? And what has Guadeloupe to do with it?"

"No," returned Blanchard, in a quieter tone. "In the beginning our Saint Barthélemy was French. Nearly three hundred years ago, I have been told, it was first settled, and for about a hundred and fifty years it was a land of France. Then Sweden took it. Then, in a hundred years, France took it back. But France cared nothing about us. France told Guadeloupe to govern us. And Guadeloupe— You have visited that island? Yes? Then you know it is an island of blacks, or of bastard half-whites. And Guadeloupe sent us what might be expected from Guadeloupe. The officials from there stink to the heavens. They do nothing but drink, ruin our little girls, grind us to death with taxes, bring death and desolation on all this land. They may be white or nearly white outside, but they are all black—black under the skin.

"And we, monsieur, we of Barths, all are white! White, all of us—except in the town, where the negroes live—all white men and women, all over the island. But we are crushed under the filthy heels of drunken, diseased, illegitimate offspring of black swine! We are——"

93

He broke off again, striving to subdue his rising rage. After smoking morosely for a moment he concluded:

"We should thank God on our knees, monsieur, if your America would come here and kick those beasts into the sea and give us a decent government. We are French of the old time, but we want no more of France."

He looked again at his daughter, a somber shadow deepening on his sallow visage. Thoughtfully the outlander followed his gaze, again reading his thoughts. Under such misrule, what future lay before this girl?

"We who are old and ailing have not much more to endure," added Blanchard, his voice solemn. "But for the young people there are long years of misery and want, and nothing else—thanks to Guadeloupe, and France, and the good God who has not forgotten us!"

Céleste looked reproach, as if she felt this combining of names to border on blasphemy; but she made no other answer. To Spearman it was significant that she made no attempt to gainsay her father's savage arraignment of the existent régime. Apparently there was no refuting these accusations.

"Céleste is your only child, sir?" he broke the silence.

"Now," nodded the old man, his expression darkening still more. "There were two sons, monsieur, fine strong men. When the war came—France remembered us then! She took my boys, both of them. They were shot to death by the Germans, fighting for la belle patrie which had graciously permitted them to be born on this beautiful island. Now none is left but the baby girl. And in time, perhaps, our noble France may honor

her too, by allowing her to scrub the floors of some
black bawd of a Guade——"

She sprang up, half tearful, red with shame, and
poised an instant twisting her interlocked fingers; then
ran to the door and stood there with her back to them.
The guest changed position, knocked out his pipe, and
frowned over the job of refilling it. Blanchard, scowling
heavily, set his teeth and said no more. One hand laid
itself involuntarily over his heart.

Pipe once more aglow, the American looked searchingly at him, around the barely furnished room, and
thence out through the window at the broiling hills.
The old fellow's bitterness against France and Guadeloupe manifestly arose from hypochondria, but his
charges rang true. His home, his own person, bore elo-
quent testimony of a gruelling struggle for mere existence in a misgoverned land. His fields, untended save
for the tiny patch of drooping plants cultivated by the
girl at the door, spoke mutely of the young colonials
seized as cannon fodder by a thankless republic. His
environment, waterless except for the salt-soaked ocean,
rainless but for the annual deluge which often swept
away both crops and soil, could hardly be considered to
be under the watchful care of any beneficent deity.

Could the visitor have looked through the hard-
hearted hills, he would have seen, at the port of Gustavia, or down in the curving bay of L'Orient, or wherever else a horse could carry them, a pair of Dutch
priests indefatigably laboring to educate the children,
relieve distress, comfort the dying—and opposed, ham-
pered, and maligned by the Guadeloupe-French officials.

But he did not need to look that far to accept the truth of the assertions he had just heard. This little isle, with its white men and women, was forgotten by France, forgotten by the world, and, in so far as loving kindness was concerned, forgotten also by God.

Chapter VIII

CROSS CURRENTS

After an interval Lawrence broke the brooding silence which had fallen on the little home.

"Well, sometimes a path opens before us when we least expect it, you know," he hazarded. "And speaking of paths, who is the woman living on the path leading here? Over at the west, you know, on the other side of the Boîte du Mort."

The name dropped unconsciously from his tongue, as he sought to divert Blanchard's mind to some topic less mordant. In this he succeeded, but with unexpected results. The clay pipe, rising to the white-fringed mouth, halted in mid-air; and into the wrinkled face came a strange expression.

"What place did you say, monsieur?"

"Boîte du Mort. Over the hill, you comprehend."

Slowly Blanchard nodded, watching him oddly.

"Oui, I know. But where did you learn that name, mon ami?"

Lawrence squinted into his pipe bowl, mentally scrambling for an answer.

"Why, I am not sure," he hesitated. "Perhaps I heard somebody speak it. Isn't that the name of the place?"

"An old name. Very old." Blanchard continued to study him. "Nowadays that place is called Chaurette." A pause, during which the visitor felt the gaze of Céleste from behind him. "The woman beyond Chaurette is one named LaFlamme, who is not long in the country."

"Oh, I see. She is from some other place?"

"From some other island. Some say, from S'n Domingo. And some say she brought with her the plague that killed Chaurette."

"No! Truly?"

"I do not know. That is what some people say. But the pest did not come until she and her man came to live at that house. But then, neither she nor her man—Montez, that one—neither of them was sick then nor later, when everyone else died. It is not possible for well people to carry disease to others, is it, doctor?"

"Possible, but not very probable. Why did they come here?"

"None knows."

Blanchard drew at his pipe, found it smoked out, and helped himself to a new charge. Céleste quietly returned to her chair.

"Well, tell me something about this Boîte du Mort yonder," requested Spearman. "It is a strange name. Why did people call it so?"

"People did not, monsieur," dryly replied the oldster, an enigmatic smile lifting his mustache. "Not the people of Barths."

He scratched a match and ignited the tobacco, shooting a keen look at his guest.

98

"Then who did?" coolly persisted the questioner.

Blanchard seemed disinclined to enlighten him at first. As he rested an elbow on the table, however, he knocked over the bottle of tablets; and its sharp clink perhaps reminded him that this man, actuated only by kindness, had toiled over the hills in the midday heat to bring it to him. All at once he began talking freely.

"Once I was told by my father, who was told by his grandfather, who was a sailor and traveled far on the sea, that somewhere—at Martinique, or perhaps at Margarita—I have forgotten—at some such place he chanced to meet men who, finding that he came from Barths, spoke of a Boîte du Mort. And when he said no place of that name was here, they said he lied. There were a bay and a valley, they said, and the bay was the second one south of the harbor, and the valley was very stony, and that valley was La Vallée de la Boîte du Mort. And it was called so because somewhere in that valley was buried a great box of gold, hidden there many years before by a pirate. And nailed over the top of that box was a Spaniard, who had been buried there with it—buried alive, with spikes driven through hands and feet to fix him to the wood. So, you see, it is a veritable box of a dead man.

"They wanted my grandfather to bring them here and help them hunt for the box. And he said he would, because they were dangerous men and he had fear of them. But he tricked them and got away to sea without them, and he never saw them again. And when he was here again he looked about, but he found nothing. And later his son looked, and afterward the son of his son looked, but also they found nothing. And then came men from the sea who looked—and found only their death."

He paused, puffing reminiscently.

"Death?" prompted Lawrence.

"Death. It was when I was very small; perhaps fifty years ago. Three men came by night on a sloop. What they did before the explosion, none knows. They worked quietly. But some mischance happened, and there was a terrible noise as if the island had blown up. And when we gathered from round about there was a great hole in the ground, and the pieces of three men scattered around, and the little sloop anchored in the bay, and that was all. So when the sun rose we gathered the pieces and dropped them into the grave they had made for themselves, and covered them up."

"And there was nothing in the hole they made?"

"Rocks. Nothing else. Their powder must have blown up while they were carrying it to some place above. One of them may have been smoking; we found a broken pipe. At any rate, they died like the fools they were."

He puffed again, then added in a tone which seemed significant:

"All who come to this island to hunt gold are fools."

Spearman laughed easily.

"A good story!" he said. "I always like to hear stories of the old pirates and their buried treasures. If half of them were true we all might become rich, eh?"

"That is so," agreed the other, nodding sagely. "There

are tales and tales, but few treasures. And as for gold on Barths— Pah! One might better seek it in the bellies of the fish. He could sell the fish, and so make a little silver."

He chuckled shortly at his little joke, but his eyes remained shrewdly speculative as they rested on the self-styled student of herbs. The latter, sensing half-born suspicion behind that observant gaze, feigned lack of further interest in the subject and began talking humor-ously of various happenings in Saint Thomas and other islands on the steamship route. Most of the incidents which he narrated were years old, but these out-of-the-world islanders were unaware of that; so they accepted them as recent occurrences noted in the course of his travels. At length, feeling that he had thrown out an effective smoke-screen of words, he arose and took his helmet.

"Well, it's time to be moving back to my leaves and roots," he announced. "And I have a rather long walk. So au revoir."

"Where are you staying?" Blanchard quizzed.

"Ah, that's a secret. When I am at my work I don't like to be disturbed by callers, so I have taken a little house outside the town, and I tell nobody where it is. And you will oblige me, my friends, if you say nothing about me to anyone calling on you."

Both regarded him queerly.

"You have one of the houses at Grand Bois, perhaps, on the top of the hills?" persisted Blanchard.

"Perhaps," grinned Lawrence. "Who knows?"

The bushy brows drew down at the rebuff. There

was a short silence. Then, glancing again at his medicine, the oldster conceded:

"Well, we shall say nothing. We see few people. Very few think enough of Pierre Blanchard to walk here. Let the old dog die as he may, for all they care!" His voice grew grumpy.

"Oh, they're probably busy with their own work," soothed Spearman. Then, smiling at Céleste, he added: "And there must be some young men who think enough of the Blanchards to come here—by moonlight——"

"Sacré!" barked the invalid, so sharply that both of the younger folks started. "Love-sick moon-calves? No such creature comes here to slobber! Not while I live!"

Sudden ire darkened his face. Amazed and somewhat irritated by the unexpected outburst, the visitor stared at him. Then he felt the warning touch of Céleste on one arm.

"Don't let a little joke annoy you," he advised. "Bon jour."

Turning from the peppery invalid, he moved doorward, glancing down at Céleste. She, too, looked rather displeased, and somewhat humiliated, by her father's choler. And now, though she had involuntarily suggested his speedy departure by that touch, she sought to vindicate the courtesy of her house. Pausing, she said hesitantly:

"It—it is still very hot, mons—doc—Laurent! Can you not stay longer—until the sun is lower?"

"No, thank you, Céleste. I have other things to do. Perhaps I'll spend a little time at the other house and talk to—Mademoiselle LaFlamme, or Madame Montez, —which is it?"

The random remark was meant more for the ears of Blanchard père than for her; but the effect was not especially happy. Behind him sounded a satirical grunt. Beside him, his companion drew away. Looking straight ahead, she walked to the portal and stood there, waiting for him to pass out.

In the doorway he paused, regarding her searchingly. Despite his habitual nonchalance, he found himself somewhat nettled by this turn of events. Nor did her present attitude tend to mollify his sensation of pique. She returned his gaze unswervingly, but with an indefinable absence of cordiality.

After a dragging minute or two he quietly remarked:

"I seem to irritate your father. So perhaps I had better not come again."

A faint flicker of the eyelids was her only sign of feeling. Impersonally she answered:

"As you please, docteur."

There seemed to be nothing further to say on that point. So he stepped out.

"Adieu, Céleste."

"Adieu, monsieur."

The tone of response was decidedly cool. His lips hardened. With a formal bow he amended his leave-taking.

"Adieu—Mademoiselle Blanchard."

He walked away. Twenty steps he took, unhurried but unhesitating, without a turn of the head. Then on the hard earth behind him came a patter of shod feet.

103

Still he did not look back—not until a voice spoke at his shoulder.

"Laurent—I am sorry———"

He slowed, and swung to face her. Flushed, breathing fast, she looked appealingly up at him.

"I—I did not thank you for the medicine," she quickly added. "And I am sorry that—that father was not more agreeable———"

"That's all right." He smiled again. "He is sick, and I understand. But is that all you are sorry for?"

She laughed, and frowned, and looked at him and away from him, and intertwined her fingers and unlocked them, all at once. Then she dropped her head and gazed at her hands, folding one within the other and seemingly deeply interested in their fit. He laughed down at her.

"I'm sorry too, Céleste," he told her. "It's not adieu but au revoir, yes? And I don't believe I shall stop to visit Mademoiselle—Madame LaFlamme—Montez. Now you must not stand here in the sun without a hat, or you will turn black. Run along home."

The downcast head lifted again, and the rosy face dimpled in another swift smile.

"Au revoir," she said softly. Then she turned and walked buoyantly back toward the house.

He stood a moment watching her go; then resumed his own progress, moving now with his usual looseness of muscle instead of the stiff-backed gait of the recent few yards. Upward he toiled until he reached the knife-edged boulder which had become his halting place. Once more he looked for her in the doorway, and found her there; and this time his swing of the helmet brought instant response. With that farewell flutter of the hand she faded from sight.

Through the pass he returned, to swing from the path at the point where he had entered it and ascend, behind the brush screen, to the divide overlooking the valley of the salt pond; thence to retrace his way to the edge of the Box and reappear on the sky line at the same point where he had vanished from the surveillance of Van Horn. His precaution proved needless. No watcher was visible at the camp.

His eyes roved to the western notch, beyond which lived the woman said to be from Santo Domingo. The Blanchards evidently had no exalted opinion of her, and any gentleman enjoying her society needn't look for much cordiality at their home; not from Céleste, anyway. He chuckled. Then, sobering, he moved to the shady side of a stone jut, sat down, and looked seaward, removing his helmet.

Santo Domingo, eh? Spanish Santo Domingo, with French Haiti, formed the old-time island of Hispaniola: birthplace of the buccaneers, and, if tales were true, hardly an abode of angels even now. Plenty of smallpox there, too, it was said. And this woman with the Spanish-French name came from there with a Spaniard and took a house next to the Boîte du Mort, where French pirates once had crucified a Spaniard to the lid of a treasure chest; and then smallpox destroyed all the people of that Box; and, according to MacLeod, the woman hinted at knowledge of that treasure. It all looked queer.

It looked, at least, as if they had come to unearth that treasure. But, with the "brother" working as a laborer at the town, it was self-evident that they had not found it. As for the pestilence, there was little sense in supposing that these outlanders, themselves immune, after traveling four hundred miles across the sea and living at the town without harming anyone, would infect the meager population of Chaurette. They got the blame simply because the habitants felt like attributing the calamity to the presence of foreigners. And if they had any knowledge of the buried loot it must be fragmentary. Probably it was mere legend. Men had known of the cache in the time of old Blanchard's greatgrandfather. Others had come and killed themselves. The tradition must be fairly well known, then. But it would take something more than tradition to locate the correct spot amid all that chaos down below. The box would belong to whoever could find it.

But could anyone find it? Three generations of Blanchards had failed. Those fools with their powder had failed. Likely as not, it was that explosion which had obliterated the landmarks sought by the present expedition; the concussion had rolled the banded boulder into the sea, toppled over the fer-de-lance, loosened many stones on these heights to be afterward tumbled down by the rains and strewn above the markers depicted on the chart. At any rate, the quest seemed virtually hopeless, and Blanchard's pessimism well founded. All the same, there was no use in quitting until every foot of ground had been covered by the slow sweep of the drag net; no sense in revealing any of these discouraging surmises to the fellows, either. The less said, the better all around.

With this conclusion, his mind reverted to the humble home on the headland. Crusty old codger, Blanchard. Considering everything, though, his crochety temper was natural enough. A lifetime of toil and poverty; wife dead; sons conscripted and killed; himself helpless, tottering on the brink of the grave, cankered by fear for the future of his one remaining child—it was hardly strange that he should be a bit crabbed. How he had exploded, though, at the suggestion that men might seek his girl! Savagely jealous of her, determined to keep her to himself to the end—how his trenchant tongue would flay any rustic swain who came to "slobber" over her!

The thinker chuckled again. But the old fellow might be right enough, at that. His daughter was well worth guarding; a fine, honest girl, modest and sweet, and quaintly charming. Very wholesome and refreshing, by contrast with the loud, lipsticking, leg-showing, cigarette-smoking flappers up home.

"Hey! Snap out of it! Time to get to work!"

The hail rang from below. There in the doorway was Devlin, peering up and waving a sun-browned paw. Outside stood Mallory, watching him through the binoculars by which they had found him.

"Oh, to the devil with work!" muttered Lawrence. But he arose and began picking his way downward. Recess was over, and another lesson in futility was at hand.

CHAPTER IX

ENTER EVE

Another sunset flamed.

Shadows, sweeping from the western wall of the Box, enveloped the camp. Shadow seemed also to rest on the spirits of the men seated around the table within the shingled barrack. They ate moodily, voicing no thoughts. Outside, their bath towels dangled dejectedly from a sagging line. Down the slope their line of pegs marked off a widened field of squandered endeavour.

Devlin, finishing first, shoved back from the board, lit a cigarette, blew smoke at Van Horn, and sardonically met the retaliating scowl. With one hand he derisively stroked his bald crown as if slicking down hair to match the smug set of the straight blond locks of the "Dutchman." Although the absconder wished nobody to suspect that he was a former bank employé, precise habits still clung to him; and the exact parting of the hair, the shiny sleekness imparted by habitual palm-smoothing, had become eyesores to the ex-teacher— perhaps because they reminded him of his own bygone subservience to outward impeccability. Now his mocking gesture carried a plain imputation of contemptible foppishness. Van Horn's glower became a hot glare.

Mallory, observing the offensive motions and the resentful response, threw a switch in the track leading to immediate collision. To him, as to Spearman and MacLeod, it was plain that these two were likely at any moment to crash head-on, with disastrous results; moreover, that a perverse imp was continually goading the restive Devlin to precipitate the impact.

"I've got a hunch," he asserted, "that we're wasting time in pawing over this rocky hillside, and that we ought to look for our box somewhere along the beach. Wouldn't that be the most natural place for a pirate to bury his stuff? Sandy soil, easy digging, and easier transportation for the load. What do you think, Dan?"

The ruse worked. Although the hypothesis contradicted the reconstructed chart, work-weary minds momentarily snatched at the easier prospect thus proffered. Devlin's provocative scalp stroking ceased, and he squinted meditatively at the speaker.

"Might be something in that," he conceded. "It sounds sensible, anyway. What d'you think, Larry?"

"Well, one guess is as good as another," deliberated Lawrence. "We can spend a day down there, if you like. But the more I look at this place the more I believe that beach was under water in pirate days, and this whole coast was lower than it is now."

"How come?" queried MacLeod.

"Oh, upheaval or tilting or volcanic disturbance. All these islands are likely to move a bit in two or three centuries. There was old Port Royal, over in Jamaica, the buccaneer's headquarters, that dropped into the sea with all hands aboard when a quake broke loose. And over in Nevis, about fifty miles south, old Jamestown did likewise. All these Antilles are more or less volcanic, and they rise or sink or tip as they happen to. Likely as not, the whole lower end of this Box was inhabited by fish when that treasure came ashore, and the place we're hunting for is up above somewhere."

"And just as likely," grumbled Van Horn, "the island's sunk, not risen. That means the treasure is out there in the bay, where we'll never get it!"

"Oh hell, there goes the vinegar barrel again!" growled Devlin.

"If you don't like it," rasped Van Horn, "you know what you can do about it!"

Devlin's temper snapped. Like a released spring he shot up from his chair, his under teeth agleam. Instantly every other man came to his feet, Van Horn leaning forward as if welcoming attack, Mallory leaping in front of Devlin with arm outstreached, MacLeod and Spearman sharply scanning both belligerents. And then, just outside the doorway, sounded a low laugh.

MacLeod's eyes swerved toward the sound, and then he chuckled. Spearman shot a sidewise look, and kept on looking. Mallory took another step, blocking Devlin completely; then glanced at the door, and exclaimed in joyous surprise:

"Red-hot mamma! See who's here, Dan!"

Still glaring, Devlin involuntarily obeyed—and forgot his truculence. Outside stood a woman, and on her head balanced a basket, and from the basket peeped the necks of bottles. Moreover, the woman was decidedly good looking, and she was smiling at him. His wrathful visage smoothed out, soon to crinkle into a grin of responsive good humor.

Van Horn, too, relaxed from his ready posture, turning away to let his eyes dwell on the shapely Hebe and her revivifying burden. His first lowering stare brightened into live interest, which in turn became more than a little covetous. An alluringly exotic figure was Lolita now, her slumberous eyes drifting from man to man, her smile seeming to each a sensuous caress, her languorous poise suggestive of fathomless fires of passion carelessly controlled; her dress a seductively revealing, yet tantalizingly concealing drapery of red, short sleeved, low bosomed, falling in clinging folds to silky golden calves.

Stockings she had none; and her footwear was only a pair of heelless Spanish sandals. Such women as she might often have walked, centuries ago, to meet pirate and privateersman, and might even now be wantoning in the hot-blooded isles away at the west. But never before had so live a flame glowed before the vision of Van Horn.

"Hullo, Lolita," called MacLeod. "Come in and look at the pirates."

"Oh, but I am scare, Cap'n Jack," she laughed, raising her brows. "They too rough, they mos' fighting now, an' I am 'fraid for myself. I am so-o-o 'fraid of men!"

"You misunderstand us, babe," chuckled Mallory. "We just stood up to sing a hymn. Bring in the holy water and have some with us."

"And, for the love of Bacchus, don't drop it," besought Devlin, seeing the basket sway slightly on its seemingly insecure perch.

With an amused glance at him, she sinuously moved her body, making the wicker box dip at alarming angles, yet preserving its balance as surely as if it were fastened to her head. Dan's involuntary grunt of anxiety was echoed by others. MacLeod strode to the doorway and seized the apparently tottering receptacle.

"Some day," he threatened, "I'm goin' to spank you hard, you little devil!"

"Mais oui?" she mocked. "Some day when you feeling strong, eh? How soon?"

"Right now!"

Passing the basket to Spearman, he swooped at her and swept her off the ground. Startled, half angered, she resisted furiously for a few seconds; then, with a flutter of laughter, threw both arms around his neck and clung tight, her eyes burning recklessly up into his.

"You are brute!" she cooed. "An' now you going beat me, eh?"

"Not yet, but soon," he promised.

Carrying her across the floor, he sat her down firmly in a chair.

"Now sit there and do penance until I attend to you further," he grinned.

"Ah, oui? 'Fore you 'tending to me you mus' have a drink, yes?" she taunted. "You fin' cognac in the basket, capitaine!"

Van Horn laughed loudly, a jarring note in his unexpected mirth. MacLeod turned and surveyed him with narrowing gaze. The other men chuckled, giving scant attention, however, to either Van or Jack; for both Mallory and Spearman still watched their saucy visitor, while Devlin gloatingly removed straw coverings from wine bottles and avidly eyed twin quarts of brandy. After that one chilly stare, the tall man wheeled to the table, drawing his pocket knife and opening from it a stout corkscrew.

"What'll you have, Lolita?" he asked casually. The cool tone brought her mischievous gaze from Van Horn to him, and when she found him not even looking at her she lost her smile.

"Oh, nothing," she pouted. "I not caring about it."

Without reply, he opened a bottle of red burgundy, filled a pair of short tumblers, and extended one to her. The girl looked at him.

"Don't you be sulky," he advised. "We've got enough bad tempers here now, without you bringin' another one."

"Eh bien," she accepted, smiling again. "Maybe if I drink you not beating me, no? But who have the bad temper, eh? An' why?"

"Oh, everybody but the minister here." He grinned at Lawrence, who was pouring from a bottle of sauterne. "And we're all mad because we haven't any girls."

"Ah, so? It is great pity, yes?" She looked shrewdly at Spearman. "An' that one, he is minister? Ha ha! An' this one, he is pries', eh?"

A nod designated the naturally tonsured Devlin, now wrestling with the tight cork of a brandy bottle. Again Van Horn snorted; and this time everyone laughed with him—even Dan himself.

"That's right, girlie," Devlin chuckled. "Confess all your sins to me and I'll give you absolution."

"But me, I never do any sin." She drew a demure face.

"Umph!" He grunted cynically, yanking out the cork. "Well, any time you feel like committing one don't hesitate. This church forgives anything to a pretty bootlegger."

"Them's my sentiments too—especially the first," coincided Mallory. "And here's to the new member of our congregation!"

Glasses rose. Lolita, luxuriating in the broad homage, raised her wine with practiced surety, openly coquetting with the latest speaker. MacLeod, observant but imperturbable, smiled lazily at Mallory; then, catching a sidelong glance from her, laughed aloud.

"No, you're not makin' me jealous," he informed her. "Go as far as you like."

"Pouf!" she retorted, with evident pique. "What I care about jealous?"

He laughed again and drained his glass; refilled it, moved to a cot near her, and sat down.

"My dear young lady," he rejoined, "that's just the point. You don't care if I do get jealous; so what's the use? And besides, the whole camp is your debtor for fetchin' this joy juice so soon and unexpectedly, and so the house is yours, and everything in it. So if you see a man you fancy, just help yourself. Look 'em over and take your pick.

"The worst one in the lot is that long loose-jointed scoundrel with the mustachio. We call him Larry, but

114

he's really Blackbeard in disguise, and he's killed seven
wives already at his tower over in Saint Thomas. Look
out for him; he's a deceivin' devil. The best man in this
gang, of course, is me, Montbars Junior, meek and mild.
That one you took for a priest is a hard-boiled yegg by
name of Captain Kidd, so called because he tortures his
women to death by kiddin' 'em all the time. This curly-
headed pirate you were just lookin' over is Harry
Morgan, the scourge of the Spanish Main. He takes a
new wife every night, and she's always found dead in
the mornin'. I don't know just how he does it, but you
might find him interestin'. And yonder there, with the
bullet head and the death clutch on the neck of the
cognac, is Roche Brasiliano, called Van for short. A gay
blade, he is, always dancin' and singin' and throwin' his
money with both hands to the girls. And that's all of us.
Drink up, and have another. Oh, and have a cigarette."

"Maybe," she assented absently, looking with languid
yet penetrating gaze at each of the men slandered by
MacLeod.

All except Van Horn, who scowled at the obvious
ridicule underlying his portrayal as debonair spend-
thrift, laughed easily and returned her regard, though
with varying degrees of intensity. In the momentary
glance of Devlin, who speedily transferred his attention
back to the bottles, she saw indifference to her fascina-
tions.

In the steady observation of Spearman she found
a speculative appraisal which gave her a second's pause,
then led her to lower her lashes defensively. In the danc-
ing pupils of Mallory she perceived a touch of deviltry,

and in the blue watch of Van Horn a furtive hunger, which she read with ease.

With the four strangers mentally catalogued and classified, she emptied her glass and negligently accepted a second measure poured by Mallory, as well as a cigarette proffered by MacLeod.

"You are bad man, Jack," she reproached, her gaze meanwhile roving about the crude house. "You always telling big lies, always deluding poor little Lolita. You not the bes' man here. No, you are the wors'! An' the things you say, they making me blush for shame. Maybe I not bringing you no more wines if you talk so. Now today—soon as my brother come home—I make him walk——"

Her tongue stumbled, then stopped a moment. Her wandering attention had come to rest on a sheet of paper pinned on a wall near a window. In the rapidly thickening shadows the inscription on that rectangle was barely visible and, from her position, illegible; but for several seconds she looked hard at it, suddenly alert. It was Spearman's incomplete copy of the chart of the Boîte du Mort.

"——I make him walk back to the town an' buy this basket full," she caught herself, "an' fetch it tout de suite, jus' for your pleasure Sat'day night, now. An' you thank me with the big lies and' make fun of me. I am mad."

She pouted again. Under the mask of her lashes she covertly peered at the map.

"Well, supposing we thank you with a kiss," chuckled Mallory. "How would that suit?"

116

Her eyes left the paper and flashed up at him daringly. Slowly she sipped more wine, still ogling him over the glass. Then, with a puff of smoke, she declared:

"Me, I know nothing about kissing,—eh—what your name?"

"Bill. Well, now's a good time to learn, if you feel that way."

"No no, I don' think so. Maybe some other time— some other place——"

She shot a glance at MacLeod, who carelessly quaffed more wine, giving not the slightest indication of jealousy, or even of interest. So pronounced was his outward apathy that her eyes snapped with spite.

"Poisson!" she hissed at him.

"What's a poisson, Larry?" drawled Jack. "I don't comprenny fransay."

"The lady calls you a fish," laughed Spearman.

"Wrong," denied Jack, taking another swallow. "A fish drinks water."

Devlin cackled. The cachinnation, unmusical and metallic, seemed to jar on the temper of the mercurial woman, already nettled by MacLeod's phlegm. She threw her wine down her throat, arose, flung away the glass.

"You all making fun of me!" she flared. "Trés bien, you all go to the devil! An' you wait! You all drink water! Warm water, ol' water of cistern! No more wine you get from Lolita!"

Head high, she swept toward the door. For a second all looked blankly at her. Then spoke Devlin, alarmed by her threat.

"Oh, hold on, there! Nobody's laughing at you, girl. It's the poor fish yonder that I'm snickering at. Don't go away mad."

At once she paused. By accident or design, she now stood much nearer the sketch of the Box. For a moment she regarded Dan with calculated hauteur. In that brief interval Spearman moved casually aside and leaned against the wall, one shoulder completely covering the map.

"Now you know, Lolita," came Jack's plaguing voice, "we're all desecrated—I mean desolated—with love for you. Only we're bashful about letting you know it. But if you're going to high-hat us we'll just have to find another girl. So have a care, me proud beauty, have a care!"

"Bah!" she retorted.

Turning her back on him, she faced toward the window—to find Spearman blocking all view of the chart. For a second she looked nonplussed, meeting his saturnine gaze with a blank expression. Then she stepped on toward the exit. But she moved much less hastily than before, and in the doorway she paused again, looking back at the group. In her hesitance now was a subtle invitation.

Her gaze drifted in turn from MacLeod to Mallory, and from him to Van Horn. Mallory, glancing at MacLeod, found him lounging inert.

"How about it, Jack?" he muttered. "I don't want to trespass, but——"

"Look alive," prompted MacLeod, in the same tone. One thumb moved toward Van Horn, who had set down his glass and stood irresolute. Mallory wasted no more time. He stepped briskly toward Lolita, who smiled and sauntered out into the gathering night.

"Now there's no sense in your going home all alone, Lolita," his cajoling tones drifted back. "And we were speaking just now about a kiss——"

"Oh, but I mus' hurry home," came the laughing evasion. "My brother he is waiting for his supper——"

"The longer he waits the better he'll eat. And besides, I'm a fast worker——"

The voices receded. In varying keys, Spearman and Devlin and MacLeod laughed. Under his breath Van Horn swore.

CHAPTER X

SATURDAY NIGHT

*"Oh, there comes a night when we all get tight
And the water wagon is a sorry sight!
Nobody cares if you fall downsta-a-airs,
Nobody cares how the landlord swea-a-ars———"*

Thus sang three men, beating time on the table, while the fourth sat silent and sour. MacLeod and Spearman, pleasantly mellowed by wine, and Devlin, exhilarated by brandy, blended their voices in harmony which should have cheered Van Horn but did not. Nor did the cognac, of which he had imbibed fully as much as Devlin, sweeten his sullen temper. Fixedly morose, he stared at his drink as if seeing in it only acerbity.

The song ended on a high note which Devlin, with a wink at MacLeod, made raucously dissonant. The cacophony of it rasped intolerably on Van Horn's present mood. He kicked back his chair and sprang up. The look he gave Devlin bordered on ferocity.

"Shut up!" he snarled. "All of you! That hellish noise you're making sounds like a cat-fight! If I couldn't sing better than that———"

"Well, it's the best we can do," MacLeod cut in.

"Suppose you sing awhile and show us how. Hop to it, kid!"

An inarticulate mutter was the only rejoinder. Van Horn flung toward the door, eyed the black night, and stopped. Outside waited nothing but gloom and rocks.

"He won't sing," Jack mourned. "Now I leave it to you, Larry, what can we do to entertain the gentleman? Here's fine liquor, and he doesn't appreciate it; good singin', and he doesn't like it; and there was a woman, and he let her go off with a handsomer man. Wine, woman, and song. What else could a normal male want for a pleasant evenin'?"

The man at the door turned back, glowering. Without a glance toward him, his tormentor continued:

"You don't suppose, now, do you, that he's sore because he let the woman get away from him? He had his chance, and didn't take it, so he evidently didn't want her. But if he only knew what he was missin'——"

"Huh! What about you?" barked Van Horn. "You let Mallory take her right out from under your nose!"

With a saturnine smile, MacLeod poured another drink, leisurely quaffed it, and answered:

"That's right. So I did, so I did. But there might be a couple of reasons for that. One might be that I never like to be a hog, and I was willin' to give you boys a chance. And another might be that I'm feelin' lazy tonight and wasn't interested. I take what I want when I want it, son. And then I don't wait for some other chap to grab it before I can get started. Write that down in your copybook and profit by it."

Van Horn's scowl deepened. Before he could retort—

if he intended to—Devlin took a hand. Grinning wickedly, he began waving his fingers childishly in air and, in a ridiculous treble, chanting kindergarten doggerel:

> "Van's mad, and I'm glad,
> And I know what will please him:
> A jug of rum, and a sugar plum,
> And a little vamp to squeeze him!"

So absurd were his antics and his infantile tone that both MacLeod and Spearman burst into echoing mirth. MacLeod, recovering breath, roared the same puerile rhyme, while Devlin repeated it with cackling glee. They were on the last line when Spearman, glancing at Van Horn, yelled:

"Look out!"

Goaded to fury by the mockery, Van Horn had snatched the first missile at hand—a tin of beef on a near shelf. Now he hurled it with murderous force. Devlin ducked to the right, MacLeod to the left. The can flew between them, thudded on the farther wall, tumbled to the floor. Instantly both were on their feet and leaping at the assailant. But Spearman, jumping a second sooner, was there before them.

"That'll do! No more rough stuff!" he snapped. "What the devil ails you, Van? That can would kill a man if it struck fair. And you there, Jack and Dan, pipe down! You started it. Now stop it! All hands stop it right here!"

The incisive commands bit deep. Van Horn, though half berserk, blinked and stood still. MacLeod caught himself, stopped, grasped the red-faced Devlin. For a second Dan struggled to free himself; then, mastered by MacLeod's powerful grip and Spearman's stern gray gaze, grew quiet.

"Correct," clipped Jack. "Our error."

With which he turned Devlin about, sauntered with him to the table, pressed him down into his chair, and calmly took his own seat. Spearman eyed Van Horn, who, after a sullen attempt to combat his uncompromising disapproval, turned again to the door. There he slouched and stared moodily outward.

For a few minutes strained silence ruled the house. Then Devlin, outwardly composed, glanced at a vacant space on the wall where, until tonight, had hung Spearman's sketch of the Boîte du Mort.

"What's the idea of hiding the map, Larry?" he broached a new topic.

"Oh, there's no particular use in keeping it in sight. We've all memorized it. And now that visitors are coming and seem sort of inclined to inspect it——"

Lawrence left the sentence unfinished.

"You've got the right idea," approved MacLeod. "Our ewe-lamb is a curious little critter. I was watchin' that maneuverin' of hers. She's givin' Bill the third degree right now, I bet, tryin' to get all the dope. If he's wise—and I think he is—he'll kid her and tell nothin'. That's the secret of keepin' her interested. And the same goes for all of 'em. If you've got somethin' that a woman wants you'd better hang onto it, because as soon as she gets it away from you you're a dead one."

"Thus speaketh the sage," intoned Lawrence. "But

123

something tells me that she already knows pretty well what we're after, and that her main object just now is to find out what we know about it; likewise that she and her obliging brother are after the same box."

"Oh, yes, she practically said so the other day when she was tryin' to pump me. But as long as we tell nothin' she'll keep comin' back for more, I'm thinkin'."

"I hope so!" fervently declared Devlin. "We don't want to lose our bootlegger. That threat she made about the cistern water gave me a horrible sinking sensation."

"Oh, that'll be all right. I can kid her into gettin' another lot any time," MacLeod placidly assured him. "She's right obligin' when she's in the mood. For instance, I wasn't expectin' she'd get this shipment so quick, or that she'd deliver it right on the door-step——"

"By the way, that seems odd to me," interrupted Spearman. "That she would come down here, I mean. How did she know where we were living? And how would she dare come into this old pest hole when all the natives dodge it?"

"Well, answerin' in chronological sequence, old thing, she must have done a bit of spyin' to locate us, because I told her exactly nothin' about our palatial domicile. Come to think of it, though, our towels hangin' outside are about as good advertisin' as we could put up. And as for the smallpox, she's immune."

"How do you know?"

"Easy. Vaccination mark."

"I didn't notice any."

"You wouldn't, deacon. It's not on her arm."

"Oh!"

Dan snickered. Glasses were refilled. At the gurgle of the flowing wine Van Horn turned, licked dry lips, and marched to the table, where he tossed off his neglected drink. His bearing was defiant, but his eyes avoided those of the other three. Spearman, after studying him a moment, arose, rummaged in an open box, and produced cards and chips.

"Let's shoot a game or two of something," he proposed.

"Not bridge," refused MacLeod. "No partner games tonight."

"Not poker," declined Devlin. "Too much concentration."

"Oh, come on, Dan," urged Jack. "Poker's a good cutthroat gamble. Shoot some jacks."

"Not me. Not in the same game with you, you shark. You'd have my shirt in half an hour. Make it something simple and ladylike, Larry."

"Well, how about rum or fantan or hearts or— What do you like, Van?"

"Hearts are all right," grudgingly conceded Van Horn.

MacLeod snorted. Spearman, with a warning glance at him, accepted the expressed choice.

"All right. Make it blackjack hearts, straightaway, spots not counted. Chips a nickel apiece. Let's go."

He sat and shuffled, while MacLeod indifferently apportioned the chips.

As the cards flipped around the board, Van Horn snatched up each of his own on delivery, watchfully intent on the building of his hand. The others observed this avidity with varying reactions. Spearman, glad to see the mordant mind biting on something else than wormwood, smiled with relief. Devlin and MacLeod exchanged sarcastic glances; and the former drew from a pocket a nickel which, after exhibition to Jack, he squeezed tight in one fist. Jack nodded, his lips twitching contemptuously. But nothing was said.

For the first few minutes the poker-loving MacLeod played with an air of boredom; but then, as ever, his gambling spirit awoke, and he followed the game with zest. Devlin, on the contrary, evinced mysterious pleasure at the first inspection of his hand, in nowise dampened by the receipt of a formidable red discard from Spearman. The latter, tossing out his cards with his usual languid motions, seemed hardly interested in his luck. Van Horn played slowly and warily, his face lightening at each opportunity to throw off, darkening when he was forced to chip.

The cards were nearly all out when, on a hand which Van Horn inevitably must take, Devlin slapped down the sinister black jack. Then he leaned back and chortled.

"Ten black nickels going to the pot, ten black nickels going to the pot," he chanted. "Ten of 'em at one swell foop—hic—I mean fell swoop—the generous contribution of Mister Van Horn. And that gambolier of a Mac-Leod wins as usual, unless that one card he's got left is a sticker. No, there it goes! Ten black nickels to Mister MacLeod, Mister Van Horn, plus half a dozen red flannel ones."

The unwilling recipient of the ebon knave scowled long at the card, and longer at Devlin, before he counted and recounted his forfeit and pushed it out. But he kept his lips tight shut, except to suck in another measure of brandy. MacLeod gathered in the pool without comment, but his eyes twinkled. Devlin, getting no rise to his baiting, shuffled and dealt. Each time he looked at Van Horn, however, his teeth gleamed.

With varying fortunes, the game continued for some time. Luck seesawed, one after the other of the gamblers accumulating a pile only to see it shrink. From time to time glasses were refilled, the taller pair taking wine, the shorter antagonists sticking to cognac. Devlin's eyes grew glassy. Van Horn's temple veins stood out, congested and purple. A haze of tobacco smoke, thinned but not dissipated by the night breeze, drifted over the room.

At length, by a freak of the game, the black jack came three consecutive times to the hand of Devlin— twice on the deal, once by discard; and each time, by reckless retention which cost him more than one chip, he nursed it until he could pitch it upon Van Horn. The third fall of that hated card not only wiped out Van's last chips but put him in debt. And the unholy mirth of Devlin, plus the sting of utter defeat at the game which he himself had elected, broke his grip on his temper.

"Funny, hey?" he panted, leaning far forward with face contorted. "You dirty crook, you played it low down to work that! You chipped when spades were called! And what's more, you've held black jack out of

127

the deck on the last two deals, keeping it to ring it in again on me! A dirty Irish trick, you monkey-faced son of the dirtiest race alive! You lousy mick! You damned——"

"Hey there!" broke in MacLeod. "Cut that out!"

"Go to hell!" snapped Van Horn, red eyes still fixed on Devlin.

Devlin, lying back in his chair and laughing all the louder at the maddened man's outburst, suddenly came forward, snatching off his spectacles. He still grinned, but into that grin had come menace, and into his eyes a devil. With face hardly a foot from Van Horn's, he began singing, in tones slurring, sneering, deliberately provocative:

"Oh, the Irish aren't much,
Oh, the Irish aren't much,
But they're a damn sight better
Than the damn dumb Dutch!
And the Irish company
Is the best comp——"

Van hit him. Up on his toes he came, and both fists shot from the table to the jeering mouth. And then, while MacLeod and Spearman sprang clear, he went head-first over the board, taking a short-arm punch in the jaw from Devlin as he went, but clutching with one hand and hitting with the other. Table and combatants all went over in a heap, Devlin underneath but fighting upward with savage joy.

Spearman and MacLeod grabbed the upturned legs of

the able, pulled it away, and pitched it out of doors. Then they looked at the grappling forms and at each other. Spearman nodded backward. They stepped to the doorway and out; walked to the nearer window, and there leaned on the sill, watching.

"Let the heathen rage," chuckled Jack. "This thing is overdue."

"They have to have it," Lawrence agreed wearily. "Now they can go the limit."

And, though keenly observant, they lounged at ease. The fighters were evenly matched in weight, in build, in enmity, and in alcoholic condition. The whole house was theirs. They could thrash out all animosity unchecked.

They fought terrifically. Of science there was none. Both were down, both battering with fist and feet, snatching for disabling holds, blocking or guarding or breaking as best they could, in a rough-and-tumble grudge fight. Blows sped too fast for the eye to follow. Kicks landed with fierce impact or flew wild. Throttling hands shut hard on windpipes, only to be wrenched away or involuntarily relaxed by some brain-jarring punch to the jaw.

Devlin clenched a hand in the hated hair—no longer smooth—and, holding his man by a leg lock, pounded ferociously at the face. Van Horn achieved a partial block with one forearm, hammering the other fist into the unprotected stomach. As Devlin at length broke away, gasping for breath, Van slammed a knee to the groin. Devlin doubled over, grunting with pain; then, as his foe arose to his knees, straightened and shot a vicious blow to the plexus. Van Horn caved in and fell, drawing loud, shuddering breaths. For the moment both sprawled helpless, unable to strike again, but watching each other with undiminished venom.

Then Devlin dragged himself shakily to his feet, and Van Horn lurched up to meet him. Toe to toe they stood, to slug unceasingly at face and body. Defense had gone by the board; each fought on the offense, taking a blow to deliver one, and speeding every smash with knockout force. Yet neither was knocked out, since neither maneuvered for the proper placement of the punch. It was straightaway bruising with bony, red knuckled sledge-hammers. And it went on and on with never a pause for breath.

After a time those mauling weapons began to swing more slowly, to land with less power; then to glance or miss altogether, while the duelists staggered on weakening legs. Both were battered groggy. Both were almost blind, their vision dimmed and blurred by lids swollen nearly shut. Yet still they fought, stumbling and fumbling, striking with uncertain aim, striving each to beat the other into insensibility.

Devlin stubbed a heel and tottered backward. A bump—it was hardly a blow—from one of Van Horn's leaden fists knocked him flat. He lay inert, still peering upward between purpling lids, but powerless to rise. Toward him, with a grunt of triumph, lunged Van Horn to pound him into oblivion. But, as he came, Devlin drew his knees up to his chest; shot both legs out with the last dregs of his strength, and planted both heels solidly in Van's midriff. With an explosive groan, Van Horn collapsed like an empty sack. And he stayed where he fell.

"And that," judicially announced MacLeod, "concludes this evenin's entertainment. One—two—three—four—five—six—seven—eight—nine—*and* ten! You're both out."

Devlin's bloated visage writhed in a vague grimace. Through his lacerated lips burbled maundering defiance.

"Irish—aren' mush," he wheezed thickly. "But damsigh'—better'n—da' dum' Dush. Hear 'at, V'n 'Orn?"

Van Horn made no response. He had no voice to respond with.

MacLeod snickered. Spearman straightened up, and together they returned inside. There Jack picked up the water pail and dumped half its contents on the wrecked countenance of Devlin, the rest on the mangled visage of Van Horn. Both sputtered, rolled over, and slowly pushed themselves to a sit; then, swaying and blinking, peered toward each other.

"Get up and fight!" sarcastically prompted Lawrence. "You've been spoiling for a scrap so long that you'd better make it good while you're at it. Round one is even. Now let's see some action."

"Good night!" croaked Devlin. "More? I've got 'nough!"

"Me too," gargled Van Horn, expectorating a broken tooth.

"Sure you've got enough?" pressed Spearman. "If there's going to be any more trouble between you now's the time for it."

"Got 'nough," repeated Devlin. "But if V'n 'Orn wants s'm more——"

"Not me." Van Horn dragged himself up and stumbled to his cot.

"Nor me." Devlin crawled toward his own bed. "There's 'n Irishm'n somewhere 'n your fam'ly."

Moving with difficulty, both got out of their torn clothes and into bed. Spearman and MacLeod surveyed the littered floor, shrugged, and left the clean-up for morning. Leaving the lamp burning on its high shelf for the absent Mallory, they, too, turned in.

Some time later, Mallory came stepping softly in from the dark. Within the door he halted, scanning the confusion of cards, chips, bottles, and tumblers bestrewing the floor, the splotches of water, and the smaller, redder wet stains here and there on the planks. Then he studied the misshapen, discolored countenances, the puffy hands, and the abraded knuckles of Devlin and Van Horn, who lay shut-eyed and motionless; the peaceful expression of the slumbering Spearman, and the faintly satirical smile seemingly playing on the lips of the somnolent MacLeod. Once more he looked at the empty bottles, counting them.

"Oh boy!" he muttered, with a wide grin. "This sure has been one real old-fashioned Saturday night!"

CHAPTER XI

THE MORNING AFTER

Morning sunlight shone across the floor, revealing to the full its unkempt disorder. Wind swooped through the openings, lustily tugging at thin blankets, tousling hair, blowing in faces, skittering cards along the planks, playing a mute reveille for the slothful mortals snoozing in comfort or discomfort. Spearman stretched, sat up, looked about. MacLeod yawned and reached for a cigarette. The other three remained torpid.

"A fine bunch of bums!" soliloquized Jack, in no subdued tone. "Scum of the earth. Makes me feel contaminated just to look at 'em. Especially that yellow Devlin. Remember, Larry, how he whined for mercy when Van got him down——"

"You're a cock-eyed liar!" erupted from Devlin himself.

"Oh, did I say Devlin? I meant Van Horn. The way he crawled and sniveled——"

"Who, me?" snapped Van Horn. He twisted over, then grunted from twinges of lame muscles.

"Wrong again, Jack," drawled Spearman. "It was that sentimental Mallory you're thinking of. He came home blubbering with lovesickness——"

"Where do you get that stuff?" broke from Mallory's cot.

"All present or accounted for," chuckled MacLeod. "Now you three delinquents can roll out and police the grounds. Shake a leg!"

Three simultaneous grunts of refusal replied. Mallory, however, sat up and looked at the beefsteak faces and liver-hued eyes of the recent combatants. In return all four contemplated him.

"I wonder, now, Larry," drawled Jack, "if our unsophisticated little Billy spilled the whole story of his life last night into sympathetic ears."

"Not me," denied Bill. "I even forgot my name."

"Good boy! Just for that, you're excused from fatigue duty. But these two birds here have got to do penance. They spilled good liquor, and that's punishable by the boot."

"What was it all about?" queried Mallory.

"Oh, nothing much. They just couldn't handle their drinks," explained Spearman, slyly adding: "And if you want to know who got the worst of the argument, watch and see who gets up last."

Forthwith Devlin and Van Horn arose as one man, moving stiffly, sorely, but speedily. The three beholders laughed. And the other two, when they had taken time to look at each other, grinned. Their faces had become grotesque masks, and Van Horn's hair stuck awry from bumps which would not shrink for days to come. They were a sorry sight.

"Hullo, mick!" snickered Devlin. "Who put that head on you?"

"A Dutchman," grinned Van Horn. "And an elephant has walked on your mug."

"Feels like it," admitted Dan. "Let's have some hair off the dog that bit us."

He limped toward the shelf on which stood the second bottle of cognac, Van Horn hobbling after him. MacLeod and Mallory snickered at the halting gait of the pair of scarecrows. Spearman, on the other hand, regarded them soberly, then walked to the shelf and seized the bottle before Dan's stiffened hand could reach it.

"I'll open this," he volunteered. "The two of you together haven't enough steam to yank a cork this morning, and you'd probably drop the bottle besides. Now listen: You'll get one shot apiece, a good stiff one, and then you'll go down to the beach and take a good soak in the sea. It'll sting, maybe, but it'll loosen you up. Otherwise you'll be cripples for two or three days. Also, otherwise you'll get no drink. How about it?"

A moment of silence, while he held the bottle out of reach and the shaky pair glumly eyed the rough ground outside. Then both muttered assent. And, when the bracer had been poured and eagerly drunk, they imbibed freely of water and went forth, lowering themselves gingerly from the doorstep and picking their way slowly down the path.

"Well, those two babies certainly did one swell job!" commented Mallory. "And it's a good thing all around. Now that they've knocked the ugliness out of each other I bet they'll be fast friends."

"No chance of that," differed Spearman.

135

"Why not?"

"Because they're natural enemies. Their natures are as antagonistic as flint and steel, and when they clash a spark is bound to fly. And they can't help clashing. The whole environment here is against them. This dismal hole, and the sun and disappointment and monotony, all work on them and wear them raw. Dan's nervous anyway, restless, fidgety, so used to a swift life in the city that he's forgotten how to relax; and this tropical sun just draws his nerves all the tighter. And Van—well, he's worried about something up home."

"I know," nodded Mallory. "His folks."

Both Spearman and MacLeod smiled slightly.

"Maybe," granted the former. "Anyway, something is on his mind all the time, and this dreary hunt among the rocks without results is making that mind no better. So, unless we find what we want very soon, there'll be another explosion between those two. It's inevitable. They'll be a bit careful for awhile, now that they've both been damaged by last night's eruption. But there's another blow-up coming."

MacLeod nodded agreement. Mallory sat with troubled countenance. Spearman drew off his pajamas and began dressing.

"Well, I can see just two ways of cheering them up when they get grouchy," declared Bill, after some consideration. "Liquor for Dan, and Lolita for Van."

Jack chuckled.

"Every gentleman must work out his own salvation," he opined. "And far be it from me to interfere with any innocent amusements contributin' to the general welfare. But, speakin' of Lolita, and rememberin' that I introduced you as a tough egg who killed his woman, I yearn to know if you left her livin'.''

"Why, sure, you cynical cuss! I led the young lady straight home, planted a Platonic kiss——"

"Plutonic, you mean."

"Avast there! A Platonic kiss on her brow, and went right away to sit alone and commune with my holy thoughts."

"Amen! The Lord loveth a cheerful liar, brother."

Spearman laughed. Mallory grinned.

"I'm a lot more truthful than you think, Jack," he countered. "And, much as I regret it, the lady is all yours. I made no headway at all."

Jack eyed him skeptically.

"Awfully gallant of you, old toppy," he derided. "Congratulations on your chivalry, and all that. But——"

"I mean it," insisted Bill. "I didn't even get the Platonic kiss I just bragged about. I tried hard enough, but I couldn't sell the proposition. All she wanted from me was a history of why we came here and how we were making out, and so on. All of which she didn't get. We sat for hours up above here, and neither of us got anywhere. As a fencing match it was gorgeous, but as a tropical romance it was a complete frost. And I'm through. She hits too hard to suit me. I like 'em docile."

"Hey? D'you mean to tell us she swatted you?"

"She did. With vim, vigor, and vitality. Lost her temper and knocked me clean off the rock we were sitting on. When I got up she had flitted from the scene. Yep, you can have her. I never was much good at the manly art of self defense."

Jack lay back and chortled.

"There's somethin' wrong with your technique," he bantered. "Speakin' from my own limited experience, I'd say you got off on the wrong foot at the start. You let her know you wanted her. That's a social error. When you want a woman, don't run after her. Make her run after you."

"Easier said than done. But I'll bear it in mind when I get back home. Till then, I'm cured."

With that Mallory arose and began collecting the scattered bottles and tumblers. Jack followed his example. Spearman grasped a stubby broom, heritage from the deceased owners of the house, and started sweeping up cards and chips.

"Lucky that none of this glass smashed last night," commented MacLeod. "If our bad boys had rolled onto a busted bottle there'd have been a job for the doctor."

"And not a doctor on the island," informed Mallory.

"Hm! Sure about that?" Spearman halted the swinging broom.

"So Lolita says. There was one government sawbones at the harbor, but he quit his job and sailed for Guadeloupe. So anybody that gets hurt or sick is out of luck."

"Well, we're all healthy," yawned MacLeod. "Unless Dan gets D T's, or that cursed canned stuff goes bad on us——"

"Oh say, I fixed it to get some fresh grub," interrupted Bill. "Also another shipment of hooch. Lolita's obliging brother will be the truck horse—unless she forgets to tell him."

"I'll see that she remembers," promised Jack.

Spearman resumed sweeping. MacLeod strolled out and retrieved the table from its resting place of the night. Mallory took dishes from the shelves. With the morning chores engrossing attention, conversation lapsed.

Down at the beach, with heads just out of water, Devlin and Van Horn swayed gently in the warm wavelets of the caressing sea. Except for the sting of salt splashed into smarting eyes and laving numerous abrasions, they were luxuriously comfortable, gradually losing the torturing stiffness which had wrung more than one groan from them on their way down. Yet they were not lying side by side nor exchanging further persiflage. On reaching the sand, Devlin had gone straight to the water; Van Horn had turned and traveled to a spot twenty feet away. And now between them passed no words at all.

CHAPTER XII

UNINVITED

Monday evening.

MacLeod turned from the shaving-glass, bathed and toweled his face, and reached for his helmet. With an uninterested glance at the supper taking shape on the table, he announced:

"You friendless shrimps can eat my share this evenin'. I'm dinin' out."

"How come?" queried Mallory, looking up from his task of apportioning canned beans.

"I'm invitin' myself to eat with Lolita, if you insist on a categorical answer to a damn impertinent question. By the mental telepathy known only to soul mates I'm informed that she's yearnin' for my company at a strictly exclusive affair."

His gaze traveled to the improved, but still battle-scarred countenances of Devlin and Van Horn. The former was agrin; the latter somber. His lips twitched, and as he left the house behind he grinned wide.

"Give my regrets to the hostess," called Devlin. "And swipe a bottle if you can."

"Deliver that Plutonic kiss of mine," added Mallory.

"And let joy be unrefined," concluded Spearman.

The departing gallant laughed. Without looking back, he knew Van Horn was jealously watching him climb the hill; and he listened to catch any provocative banter from Devlin. None came to his ears, however. For the past two days the remarks exchanged by the erstwhile opponents had been notably lacking in either bedevilment or acrimony. Thus far, Spearman's prognostication was proving correct.

As he wended his way upward the amusement soon faded from his face, giving way to a hostile look at the terrain stretching away at his right. That inhospitable expanse might hold gold, but it was becoming hateful to him, as to the rest. An ugly cemetery of dead hopes, it seemed; a ground accursed, which never would breed anything but discord and despair. His stride lengthened and quickened, carrying him faster toward the one spot where might be found relaxation and temporary relief from monotony.

Through the brushy entrance he walked eagerly, and on to the open doorway. There he stopped, glancing in and around; stepped inside, and stood at a loss. Lolita was not there.

"Cursed inconsiderate of you, young woman, I must say," he complained to the emptiness. "Here I shave and abandon my supper, and you walk out on me. You need a little trainin'."

Again he scanned the darkling interior, now discerning on the table several dishes and a short wine bottle. Walking to the board, he found the dishes clean and the bottle full. She had not gone far. So he coolly opened the bottle, drained it, returned to the doorway, sat, and filled his pipe.

Minutes crept away, while he smoked and idly contemplated the wall of sheer stone at the end of the short vista. Funny, these rock formations, he thought. This one looked as if carved away by a semicircular sweep of a titanic knife; a knife with a nicked edge, leaving odd projections here and there. How had it gotten that way?

Without debating the unimportant question, he turned thoughts and eyes toward the right, where the wall ended and the earth-clad slope led off among the trees. Was Lolita out there somewhere gathering goats to herd home, or what? For a few minutes he watched in that direction. Then something drew his attention back, and he grunted in surprise.

As if dropped from the sky, Lolita had appeared in the open. She was coming from that blank stone wall, bearing on her head a wide basket tray of food. Peering beyond her, he discerned a narrow shaded space on the stone which might be a fold, rounded and unnoticeable to casual gaze. Some small repository there, cooler than the sunbeaten house, served as pantry.

She was watching him intently, and came on without a greeting. He regarded her in equal silence, puffing casually away at his pipe. Not until she was close at hand did she speak; and then her salutation was a searching question.

"What you doing here, Jack?"

"Smoking. What you doing?"

"Getting the supper. What you think?"

"I think it's about time, seein' I've come to eat it."

"Oh. So?" She paused before him, her face none too friendly. "An' who inviting you, eh?"

From under his hatbrim he surveyed her with eyes twinkling.

"Gettin' stingy, aren't you?" he grinned, blowing another slow drift of smoke.

"Maybe I not like you no more," she countered, heavy brows drawn.

"No? That's sad."

"Maybe I liking better your frien' Bill."

Her tone was a trifle hard and edged with malice. Remembering Mallory's account of her assault on him, Jack chuckled. Then he teased:

"I don't blame you for likin' him. I like him myself."

His complaisance proved vexatious, as he knew it would. She tossed her head, nearly unbalancing the tray, which she caught with a hand just in time.

"Oh oui?" she rejoined spitefully. "You thinking, maybe, he's good frien' to you? Maybe you don' know!"

"Know what?"

"Oh, me, I'm not saying. You can be finding out for yourself."

He smiled inwardly. Trying to start trouble, the little rascal, he told himself; resentful because he had let her go the other night, jealous because he spoke well of someone other than herself. Well, he'd soon fix that.

Suddenly he arose; so suddenly, and with so swift a hardening of expression, that she fell back a pace. Harsh voiced, he attacked.

"That'll do for you! What d'you mean, anyway, by comin' down to my camp all dressed up and takin' out another man? You didn't dress like that for me—'twas for the other fellows! And you were playin' for Bill right from the start. And because I gave you plenty of rope to see how far you'd go, you went the limit, didn't you? Now what have you got to say for yourself? Speak up!"

Startled, she eyed him defensively, a spark of temper glimmering in the dilated black pupils. But soon that glint warmed into a glow, and the long lashes drooped in that caressing manner so natural to them when watched by a man, while the uncompromising unfriendliness melted into a smile.

"So-o-o! You caring a little about Lolita, then, Jack? Me, I been thinking you not caring what I do; an' Lolita LaFlamme, she not the girl to be throwing 'self away on dead man! But I not caring about those other man, Jack. They nothing to me, no, not Bill or no other man—only you!"

"Huh! A lot you care about me!"

"But I do so, Jack. Now you come, you see, I making you fine repas' to eat, an' then—then we be good frien's again, eh? You not mad no more with Lolita then, I bet you!"

"Well, you make my supper, and be quick about it!" he commanded, stepping back to yield ingress. With an impudent lift of the brows she entered the house. He sat down again, back to her, and winked solemnly at the nearer tree.

Several times during the preparation of the meal she

spoke to him, but he sat stonily silent. The sun vanished, and semi-twilight set in below the crest of the wall. At length her soft tread sounded close behind him, and he turned his head, to find her holding a large glass of wine.

"Come, bad man, you have little drink to make you sweet," she invited. "An' then big meal to make you strong. You getting weak an' cross 'cause you all time eating tin can like bouc—like billygoat. I not liking my man weak, Jack."

Without reply, he drank off the wine, which tasted unduly strong. A meditative aftertaste and a sniff at the glass convinced him that the full-bodied ferment of the grape had been slyly laced with brandy. By the time he reached the table he could feel the mixture tingling in all his veins. He preserved his taciturn austerity, however, until the meal—of sweet turtle flesh and yams and rice and strange but delicious fruits— was finished. Then, lounging back in full-fed comfort, he smiled and passed her a cigarette.

"Now you feeling better, eh?" she cooed, leaning toward him in the gloaming. "How you liking my cuisine, mon capitaine?"

"It's all very good," he graciously conceded. "You're all right, even if you are a little devil with the men. Maybe if you behave yourself from now on I'll take you away with me when I go."

"But yes?" She leaned nearer. "When you going, Jack?"

"Oh, by and by," vaguely. He tapped his own cigarette on the table and struck a match. In its light she scanned him as he drew at the flame. When it was extinguished and the tobacco smoke was drifting away, she drew her chair close and slipped an arm around his neck.

"I wan' to go somewhere, Jack," she confided.

"Where?"

"Anywhere! Anywhere away!" Her red cigarette-fire moved impatiently. "I so tire, so sick an' tire of this islan'! When your ship coming back, Jack?"

"Why, I don't know exactly. When we're through here."

She said nothing for a minute. Her cigarette glowed repeatedly as she drew quick puffs. Then she spoke out —quickly.

"You listen, Jack! You be here long time, you be old an' gray, yes, you be dead, 'fore you finding that thing you want, 'less you trusting Lolita. Me, I know; you hunting for box, box buried long 'foretime. But you not finding it. No, you not finding it in hundred year —not without me! But you tell me all you know, maybe I tell you something I know, an' we find it together then. But jus' you an' me, Jack, nobody else. An' we go 'way when your ship come in, yes? Jus' you an' me."

He laughed tolerantly.

"All right, why not? But how can we dodge the other fellows? And what about your—ah—brother?"

"My—ah—brother?" she mocked. "Pouf! What we care about him—an' them? We give them what you call the slip, oui! Listen, Jack, there is bay jus' north from Gouverneur, jus' down the hill from this very house, behind long point, an' nobody living there, no house, no nothing. An' your ship prob'ly coming by night, yes? An' you got some signal for sailors to see, maybe, yes? Fire on beach, lantern, rocket, something like that? Eh bien, you show signal in that bay—I show you good place—an' your ship come in there, we go aboard, we sail, we gone! Voilà tout!"

"Uh-huh. Clever idea," he drawled. "But where do we get the box from?"

"Mmm! You trus' Lolita. You bring ship, Jack, maybe I bring box."

"Ah, yes." He laughed again. "Maybe. And then again, maybe you'll forget where it is. You'll have to tell me a better one than that, kid. If you know where there's any such box, why don't you get your own little ship and get out? You don't need mine. And what box is this you're talkin' about?"

"Oh! Imbécile!" She snatched her arm away and threw down her cigarette, which spattered sparks on the dull floor. "You don' believe! You laughing at me! But you wait, you see, big fool! You not finding box! An' some day you coming here, you not finding Lolita, you never seeing me no more. You wait!"

Drawing again at his smoke, he regarded her with a touch of seriousness. Was it possible that she actually knew the whereabouts of that elusive treasure? But if she did, why was she living in this hovel, and why was that—ah—brother of hers working for day wages? Miserably small wages, too, they must be, on this poverty-stricken isle.

The whole supposition was absurd. She was just

147

trying again to ferret out his own supposed knowledge. And he had had plentiful experience with women who used him as a catspaw.

"All right, honey bunch, I'll wait," he cheerfully acquiesced. "Anyway I'll think it over a little. Maybe, now, I'll come around to your way of thinkin' before long. You never can tell. But still, I think you're just tryin' to play me for a sucker."

"Sucker? Play you for—— What's that meaning? I don' know it."

"I mean you just want to get away on my ship. You don't care anything about me, personally. Bill would do just as well, if it was his ship, or any of the other boys. All you want is——"

"Oh no no no, Jack!" The soft arm darted again around his neck. "You not believing that, Jack, you knowing that not so! Me, I don' want Bill or any them other man. Only you, you!"

The arm tightened so suddenly that he dropped his cigarette; then, slowly, caressingly, drew away. She arose.

"Some time, very very soon, bad man, you going believe Lolita meaning what she say!" she predicted, running fingers playfully through his hair. "Ve-e-ery soon, I bet you! I make you believe! An'— See, it makes dark very fas', now. An' me, I am so-o-o lonesome in the dark. An' you, you might break leg or something if you go home. An' so——"

Stepping away, she walked with lithe grace and noiseless tread to the doorway. A hand reached, grasped the edge of the door, and swung it half shut. At that instant

148

she halted the motion, took another swift step forward, and looked outside.

"Goin' to keep me a prisoner here, cruel damsel?" lazily inquired her visitor.

No answer came at once. She stood motionless, looking to the right. Then, drawing back, she closed the portal tight.

"Maybe," she replied, with a laugh which sounded a little forced. "Why not?"

"Quite right. Why not?" He grinned. "What were you lookin' at out there?"

"Oh, nothing. I jus' taking look aroun'."

Dim in the dark, she passed to a shelf, fumbled about, scratched a match, and lit a small, weak lamp. It was a simple task, yet one which bothered her, for her fingers trembled from momentary shock and repressed anger.

Just outside that door, lurking and listening, had been a man. Caught unawares by her silent approach, he had gaped a second, then fled into the dark. His face had been discolored by bruises, obscured by the gloom while he stared, and obliterated when he turned to retreat; but, for all that, recognizable as that of Van Horn.

CHAPTER XIII

A FALLEN STONE

It was a queerly furtive yet sullenly defiant Van Horn who, down in camp, met the casual gaze of the returning MacLeod; a culprit inwardly apprehensive of verbal excoriation or physical punishment for his eavesdropping, yet determined to defend himself to the best of his lame ability. When the dreaded denunciation failed to materialize, when, instead, Jack greeted him with impersonal good humor, he masked his surprise and relief as he had concealed his fear. And when day succeeded day without change of demeanor by the man on whom he had spied, intermittent recurrences of uneasiness subsided into conviction that that man knew nothing of the spying.

Manifestly Lolita had not revealed what she had seen. Perhaps she had not recognized him in the dimness. Or perhaps she secretly liked him. He gloated on the thought, and vowed that whenever she should come again to the camp he would make himself her homeward escort.

But Lolita did not revisit the barrack. Whether she had taken to heart Jack's assumed jealousy, whether she disliked Devlin or feared Spearman, whether she harbored some unrevealed grudge against the party as a whole, was known only to herself. At the end of the week, when the promised supply of fresh food and liquid cheer arrived, it rode not on her head but on that of her "brother." The food comprised goat meat, jackfish, sapodillas and custard apples; the drink, brandy and wines. The bearer was unprepossessing.

Miguel Montez was the name he gave. Not only in name, but in frame and feature, he seemed the antithesis of the fiery woman who called him kin. Solid of build, stolid of manner, he appeared a thickwitted laborer. Dull eyed, heavy mouthed, swarthy, pitted by smallpox, clad in threadbare garments and ragged straw sombrero, he stood incuriously at the door, answered the questions addressed to him in French by Spearman, accepted silver money and a drink of brandy, and went his way back up the hill. To a direct inquiry regarding his relationship to the woman he gave a laconic reply which served as complete (though not necessarily convincing) explanation of the dissimilarity between them. He was, he said, her stepbrother.

"Solid bone," was Devlin's contemptuous judgment of him.

"As dumb as they come," agreed Mallory.

The others concurred; then forgot him until his next week-end appearance with laden basket.

During his absence MacLeod saw to it that Lolita did not grow too lonely. Aside from his errantries, the life of the five remained celibate. Mallory, though more than once teasingly told that Lolita had asked about him, remained in camp. Devlin desired no feminine

society other than that of the invisible but vivacious
bacchantes inside the long-necked bottles. Van Horn,
desirous though he might be, lacked the initiative requisite to the realization of those desires; fettered by secretive repression, he awaited opportunity instead of boldly
faring forth to create it; waited in vain, and, waiting,
grew all the more odd in his moods. Spearman, on the
other hand, possessor of a wider range of acquaintance
than any of his partners, held aloof from neighborly
visits through voluntary decision to remain within his
own confines.

Although not a misogamist, and still less a misogy-
nist, Lawrence was attracted by few women. Lolita was
not one of those few. Céleste was an admirable little
lady, but her cool congé on his second visit still nettled
him a bit, even though she had made quick amends.
And her father was an uncomfortably suspicious fellow
at times. Moreover, the pseudo-physician could do nothing more for him. So there was no valid reason for another call, while there were excellent reasons to attend
strictly to the business of grubbing for gold. Conse-
quently, he refrained from again crossing the divide.

Days dragged away in monotonous routine, becoming weeks. The moon waned and waxed and waned.
Tenaciously the party pored over the baffling expanse of
stones and earth, and slowly the peg line climbed the
slope. Swims and siestas and meals came at their ap-
pointed times; cards and drinks and songs killed the
evening hours; and that was all. From the faces of
Devlin and Van Horn faded all traces of their duel.
More slowly, but none-the-less unmistakably, the vivid

memories of that combat dulled and unconquerable antipathy sharpened. In unguarded moments they snapped at each other; and those moments came more and more often. The others, though foreseeing the explosive culmination of the increasing friction, refrained from interference. Whatever must come must come.

When the gathering storm did break, however, it caught everyone by surprise—even the participants. It came at midforenoon of a sunless day; the day when, unexpectedly, they found the fallen stone.

For once, the Box was comparatively cool. Heavy masses of cloud, bearing deceitful promise to rain to the parched isle, blanketed the sun, while the trade wind blew lustily over hill and down dale. In the unusual half-light the five were snailing away at their tedious search when Spearman called:

"Come here a minute. What do you think of this one?"

Mallory, nearest, stubbed across intervening stones to join him. The others turned their faces, but held their positions. The days when all would hurry to inspect and discuss anything remotely resembling a clue—those days were past.

"This rock," Spearman pointed out, "looks more like a lance-head than anything we've turned up. Odd, isn't it?"

It was odd. It was a slender, tapering, pointed, gray-white formation which, if set on end, would be a capital marker. Now it lay almost prone, its tip on another rock, its base obscured by clay washed down by sluicing rains. Beside it was a small depression, free of all stones except a few waterborne pebbles; a sunken spot perhaps six feet in diameter. As Mallory surveyed the place his optimism, lately rather subdued, bubbled up.

"By Jeebus Creebus, it looks good to me!" he averred. "Good enough to sink a pick and shovel into! Hey, bottle babies, come take a peep at this!"

They came with some alacrity; studied the freakish stone, and looked at one another with faces brightening. A brief conference ended when Mallory started excitedly for the camp, where the digging tools had been slowly accumulating rust ever since the landing. Devlin and Van Horn raced after him. MacLeod remained with Spearman, scanning the ground, puffing at his pipe, which he had neglected to fill. At length he drawled:

"I guess you've found the right stone, Larry. But some way I can't get much intrigued by this little old hole beside it. Fact is, it looks to me as if somebody'd done some diggin' here before we came, and not many years back, either. They got what they wanted, shoveled the loose dirt back in——"

"Why should they do that?" interrupted Lawrence. "Who'd bother to refill a useless pit?"

"True enough. It doesn't sound sensible. Well, it's a good day for diggin', and we'll soon see whatever we'll see. Golly, look at Van Horn run! You'd think he was tryin' to preempt this place by gettin' back first."

The blond fellow was bounding recklessly back down the bouldery steep with shovel and pick, followed by the other two, who watched their footing with more caution. Arriving, he flung himself avidly on the sunken spot, sinking his pick to the handle at the first blow. By the time Mallory and Devlin arrived he had loosened the earth to a depth of two feet. Then he paused, breath failing.

"Root, hog, root!" jeered Devlin, half scowling. "Root it out! Then we'll take it!"

"You will—like hell!" panted Van Horn, breath hissing through his teeth. "I'll——"

"Whoa! Less talk and more work!" called Spearman. "Here, Dan, use your shovel awhile. Van, come here and catch your wind. You've done enough. Sit down a minute."

Van Horn stood his ground, tool half raised, face red, jaw set, as if determined to seize and hold everything below his feet. MacLeod's lips thinned. Calmly he reached to the defiant digger's shoulder, turned him about, looked hard into his eyes. After a moment Van Horn visibly weakened. Evading the cold brown gaze, he stepped aside and sat on a stone. Devlin, smiling thinly, took his place.

He shoveled until tired; then gave way to Mallory. In turn, MacLeod and Spearman took over the work. The hole deepened steadily. The picks hit nothing resistant. The shovels flung up only earth and pebbles. The watchful faces lengthened, the eager eyes grew somber. Then Spearman, shoulder deep, paused, stooped, examined something, and tossed it out. It was an old, worm-eaten piece of rotten wood.

Soon he found another, and, later, several more; dark, shapeless fragments of what might once have been a long box. Then he began uncovering relics more sinister: old, very old and crumbly, pieces of bone. These he dropped at one end of the excavation. So ancient were they that his spade had cut through them as through brittle shells.

Then he struck rock. Another quarter-hour of clearing proved the stone to be one irregular boulder, of unguessable size, extending beyond the sides of the pit. Obviously there could be nothing below it save the detritus of countless years of erosion from the hills. Once more he inspected the bone pile. Then he passed up the tools, grasped the lowered hand of MacLeod, and scrambled up the precipice of dirt.

"Well, you fellows can shove it back," he said, gesturing to the bulky parapet of soil. "It's your turn, Van. You've had a good rest——"

"Shove it back yourself, you slob!" snarled Van Horn, leaping up from his rock. "Who do you think you are, anyway, ordering me around? You damned false alarm, you've worked us to death over an old grave, and now you can——"

"Oh, shut your fool head!" snapped Devlin, nerves cracking with disappointment and animosity. "Or I'll shut it so it will stay shut!"

Van Horn wheeled on him, face blackening, under teeth agleam in a down-curved grin of hate. With a choking yell he sprang, both fists hitting at the glasses over his enemy's eyes. Had they struck true, Dan would have been blinded for life. But they missed.

Devlin ducked forward. The blows landed on his crown, staggering him. But his own fists slammed into the midriff of his assailant, who doubled over in sudden anguish. Instantly Dan swung an uppercut to the jaw. Van Horn straightened again, toppled backward, fell into the pit which he had been so eager to dig.

At the bottom he lay twitching, stunned but not completely senseless. Devlin sprang to the edge of the hole, peered balefully down at the supine shape, then seized a spade and began hurling dirt on his fallen enemy. Half a dozen scoops of earth had dropped, and another was in air, when Mallory and MacLeod dragged him back.

"Whoa! That's plenty," grinned Jack. "You're sure thorough. But kill 'em before you bury 'em. Cool off, now, lad, cool off! Hey, Larry, restrain this wild school teacher while I resurrect the victim of his academic instruction."

"Destruction, I'd call it," remarked Spearman, advancing. "Go ahead, Jack. Dan, as you were!"

Devlin's muscles loosened, and a queer look crept over his face as one hand rose to rub his bruised head. He blinked at Jack as if astonished, perhaps by the revelation that his ultra-respectable past was known, or perhaps by realization of his own unreasoning ferocity. When Jack released him he stood quiet, then grinned, then broke into a cackle of merriment. To him the brief fight had suddenly become comic.

To Van Horn it was distinctly otherwise. As MacLeod stepped to the edge he found the vanquished assailant sitting up, shakily pawing dirt off his face and staring in dazed terror at the papery bones in the corner. Deaf to a curt inquiry as to whether he was hurt, he sat there as if numb and dumb. All at once he threw himself up, glanced wildly about like a trapped animal, and made a clumsy spring for the edge, his fingers clawing for a hold in the yielding earth pile.

MacLeod stooped, extended one hand behind him to Spearman, and lowered the other to the prisoner, who snatched at it as if sinking in a morass. A heave, a scramble, and he was out. Mallory moved between him and Devlin; but he seemed to have forgotten his enemy. Face contorted, he lunged blindly away and ran, stumbling, reeling, but holding his feet, toward the camp.

"Well, what d'ye know!" marveled Mallory. "He's scared witless."

They stared after him until he disappeared through the doorway.

"Knocked clean goofy," said MacLeod then. "And there's a gun or two hanging in the shack."

A moment of silence. Spearman began walking to the house. MacLeod strode after him, laconically advising the others:

"Stick here. Fill the hole."

Devlin and Mallory looked at each other, then began shoveling earth, though watching sidewise toward camp. When the pit was fairly well filled they gathered all tools and plodded up the slope. Before they reached the house Van Horn emerged with a pail, walked to the cistern, pulled off his shirt, and began washing himself. Spearman and MacLeod also appeared.

"All down for a swim," called Lawrence. "We've got your towels."

After a look at Van Horn, who ignored them, the late arrivals dropped their implements and diverged to the beach path. Out of earshot from camp Mallory asked: "Is he all right?"

"Bruises and shock, that's all," returned Spearman.

"Nothin' broken," added MacLeod. "And if anything's cracked it was that way before he came here."

No more was said until after the swim. Then Spearman asked:

"What was your big idea, Dan, in throwing the dirt?"

"I don't know," confessed Devlin. "I blew to pieces when he swung on me. I've been trying to keep off him, honestly. But he and I don't hitch, and we never would in a thousand years. And the only idea I can remember is that I had to get that snarly face of his out of my sight—anything to blot it out! I tell you, fellows, I dream about that sour mug sometimes at night, and it's the worst nightmare I could get. The fact that I was knocking him into an old grave and burying him didn't register on me at the moment. Then when I did think of it, afterwards, it seemed funny."

A grin crinkled his face.

"I certainly did shut him up, anyway," he added. "A shovelful of dirt in the mouth dries up loose rhetoric in a hurry. But what d'you suppose scared him so? It wasn't the fall or the wallop at the bottom. I gave him worse than that when we locked horns the other night, and he kept coming for more."

"Probably a horror of being buried alive," judged Spearman. "The slam on the rock dazed him, and the dirt tumbling in shut off his breath, and he went wild. It must have been a ghastly sensation, at that. Well, it won't happen again. And, by the way, Jack and I have locked up our guns, and you might keep yours under cover too, Bill. No use in letting them hang loose and gather dust."

Mallory nodded, as did Devlin. The latter owned no revolver. Van Horn also possessed none. Concealment of the three existent firearms now was obviously imperative.

"Mine's in my trunk, and it'll stay there," promised Bill. "Well, now what's your idea about that hole, Larry? Just an old grave, or what?"

Without reply, Spearman moved away, heading back to the house. It was not until all five were together again that he answered the question. Van Horn, clean and composed, lay on his cot when the others entered, and looked at each with a stony expression, saying nothing. Tacitly ignoring him, the four lit smokes and lolled in varying postures to discuss their fruitless find.

"My own feeling is," then admitted Lawrence, "that we've found the right place, but somebody else found it first. Who or when, I can't guess. If they left the hole open and it gradually refilled by rain wash, it would be a long time back. But that's not the big point. The question is whether those bits of wood were once a treasure chest or a coffin, and whether the bones were those of an ordinary corpse or—well, maybe of a fellow buried with the treasure——"

"What do you mean by that?" interjected Mallory.

"Pirates did that little thing every now and then, Bill," smoothly evaded Spearman. "Made a buck slave or two dig the hole and lower the chest, then knifed them and buried them with it. 'Dead men tell no tales,' and all that. Anyway, with that lance-head stone lying there I can't help feeling that that's the spot we've been hunting for. It's an unreasonable distance from the shore, but that may be due to a change in the shore line. So it looks to me, frankly, as if we were licked. But, speaking for myself, I'm not going to be satisfied that I'm licked until I've covered every foot of the remaining ground. Then when I do get out I can never say to myself afterwards: 'Oh, if I hadn't lost heart I might have found it by looking a bit farther!'

"But we're five instead of one, and some of us may want to quit, and it may be just as well if they quit now, before things get any worse. In which case, we'd all better get out together: go to the harbor, tell the gendarmes the smoothest yarn we can think up, get off the island as best we can, make our way to Saint Thomas, find out what's happened to Thirsty, and—Well, that's enough for the present. I've spoken my piece. Motions now are in order."

A protracted pause followed. Finally Jack declared:

"Speakin' personally, I'm makin' no motions. I'm standin' pat and playin' the hand out."

"Me too," seconded Mallory.

"Nobody ever saw Dan Devlin crawfish," promptly added Devlin.

Four pairs of eyes went to Van Horn. He met them with cold defiance.

"If you think you're counting me out, you're all wrong!" he asserted. "I'm staying here if all the rest of you quit!"

With that he lay back on his cot and looked up at the roof, face expressionless. Spearman studied him, tossed his cigarette butt out of doors, and leaned forward, elbows on the table.

"That ends the vote," he said. "But, Van Horn, just salt this down in your memory right now: You're here on sufferance. We're all fed up on you. You've made two bad breaks since you came, and— Well, I'll go no farther back than that. But make one more, and it'll be the last. You'll be tried by summary court martial, and when it's over you'll be sunk. That's all. Get it?"

Van Horn turned rigid. His eyes shrank to pinpoints. Spearman's grim gray gaze, bleak tone, and veiled allusion to the past told him that at least one man here knew why he had left Philadelphia. For a long moment he lay motionless, soundless, breathless. Then, hard voiced, he retorted:

"I heard you."

With that he dropped his lids and smiled; a faint, strange, crooked smile, as if he visioned something invisible to the men who now were all against him. Those men stared at him, then at one another.

A queer jigger, Van Horn. Very queer.

CHAPTER XIV

CONFESSION

That afternoon nobody worked. Despite determination to continue the search until the last stone should be inspected, all found odious the thought of further toil before the morrow. Tired physically and mentally, they lay down after the midday meal. Four relaxed so completely that they lost all touch with their surroundings. When they sat up again and looked about, the fifth was gone.

"Where's Van Horn?" yawned Mallory.

"Gone out to slip one over on us by smelling out the boodle box," hazarded Devlin, walking to the shelf to pour himself a drink. "And here's hoping he never comes back. Who wants to play a game?"

"Of what?" queried MacLeod.

"Anything. Even bridge, now that Pickleface is out of the way."

"Poker, then. Who's in?"

"I," volunteered Mallory.

"Not I," declined Spearman. "Going for a walk."

He sauntered out, leaving the others preparing for their game. Looking about for Van Horn and finding no sign of him, he trudged away uphill. On reaching the goat track above he turned eastward, walking along it without attempt at detour or concealment. Nobody was watching his movements. Moreover, he wished to survey the downhill terrain from different points along the disused route.

Several times he paused, frowningly studying the expanse below. At length he climbed the transmontane pass and left the baffling Boîte behind.

Although he was traveling toward the homestead of the Blanchards, he had no intention of visiting them. Rather, he meant to sit awhile looking out over their headland and the bay of Saline, giving vision and thought escape from the cramping boundaries within which he had of late immured himself. Tenacious and comparatively nerveless though he was, the depressing incidents of the forenoon had wrought in him a revulsion against his immediate environment, and he felt that he must break away from it for a time. On the other hand, he was in no mood to fence with suspicious, irascible old Pierre, or even to banter Céleste. His need —or so he thought—was for solitude.

But when, stopping at the tall rock, he looked down at Céleste herself, his feeling slowly changed. Some distance from the house, she was toiling at the patch of parched earth which formed the pitiable garden. With the sun still drowned behind the cloud banks, she had discarded her huge straw hat for a close-fitting white capote—the poke bonnet typical of the Barths country women. On the dun landscape that headgear formed a snowy spot which caught and held his eyes. For minutes he watched it, half expecting to see it turn toward him.

But, engrossed in her work, she gave no glance to the hillside which recently had shown no sign of life.

Almost without volition, he drifted down the path and, his soft soled shoes soundless, advanced nearly to her side before she became aware of him. As he approached, something within him rebelled against seeing her drudge at field labor which, in any other isle, would be done by blacks, and which, even here, was more fitting for some thick-wristed, dumpy-framed woman of true peasant type. This slender maiden, he felt, should "sit on a cushion and sew a fine seam," rather than fight stones and drought for bare subsistence.

Then, with a startled movement, she was looking up at him, and he thought no further along that line. The glad light of welcome flashing over the rosy face, the quick smile of lips and eyes, were charms to dispel reflections far more gloomy than these.

"Hullo," he smiled. "How are you today?"

"Oh—trés bien, doc—Laurent," she stammered. "I thought you must have gone!"

"And you were sorry?" he quizzed.

"Yes, I was," she naïvely confessed. Then her color heightened, and she looked away from him. "My father," she quickly added, "is not so well."

"Really? His heart is worse?"

"Yes. For the last two days he has been in bed. I gave him the medicine you left, and it made him feel better at the stomach; but if he walks at all he loses breath. Will you come in and see him again?"

She took a backward step toward the door, looking

appealingly at him. Soberly he regarded her. All at once the clear candor of her eyes made further quackery abhorrent.

"Céleste, I am a big liar," he admitted. "I am no doctor. There are some simple things I can do, but in a serious matter I am no good. When I called myself a doctor I was only joking; but then I let you believe it because I thought it might give you and your father more courage. Those pills really were for the stomach. I knew they could not harm him and might make him more comfortable. But there is nothing else I can do for him. So there's not much use in disturbing him now."

She watched him seriously. As he finished she looked at the empty window beyond which her father usually sat, and her expression became grave. Presently, however, she turned to him again with a faint smile.

"My father has said you must be a droll docteur, to come so many miles across the sea at the wrong time of year for gathering medical things," she told him. "He said he hoped you would not burn your fingers."

"Hm! And what do you suppose he meant by that?"

"I am sure I do not know, monsieur." She seemed to be laughing at him. "Unless, perhaps, he thought you might touch the mancenille."

"The what?"

"You do not know—docteur? The mancenille is the poison tree, with the shiny leaves that burn off your skin if you touch them when damp. And you have picked leaves so long without learning of that one?"

The blue eyes were openly deriding him now. He

smiled in answer. Although momentarily confused by her pronunciation, he knew of that tree, which, in English, was called manchineel, or, in Spanish, manzanillo.

"Oh, I know enough to let that one alone," he returned. "I've seen it a few times on other islands. And there's no danger of hurting myself with any kind of leaves. I'm not picking any."

"But no?" She showed no surprise. Indeed, as she went on her voice held a distinct note of badinage. "Yet there must be many leaves near your house at Grand Bois."

"Probably there would be if I lived there. But my house is in the Boîte du Mort."

This, he thought, she already knew, or at least suspected. Prompted by her canny father, she probably had gone over the hill far enough to peep down at the houses and thus discovered the clandestine camp. The sudden widening of her eyes, however, and the involuntary recoil from him, proved his error. Over her expressive face flitted an evanescent fright, as if on his tanned cheeks had erupted the pustules of smallpox.

"There?" she exclaimed. "One of those houses of death? Oh, Laurent! We thought you might be looking for something among the rocks—but living in that place— What house have you?"

"The best one. The largest one, with the cistern."

"That is not the best but the worst one! The home of Guillaume Therien, where the plague started. Six people—they all died."

She drew back a little farther.

"Don't be scared," he tranquilly counseled. "There's no danger. We have made the house safe and clean, and

167

we all are proof against the plague. So we can't catch
it or give it to anyone else."

She still regarded him a little distrustfully, but, after
noting anew his healthy skin and clear eyes, recovered
her serenity. Too, she caught at an admission which he
had not meant to make.

"'We'?" she echoed. "You have companions?"

"Er—yes. Four of them."

Her gaze darted to the top of the hill, a faint frown
resting on her brow, as if she did not approve the presence of unknown men so near her isolated home.

"They won't bother you," he promised. "They don't
even know that you live here. And they're decent fellows. If you need help at any time—for your father or
yourself—you must come over and let us know. We'll
do anything we can."

"Merci," she acknowledged, with a grateful glance.
"But if bad fortune should come I could go to Saline.
We have friends there."

Looking along the shore line, he saw that, although
the distance was greater, she could reach the salt pond
settlement hidden in the next valley with less exertion,
and perhaps more speedily, than she could climb over
the hill to the Box. So he nodded, making no further
suggestion of unpleasant emergency. As if she too
wished to banish foreboding, she changed the subject.

"How do you like your other neighbor, monsieur?"

"Why, mademoiselle," he evaded, with mock for-
mality, "I have not yet done myself the honor of calling on her."

"No?"

"No. And tell me, Céleste—what do you know about that woman?"

If his tone held any disparagement of "that woman" he was unaware of it; but his question evoked a quick glance and a little laugh. Her reply, though, was noncommittal.

"I know nothing more than father has told you, Laurent. She and I do not visit each other." With that she once more deflected the conversation, this time to the ever-present problem of the islanders. "How do you men get food in that place of stones?"

"It grows on the tin tree. When we are hungry we shake down a tin and open it like a nut."

"Oh. Ha ha ha! That is a funny tree. Do you like the taste of its fruit?"

"Not very well," he admitted. "It becomes tiresome."

"It must," she nodded. "And you should eat something fresh, Laurent: fish, fowl, fruit. Such things can be bought at the town, and they would be much better for you."

"Yes, of course," he agreed, smiling at her unconsciously maternal air. For an instant he thought of informing her of the occasional supply brought by Montez, but changed his mind. "We shall not be here many days more, and the tin tree must do," he said instead. "We do not care to walk to the town."

The last words brought a searching look, which he met steadily. Then she turned to the drooping plants, affecting renewed interest in their welfare, but doing nothing to advance it. She asked no more questions; nor did he volunteer further information.

Into the silence came a faint call from the house: "Céleste!"

"Yes, father!" she answered at once. Then, to her visitor: "I must go to him. He grows fretful when I am out long. You will not come in?"

"Not today. Perhaps some other day—soon—I'll come over to sit with both of you. Bon jour."

"Bon jour." She stepped away, smilingly adding: "Et bonne chance!"

"Good luck to you too," he returned. "But if bad luck should come, remember where I am."

"Yes."

He stood watching her go, oddly nun-like with the capote hooding head and shoulders and with the robe-like dress almost touching the ground. Whimsically he contrasted that virginal figure with the flamboyant picture presented by his western neighbor when she had come a-calling. The tiny, womanless world of the Boîte du Mort had its antipodes very close at hand. He was smiling over the thought when, unexpectedly, she turned.

"Laurent," she called, "would you like to dine with us Sunday?"

For a moment he was too much surprised to answer.

"Why, yes," he then accepted. "At what hour?"

"At midday."

"I'll come, thank you. Shall I bring all my hungry friends?"

"No, no! They are not *my* friends."

"Very well. I shall eat enough for all of them."

She laughed, and walked on with no further farewell. At the door she looked back, waved her hand, and vanished. And he clambered up the hill whistling softly and looking abroad with cheerful gaze.

Maybe he had made a fool of himself by telling so much of the truth to this girl, who, beyond doubt, suspected the rest of it. But he didn't care; in fact, he felt much lighter of heart. Treasure or no treasure, this rocky little isle wasn't such a gloomy place, after all.

CHAPTER XV

THE SPY

When Devlin threw out his random suggestion that Van Horn had stolen away to smell out the elusive treasure, he spoke more truly than he supposed. And now, while the minds of all his partners sought relaxation, that of the absentee was scenting for loot.

It was a queer course that he took. Instead of searching farther within the Box, he left it altogether. And, in departing, he followed no path. Traveling by the easiest gradients, looking back at times to see whether anyone had risen to watch him, he ascended the western wall. Then, hidden among the scrubby brush and cacti and disordered stones at the top, he worked toward the north, meandering past multitudinous obstacles, until at length he reached the brink of the low precipice enclosing the LaFlamme-Montez place. There, keeping behind cover, he crept to a vantage point from which, crouching beside an irregular stone, he could watch the house.

For a long time he saw nobody. Yet, as he squatted there, a hard smile repeatedly curved his lips. Thoughts kept him company; pleasant thoughts of outwitting that gang back yonder, every one of whom he hated.

He long had hated Devlin. More recently he had begun
to hate MacLeod. Now, since Spearman's implacable
warning and Mallory's cool looks, he hated them also.
They all despised him, did they? They'd sink him if he
made another break, would they? The poor fools! Later
on they would wake up to the facts that they themselves were sunk, and that he was far away with the
treasure for which they had slaved. He'd show them!

After a while he dropped imaginations to rivet his attention on actualities. Lolita had appeared.

Sleepy-eyed from siesta, she stood in the doorway,
looking about with lackluster gaze. Presently she
stepped out, sauntered away along the ravine, and disappeared. After a few minutes of absence she returned
with the same bored listlessness. If she had been looking
down at the barrack of the bachelors she had seen nothing of interest. Now she sank on her doorstep and, with
chin cupped in her hands, gazed moodily at the short
cliff on which lurked the observer.

Crouching a little lower, he kept her steadily in view.
Except for such pleasure as he might derive from playing Peeping Tom, however, his patience went unre-
warded; for she simply sat there brooding. Moreover,
she now was not so alluring a siren as when aware of
the gaze of men; a huddled shape in a drab dress, with
face empty of light or laughter, staring stonily at the
close confines of her everyday world. If he had harbored
the odd notion that by watching her he could discover
some clue to the whereabouts of the lost gold, he found
himself at fault.

Thus passed a protracted interval during which his

cramped posture became increasingly uncomfortable. At last he had to alter it. In fact, he waited overlong, and when he did change the position of his stiffened legs they responded clumsily, causing him to move in awkward, jerky fashion. He made no noise, however, and when he again became motionless Lolita sat as before, with no indication of having detected his presence.

At last she stood up, stretched herself, and stepped into the house. More time passed, with no further sight of her. Moving carefully, the spy worked back into full concealment behind the rock. There he took a much needed stretch of his own; glanced at his watch, and discovered that the sunless day was nearing its end; considered a moment, and then, his lips taking a determined set, moved away. Hidden behind brush, he picked his way eastward, skirting the homestead until well beyond it. Then he swung toward the ravine; let himself down its rocky, thorny side, and so came into the path. Now he could go to Lolita's home as if he had just come up from the camp. He was not yet through with her. On the contrary, he had hardly begun.

An adroit move, this, he complacently told himself. She would never know he had been watching her. He might not have felt so self-gratulatory had he known that he had been not only observer but observed; that Lolita had detected him up there the instant he moved, and, cat-like, had watched him continuously, both from the doorstep and from within the house, until he crept away.

After adjusting his somewhat disheveled clothing, he

stepped toward her home; then wheeled and walked toward the Box. It would be just as well to reconnoiter the camp and make sure that nobody was coming. Beside a boulder outside he did so. No man was in sight. He turned away, but halted. Voices were singing down there, singing an air old and familiar, and on the eddying breeze the words suddenly came clear and strong; words which, with the bass of MacLeod booming out the refrain, struck the listener as malicious ridicule:

> *"He left me for a damsel dark,*
> > *Damsel dark,*
> *Each Friday night they used to spark,*
> > *Used to spark,*
> *And now my love, once true to me,*
> *Takes that dark damsel on his knee—"*

"Damn you!" grated Van Horn, glaring toward the barrack. Had they seen him? Were they throwing more of their infernal derision at him? So pat was the song just at that moment that he felt every word directed at him. With another and more vicious curse he whirled away and ran from the sound. But the tormenting wind followed him, bearing more imagined mockery:

> *"Adieu, adieu, kind friends, adieu,*
> > *Adieu, adieu!*
> *I can no longer stay with you——"*

Then a shift in the breeze cut off the rest as if a door had shut.

Down in camp, the singers, grouped around open

bottles and wet glasses, finished the ditty and swung at once into another. And none of them ever knew that they had sung Van Horn's swan-song.

Van Horn himself, advancing for the last time on the house of Lolita, soon slowed from his precipitate pace, lapsing into his usual plod. With the silencing of those detested voices he forced his mind away from them, to fix it on the woman beyond. By the time he reached the door he was moving with outward calm. Without preliminary knock or word, he entered.

Lolita, seated at the table and frowningly peeling some fruit, started up in surprise. She had not anticipated his return. As she identified him, her frown swiftly deepened.

"Hullo," he greeted gruffly.

"Hah-lo. What you wanting here?" Her voice was inimical.

"You!" was his blunt response. He walked toward her.

Her right hand, holding the short knife, lifted breast high. Her eyes narrowed still more. But then, as she studied him, she relaxed a little.

"So-o-o?" she retorted, with a tilt of the head. "You wanting me, eh? An' jus' what you wanting with me?"

"Uh—well—why, I want *you*, understand?" he floundered, somewhat disconcerted, but dogged.

Her lips twitched. Suddenly she laughed outright.

"Ha ha ha ha! Tha's all, eh? Nothing but poor little me, eh? An' you jus' have to walk in an' say so, an' I am yours, eh? Ha ha ha!"

He reddened angrily. As ever, ridicule stung him. But he plunged onward, following up his blunt attack.

"Look here!" he ordered. "You hitch up with me, and you'll get somewhere. Quit fooling with that big bum of a MacLeod, and——"

"Who?" She caught at the name. "Cloud? Who is Cloud?"

"MacLeod. That big mutt. Jack. He's only kidding you——"

"Oh, ah, Jack! His name being Mack Cloud? Ah! An' your name——"

"Van Horn. Now listen, Lolita, you're a fool to fall for him. He's nothing! He'll leave you flat when he's through with you. He won't even tell you what you want to know about that box. Neither will Bill or anyone else—except me. I know as much about it as they do. And you know something about it yourself. And you want to get off this island. Well, then, let's get together."

Her face was a study as she listened. At first it turned stormy. Then it became a little puzzled, a bit crafty, and shrewdly interested, all at once.

"Jus' what you meaning, eh?" she probed.

"Just what I said. We get together, and we stick together all the way. We ditch that gang—and that brother of yours—and lift that box and fade out."

"Ah, so-o-o? An' what box you talking about?"

"Oh, quit kidding!" brusquely. "You know what I mean. And you know I heard what you said to Jack that night. He was too dumb to understand what you were getting at, but I'm wise. You know where that box is! You can't fool me. Well, now you give me the straight truth about it, and between us we'll yank it loose in no time."

Again she was quiet, watching him with a strangely penetrating look. Presently she asked:

"An' why shall I be telling you this, if I knowing so much? What good that doing me?"

"I can signal our schooner as well as Jack can. He's not the captain of our crowd."

"No? Then who is?"

"Nobody. The ship will come to me as soon as to anybody."

A cunning stroke, that, he thought, as he watched her. That ought to fetch her. And, after a brief interval of thought, apparently it did. Her gaze, which had gone to the door, came back to him, and she smiled as if yielding. But still she seemed a little dubious.

"Maybe you right, Van," she conceded. "But then, maybe you trying take 'vantage with poor little Lolita. Maybe, if I telling you what I know, you going get box an' leaving me. Maybe you jus' coming up to say all this, then you going back to tell your frien's what I tell you. You not telling *me* anything, Van, an' I don' know——"

She paused doubtfully.

"Huh! You think I'm trying to doublecross you, do you? I tell you I'm through with that bunch of mouthy bums!" The rancor of his tone left little room for doubt on that point. "And what is it you want to know? Ask me! I'm playing square with you, Lolita."

"We-e-ell, jus' why you all coming here, eh? An'
what you know about La Boîte, an' how you knowing
it? You got map, maybe, yes? What's it saying? Now
come, we sit down an' talk comfortable, eh? An' maybe
we having little drink? An' maybe we be ve-e-eery good
frien's 'fore very long. No no, not now!"

The knife, which had sunk, lifted again and hung
before her bosom as she laughingly retreated.

"Firs' we making sure we are frien's," she warned.
"You sit down!"

Van Horn, who had started forward as her tone became seductive, grudgingly obeyed. Business before
pleasure—particularly when pleasure looked dangerous.
While she passed to a shelf and selected a bottle and cups
he grinned slyly. And when she returned he grinned
openly, receiving in return a lingering glance which
nearly upset his tottering repression. But the wicked
little knife still was in her hand, and, for all her semblance of growing amiability, he sensed a readiness to
use it. So, playing for her complete confidence, he sat
stolidly and drank; then, with outward candor, talked.

Across the table, toying absently now with the fruit-
stained blade, she sat facing him and plying shrewd
question. And he, acknowledging no further allegiance
to his partners, told practically all he knew—with two
noteworthy exceptions. He failed to reveal the fact that
the schooner was long overdue, or to mention the digging of the hole beside the odd stone that morning.
The ship, he let her believe, would be available whenever needed. As for the discovery of the marker and
the subsequent failure to unearth the long sought cache,

that obviously was not the sort of thing to disclose. To let her know that he held no cards at all, that he was playing a queer hunch and running a rank bluff, would be hardly the way to win this game. Hence he ended his talk with an aggressive attempt to force her own hand.

"The gang will keep hunting till they find it," he asserted, "no matter where it is or who's got it! If they don't find it in the Box they'll look farther. And then they'll take it! And, what's more, they're almost through out there already, and it's up to us to move quick. You throw in with me, and we'll beat 'em out. Now you tell me what you know!"

For a little time she made no reply by word or look or expression. Face unreadable, she sat looking pensively down at the table top, the knife lightly jabbing the wood in restless reflex of her fingers. At length she eyed him speculatively through her lashes.

"Supposing, now, I not knowing where is that box. Supposing I only joking with Jack——"

"Cut that out!" He leaned forward with an angry scowl. "D'you think I'm a fool? You play square, or——"

"Or what, eh?" A thin smile edged her lips.

"What'll I do? I'll put the gang wise to you, that's what!"

"Ah, yes? But you lef' them already, you telling me——"

"But they don't know it! D'you think I'm simple enough to tell them that? Not much! They'll know it when I'm ready, not before! And unless you talk straight I'll go back right now and wake them up!"

Shoving back his chair, he arose as if to put his threat into immediate execution. But he took no step toward the door. Her eyes held him. She was smiling again, and into her gaze had come that leaping, luring fire which she could evoke at will.

"Don' go," she softly forbade. "Maybe Lolita jus' fooling, Van, to see what you say. Maybe I'm making up mind to trus' you, but you going too fas' for me. You are strong man, Van, very quick an' impatient, yes? An' very sharp too, eh? But maybe you more hones' with me than those man that jus' talking an' saying nothing. Oui, maybe tha's right, an' you an' me, we get along very good together, eh? Now you wait little minute, Van, you give me time for thinking."

She spoke musingly, as if voicing her thoughts and working to a definite decision, while her eyes still exerted their magnetic power. Now she turned her gaze from him, looking thoughtfully out through the doorway. The day had gone, and the fast failing light from the thick sky was dulling into dusk. A moment of silent debate—then suddenly she arose.

"You come, Van! I show you something!"

The knife dropped on the table, and she stepped toward him, motioning doorward. Instead of obeying her gesture, he seized her. An instant later he stood empty-handed, smitten by a queer feeling that he had tried to hold a snake. With a movement bewilderingly swift and sinuous she had squirmed from his grasp and moved six feet away.

"Not so fas', monsieur!" she warned. "You go now, you go see that thing 'fore it makes too dark—an' 'fore I change my mind! Quick, now!"

Imperiously she pointed to the door. And, with a short, eager laugh, he went. A step or two behind, she followed.

"Where to?" he asked, pausing in the opening and scanning the dimming field.

" 'Cross to the wall, jus' to left of the tree," she prompted. "You seeing little dark place, little darker than rock? We go in there, an' we see—what we see!"

A few seconds he stood peering at the designated spot; then, with a greedy grunt of discovery, started for it with fast strides. Behind him, she stooped and snatched up something from the darkness beyond the door jamb; stepped out, and swept one glance around. Nobody else was within sight or hearing. With quickened gait she glided after the hurrying treasure hunter.

Nearing the wall, Van Horn gave an exultant chuckle. The little dark place was an entrance—an entrance to a cave! A hidden cave—holding a chest of pirate gold! And he had been almost on top of it all the afternoon, never knowing it was there! Never mind, he knew it now, and he'd beaten everybody out in finding it, and when he got his hands on it——

His eyes glittered in avaricious triumph.

Behind him another pair of eyes gleamed, as the twice caught spy and confessed deserter baited himself onward with his own cupidity. He did not look back. For the time, indeed, that woman, so ardently desired hitherto, had become hardly more than a shadow.

Almost at a run, he reached the obscure-edged fold in the wall; found a short natural passageway angling acutely to the right; and, straining his gaze into the darkness of a small cavern at its end, pressed forward. Lolita halted a second at the edge of that masking outer shell of rock, took one more glance about, and vanished after him.

Hardly a full minute elapsed before she reappeared. Narrow eyed, tight mouthed, nostrils flaring with swift breaths, she walked rapidly back across the clearing. Into the house she darted with a sudden spring, as if evading something clutching at her from behind. To the table she ran, to snatch up the brandy bottle and gulp repeated draughts. As she set it down her face blazed with hate.

"Cochon! Espion!" she panted. "Mais oui—I show you something!"

CHAPTER XVI

THE ANT

Late, the limitless sea of cloud broke. At first in huge
fields of darkness, then in smaller segments, divided and
subdivided by cleaving currents of air, it rolled westward. In the shifting lanes of clear sky, stars gleamed
out and a lopsided moon flashed forth.

Down in the valley of L'Anse Gouverneur, another
light—an earthly light, yellowish and weak—shone
steadily from windows and doorways of a house; and
from that house broke fitful bursts of noise, swept away
to sea by the incessant wind. Now the sounds were
shouts of laughter, now choruses of song; voices of men
making merry in the night.

Up on the brush-grown, rock-strewn hill to westward of the Boîte du Mort, something moved. Slowly,
toilsomely, it snailed along an ancient, disused path.
That old track, worming away to the uninhabited cove
just north of the Box, would be hardly noticeable even
in the brilliant light of noonday; and now it was as
invisible as the random trace of a foraging ant. Yet,
even as the ant could follow its own road at need, so this
mysterious creature found its course whither it willed
to go. Too, it worked as determinedly as any ant, and

with the same tenacious purpose: to bear away and conceal something—something inert, something heavier than itself. With inflexible persistence it felt its way along, and with desperate strength it dragged its burden toward the chosen resting place. Often it paused for breath, and sometimes it turned to the spying moon a face fraught with tragedy. But ever it renewed its endeavor.

At length its labor became lighter, for now the ground sloped sharply to the sands and the waters, and the load moved with less effort. Down it worked, and down; halting, by and by, beside the beach. Yet the exertion had not reached an end. Greater stress waited beyond, for the telltale sand was not the goal.

Resuming motion, the ant worked now to the right, and, foot by foot, crawled along the steep slope projecting outward to form the northward wall of the bay—a blunt promontory, which dropped below the restless surface of the sea to unguessable depths. Out to the very tip of this projection crept the toiler, ever hauling its incubus, and, toward the last, climbing with it, pushing it, lifting it with sobbing straining effort, to the top of a vertical cliff. Then, for a time, bearer and borne lay almost equally motionless.

Finally the overworn insect resumed its task. In the thin light of the momentarily helpful moon it found a large rock, ponderous, yet movable, and rolled it nearly to the edge of the crag. In the succeeding darkness it carefully tied a short length of rope around the sodden thing it would conceal, then about the stone. This done, it pushed each to the verge. It balanced the rock—and shoved. As it staggered back, the bulky object which it had brought there whisked off the brink and was gone. Below sounded a sullen splash.

The next spread of moonlight found the bluff empty. Back near the crescent of sand, the ant was wearily retracing its course. At the end of the beach it paused, drooping, eyeing a smooth bare stone which dipped into the water. Presently it drew from its body a drab garment, dropped it, moved outward on the stone, stepped into the shallows. Knee deep, it walked along the submerged sand, then stooped and reclined. Now, lying back with head on shore, it had become a mermaid; a seductive nymph of the sea, reposing quiescent on the edge of the strand, face upturned, bare arms relaxed along the wet margin, breasts moving gently in the wavelets, body clasped in the throbbing embrace of Ocean—but unable to lose in that dalliance the haggard fear staring from deep, dark eyes.

Of a sudden she started up and floundered back to the rock, where she sprang out as if some awful thing had come groping for her beneath the waves. Panting, she looked fearfully at the water, then out at the bluff; snatched up the dingy dress, huddled it under an arm, and stepped rapidly away.

After a few paces she slowed, picking a way around saw-edged stones. Thereafter she walked deliberately back up the funnel-formed valley and onward to the top of the hill. Her dress, dangling at haphazard, caught now and then on brittle brush; but to the resultant rents she gave no thought. Unclothed as Eve, she passed through the thorn-fanged, cactus-clawed, stone-knifed wilderness, uncut and unscratched. Though still very tired, she was stronger of body, surer of movement, and clearer of mind than before resting among the waves.

At length she reached a clearing, half rimmed by stone, wherein stood a lightless house. Narrowly she scanned that gloomy cottage, and intently she listened. No sound came, save the flutter of dry leaves whispering eerily in the night wind. Her gaze went to the natural wall, dwelling on a spot where the moon, now shining steadily, cast a shadow darker than the others. Slowly, as if forcing her feet to a course from which they rebelled, she moved toward it. That shadow marked the portal to a chamber where certain things must be done.

While still a dozen steps distant, however, she shrank away; swerved, and leaped into a frenzied dash for the shelter of the house. Nothing had moved. Nothing was there which could move. But she could not enter that hole in the wall again this night.

Within doors, she struck a light, hands shaking; seized a bottle, and drained it. A minute or two she leaned on the table, while the fiery liquor coursed through her. Then, moving fast, she shut and barred door and windows, locking out the night; threw on the crude hearth her drab garment, poured on it some oil, and set it ablaze. With a brief roar the friendly fiend of fire obliterated forever that faded dress and, with it, several red stains.

Then, with a long breath, she passed to her bed. For a time she sat on its edge, her fingers automatically liberating the cone of heavy hair tightly pinned about her head, while her eyes, somewhat glassy now, fixedly stared at something, or nothing, across the room. Later she lay over and relaxed, seeking sleep. But her arms and legs kept twitching, her hands clutching aimlessly at the thin mattress, her lids jumping open despite efforts to keep them closed. And the little lamp, holding at bay the shadows lurking along the walls, burned on.

Down in the Boîte du Mort, the house which had been alight was dark and the festive voices were still. Up on the hill to westward, a few bushes were broken and others bent by the passage of a heavy body, and a number of small stones were dislodged by the same dragging weight; but no eyes save those of incurious lizards would ever note these slight alterations in the discontinued byway. On the hard soil of the upland, on the sands of the untenanted bay, were no footprints. Along the rocky promontory the waves danced as usual, bearing no trace of the plunging disturbance which had momentarily broken their rhythmic beat. Over all, moon and stars went their westward way, loftily disdainful of the creepings of earthbound insects. They alone had seen. And they told no tales.

Chapter XVII

MISSING

Four men sat at breakfast, eating rapidly. Outside flamed fast rising sun. The sky was cloudless, the gray blanket of yesterday having vanished over night. Heat was waxing minute by minute; and the erstwhile drones now were in haste to recommence their habitual search among the rocks—haste incited not by hope but by knowledge that the coolness of the shortening hill-shadows was a boon to be snatched while it lasted.

Devlin, red eyed and qualmish-stomached as the aftermath of too assiduous devotion to the bottle, was first to shove back from the board, eyeing his half-eaten provender with distaste. A copious drink of water, a cigarette lighting, a gingerly adjustment of the helmet to his throbbing head, and he walked out. Once outside, he made no further move toward the waiting work, but squinted uphill toward the LaFlamme path.

Mallory, heavy lidded and sluggish, soon joined him. MacLeod and Spearman, moving sleepily, but showing no other effects of late hours, came out together. The impromptu concert of the afternoon, starting spontaneously as a break from oppressive quiescence, had developed into an evening of wassail wherein Devlin and Mallory strove to drink each other under the table; a contest which had been inconclusively terminated by the exhaustion of the liquor supply, but which had inspired the participants to noisy antics precluding sleep for anyone before midnight.

Now, as the three emerged, each followed Devlin's example by wasting a minute or two in contemplating the closed end of the Box. Nowhere up there moved any form. No sound came on the breeze. Unspeaking, they trudged away down to the waiting line of pegs.

Throughout the morning they pursued their slow quest without result, occasionally glancing back at the camp or up at the northeastern corner beyond which stood the hidden home of Lolita. Near noon, they set their pegs and returned to the barrack with strides a little longer and quicker than usual. Within the house they stood a minute or two in silence. Everything was just as they had left it.

"I think," said Spearman, "I'll take a little walk."

He stepped out again. MacLeod, with a slight nod, followed. They turned northward, while Mallory, in the doorway, hesitated.

"And I think I'll take my swim as usual," differed Devlin, taking his towel from its nail. "No need of all of us going up there."

Again he drank thirstily from the water pail. Mallory wavered an instant longer, then reached to his own bath cloth. Together they journeyed seaward.

The taller pair said nothing until they had surmounted the slope and turned to the west. As they trod the cross path, Jack asked:

"What d'you think of it, Larry?"

"I'm not thinking yet. Just getting curious."

They walked on without further converse.

Beyond the gateway Lawrence slowed, looking about the place, which to him was unknown ground. Jack, with the perfunctory glance of familiarity, walked to the house. Several paces in advance of his comrade, he stepped through the doorway without warning.

Lolita, sitting at table with head in hands, sprang up with a sharp intake of breath. So violent was her start that her chair fell over, and a dish holding food—for which she evidently had little appetite, for it was virtually untouched—slid almost off the board. Face blanched, dark-ringed eyes wide with fright, she stared at him as at a Gorgon.

"Que diable!" she gasped. "Oh—eh—you, Jack? Mon Dieu! Why—why you jumping so sudden at me, eh? You scare me, you bad man, you!"

She forced a little laugh, and her tension relaxed a trifle, though she still stood rigid. A glance about the room showed the intruder that nobody else was present. He looked at her again, mildly puzzled.

"Pardon me for not ringin' the bell and handin' my card to the butler," he drawled. "But what's ailin' you? Gettin' nervous?"

"Oh—I—I have bad night, Jack, I dreaming very bad, I— Oh, I hating this place, Jack, it making me sick, sick! You take me away— Sacré! Who coming?"

Spearman was entering, glancing about as Jack had done. The latter, without turning his head, whimsically replied:

191

"Oh, just the minister. I was thinkin' this might be a good day for us to get married, so I brought him up to do the job at the fashionable hour, high noon. But if you've let another man cut me out it's all off."

Her gaze dwelt intently on Spearman, then came back to the lightly smiling but steadily watching fellow whose habit was to tease. Of a sudden her own lips twitched, and her head went back in a burst of wild laughter. Peal after peal rang, sharp, high pitched, hysterical mirth which seemed born not from amusement but from overwrought nerves. At the end she stooped and fumbled her chair upright, then sank into it, wiping away tears.

"Some day—some day you making me laugh to death, Jack," she reproached. "But what you meaning about another man?"

"Well, now, far be it from me to insinuate that you could ever love anybody but me, you know. But still, one of our bright young men has sort of wandered away from the parental rooftree, and we happened to think he might have been seekin' your joyous society and forgotten the way home. So we thought we'd come and get him before your—ah—brother returned. This happens to be Saturday. You know what that means."

She frowned at him in apparent bewilderment.

"What man you talking about, Jack?"

"Van Horn."

"Van 'Orn? An' who is he?"

"Er—why, now that I think of it, I introduced him to you down at camp as Roche Brasiliano. Short, broad, with blue eyes and——"

192

"Oh!" Quick light flooded her face. "Ah, oui! The crazy one!"

"Crazy?" thrust Spearman, speaking for the first time. "What do you mean?"

"I mean, monsieur, he's crazy! I see him once here, one night, here at this very house! 'Foretime, when you come here, Jack—when you come wanting supper, you remember——" She turned again to MacLeod. "When I go shutting door, that Roche is jus' there, outside. An' he looking at me, an' his face all black, all puff up, an' his eyes—mon Dieu, they crazy like the devil! An' then he go running away, very fas', very quiet, an' I never seeing him no more. An' I don' want to! He's crazy, believe me!"

They stared at her, then glanced quickly at each other. Jack's look was questioning. Lawrence, after a few seconds of thought, nodded.

"He was out of the house that night, Jack," he recalled. "Just about dark he sneaked out. We didn't watch him, of course. But he was gone some time."

"The devil you say!" muttered MacLeod. Then, to her: "That's what you saw when you said you were lookin' at nothin'? Why didn't you tell me?"

" 'Cause I thinking you run out after him, Jack, you maybe have fight, an'—an' I wanting you stay with me. I not wanting stay here. Oh, par Dieu, how I hating this place, so lonesome! An' after that, I think if I tell you you won' believe me, you think I jus' trying make you jealous. So I say nothing. An' I never seeing that man since that time. Maybe he's scare to come back, I don' know. But he not here las' night, an' if you lost

193

him don' ask me where he gone. Maybe he running wild somewhere, jumping in sea, or something. Plenty man done that in these islan's 'fore now."

Again the men looked at each other, this time with startled expressions. Her words were almost an echo of Spearman's warning—ages ago, it now seemed—to the snappish Devlin and the morose Van Horn down on the beach; a warning of which, though Jack had not been present at the time, he had later heard. Moreover, those words spoke plainly a foreboding thought which, during the forenoon hours just past, had tried to insinuate itself into both their minds, only to be peremptorily denied admittance. Even now they would not concede the probability of its truth; but they could not deny its possibility. There was a pregnant silence.

Jack turned, and, head bowed as if in thought, walked to the end of the room. As he went, he covertly surveyed everything before him: floor, walls, furniture, clothes, everything standing or lying about. Nowhere was the least indication of any visit by the absentee. Returning, he remarked:

"Well, Larry, I guess we'd better apologize and toddle along. Wherever Van went to, it wasn't here. Sorry we scared you, Lolita; but I wasn't thinkin' you'd be so jumpy."

Pausing beside her, he laid hand on her shoulder.

"Listen, girl," he went on, his voice unusually serious. "It's up to you to get out of here soon. I'd hate to have you go before I do, but you'd better be movin' somewhere—down to town, or any place where there are other folks. Your nerves are gettin' all shot; and it's no wonder, the way you're livin' in this godforsaken hole."

An uncontrollable quiver ran through her. She sprang up.

"Don' I know it?" she cried shrilly. "Sacré, one day I going crazy too, me! This place is hell! Rock an' lizard, sun an' wind, nothing else, nothing! An' when you gone, Jack—then——"

She broke off as suddenly as she had begun, gripping hard at the edge of the table, gripping even harder at her self-control. After a silent struggle she added, in a tone of restraint:

"But you never mind, now. Maybe some other time, soon, we have little talk, jus' you an' me, 'bout me going away. Now I not feeling very good, Jack. Maybe nex' week—you come see me again."

Spearman, with a slight smile, swung about and walked through the doorway, giving her opportunity to speak more confidentially if she wished. But she said nothing further; and Jack lounged outward.

"All right, girlie," he assented. "Any little old time you want me, let me know. And you take a brace. Take a drink. Take somethin' for what ails you, anyway. So long."

She gave him no answer. Rigid as a statue, she stood there in her nightgown-like white garment, watching him depart. Outside he paused to look around, his forehead creased with puzzled meditation. His roving gaze came to rest on the oddly shadowed bit of stone wall.

"Wait a minute, Larry," he called. "Say, Lolita, what's this place over yonder in the wall? A cave, or what?"

Spearman, several paces away, stopped. Lolita stood dumb. Jack continued to peer at the mysterious recess. With a dragging effort, the woman inside forced herself to approach.

"Jus' a little hole where I keeping food. Tha's all," she asserted.

"Uh-huh. Well, let's go look at it, Larry. I'm always sort of curious about caves."

"Oh, all right."

They strolled across the clearing. Lolita clenched her hands until the nails cut the palms. Then she moved swiftly after them.

"You mus' have care, Jack! Don't step on the fruits —or break bottle! It makes dark in there, an'— Wait, I show you!"

She ran ahead, entering the concealed corridor first. So narrow was it that the shoulders of the following men almost scraped against the smooth sides.

At the point where it broadened into the cavern she stopped, blocking further entrance, still keeping her face turned from the men.

"You see," she indicated with a nod. "You walk care-less, you spoiling something. An' food mus' not be spoil'. It cos' too much."

Craning necks, they looked over her head into a prosaic pantry. Solid walls and domed roof, perhaps a dozen feet wide, it contained a jumble of red clay jars and flagons and pitchers, a few bottles of wine, some yams, an assortment of fruits, and similar foodstuffs in or out of containers. Everything was on the earth floor, virtually covering it.

196

"Uh-huh," grunted Jack, stepping back. "As a lazaret it's good, but as a cave it's a fraud. And without meanin' to criticize your housekeepin' I'll say the arrangement's rotten. Make a few shelves, now, with pole legs under 'em, and you could stack this stuff so it wouldn't be all under foot; handier to get at, too."

Although he did not suspect it, the suggested arrangement was nothing new. In fact, it had actually existed there at sunrise. Now the shelves and their pole supports lay hidden among rocks only a few rods distant. The deceptively disordered condition of the place at present was but camouflage, cunningly contrived to conceal certain dark stains on the smooth yellow soil. And the woman who had created that confusion had also invented her explanation.

"The ground keeping things cooler than shelf," she declared.

"Well, all right. It's your place, not mine. Come on, Larry. So long, kid."

The men turned, walked out, and left her. As their footsteps receded she swayed and leaned against the stone, white and trembling.

She had known that the disappearance of Van Horn must inevitably bring Jack here to inquire; she had suspected that he was aware of the existence of this grotto; she had prepared her defense accordingly, and now it had proved efficacious. But the ordeal had been much harder than she had expected. That abrupt entrance, catching her at an unguarded moment, had given her a bad start. The unforeseen arrival of Spearman had been a second shock. And there had been something in Spearman's silent appraisal, something in MacLeod's lazy but searching glances, which had sent panic darting along every nerve. Now that the investigators were gone she stood weak and wan, swept by successive chills.

On the way back to camp, and thence to the beach, the men spoke no word. Even after reaching the sand, Spearman still said nothing. In an absent way he laid aside his towel, undressed, and waded into the sportive sea. MacLeod, answering a question from Mallory, briefly declared:

"No trace."

With that he, too, immersed himself. And not another word would he say until the bath was over. Then, when all had gathered in a patch of shade, Mallory and Devlin, sober faced, listened to a short recital of the incidents of the call on Lolita. It was MacLeod who talked. When he finished, Spearman sat looking far out to sea; Mallory picked at the sand, his expression worried; Devlin rubbed his jaw and scowled. At length Mallory asked:

"What do you make of it, Larry?"

"I don't make head or tail of it, so far. There's nothing to get hold of."

Mallory lifted and dropped handfuls of sand. After an interval he said:

"There's this much to get hold of: He went off his nut yesterday morning; we all know that. And he made a sneak while we were asleep, for no sensible reason that I can see. And he's been away all night, and gone without supper or breakfast—or dinner, now. And it looks to me as if he was cuckoo."

198

"When has he been otherwise?" sneered Devlin.

Another long pause, broken at last by Spearman's calm voice:

"Granting that that's so, what follows? Either he's running wild or—he's killed himself. If it's the first, we'll soon hear of it. Somebody will see him; and in a little island like this, news travels like wildfire, and Lolita's man will bring it home. If he's jumped overboard we'll never find him. He'll wash out to sea.

"There's another possibility. He may have taken the notion, sane or insane, to quit us. He may have gone to the harbor and hired some fishing boat to carry him over to Kitts. He had some money. And what he said yesterday about sticking here might have been just a blind. Personally I think that's improbable. Still, it's possible."

"But in that case the gendarmes would nail him, wouldn't they?" objected Mallory.

"Most likely. And if they did we'll soon know it. They'll be over here investigating.

"The only other possibilities that I can see, besides insanity or death or a break for other parts, are that he's gotten hurt or that somebody's done him in."

"Who?" demanded MacLeod.

"I'm wondering. If this island was like most of the Antilles I'd think maybe it was some bad nigger after money. But Thirsty said this was mostly a white man's island, and the people, although they were poor as dirt, were a pretty honest and decent lot. Besides, as far as we know, nobody but us—and Lolita and her dummy—knew he even existed. And we know none of us did

him up, and we've no valid reason to say the folks up
the hill did."

"None at all," asserted Mallory. "That's too far-
fetched."

Spearman continued gazing out to sea.

"And as for his hurting himself very badly, that
doesn't seem likely either," he concluded. "There's
hardly any way he could, except by breaking himself
upon a rock; and it would have to be a mighty bad
smash to keep him from crawling back. And there
would be no reason for him to go climbing into dangerous spots, anyway. He wasn't fond of exercise, or interested in anything outside this Box. So— Well, there you
are. All we actually know is that we don't know anything. He's gone and we're guessing."

Devlin scratched the back of his neck, then jumped
up impatiently.

"Oh, what are we getting all hot and bothered about
him for?" he demanded. "He's big enough and ugly
enough to take care of himself, I'll say. Chances are that
he's made a sneak over to town to get a good souse and
a hot woman. He knew we'd kid him to death if he
tried to make Lolita, so he went A W O L, under-
handed as usual, and while we sit here frying our brains
he's giving us the horse-laugh. He'll come back, all
right, like any other bad penny. Come on, let's eat!"

So they arose and went. But, as they climbed, each
of them—even Devlin—cast glances to right and left
and up ahead, looking for the man who was missing.

Chapter XVIII

MOONSHINE

"Non, monsieur. No stranger has come to Gustavia."

Montez, standing at the door of the barrack, thus succinctly demolished two possible explanations of the absence of Van Horn. His opaque eyes dwelt unwinking on the steady gaze of Spearman, and his pocked visage was expressionless as ever.

"You are sure?" quizzed Lawrence. "He could not be drinking secretly somewhere?"

"C'est impossible, monsieur. So small is the town, and so seldom comes a new face, that the whole place would buzz at sight of one. I should hear of it."

A momentary silence. Spearman looked out across the hilltops, which were grayed by evening shadows. The other three, lounging about on cots, eyed Montez, who in turn glanced suggestively down at the basket of liquors he had brought. Nobody, however, offered to open a bottle.

"And there are no other towns?" the questioner pursued.

"Tiny villages only." The barefoot fellow shrugged contemptuously. "L'Orient, Grand Fond, Saint Jean, Flamand, a few even smaller, all on the east coast, all farming and fishing places. The fishers come to Gustavia to sell their catches, so they bring all news."

"I see. Well, have a drink."

"Merci!" The acceptance came with alacrity. "Cognac, s'il vous plaît."

After tossing a stiff measure of brandy down his throat he licked his lips, grinned, and departed.

"What's the dope, Larry?" queried Mallory.

Spearman translated the conversation into English.

"Well," said Devlin, "that narrows it down a lot. Van Horn didn't skip out on a boat, and he didn't go on a spree. And he can't be running loose, either. So he's either hurt or dead—unless——"

He hesitated.

"Unless what?" prompted MacLeod.

"Well, he may be hiding out somewhere in the brush——"

"Without food? Without water? He's got to have water, man, and he can't get it anywhere but at a house."

"I know that. But he might get it without being seen. He could sneak to a cistern at night, and maybe steal a hen or a young goat for meat. Or he might do better than that. He might locate some isolated house and terrorize the owners into feeding him and keeping him there. Some lunatics are cunning as the devil; and he always was sly. He's strong, too. Those punches he gave me yesterday nearly knocked me blind, even though they landed wrong. Now if he should get hold of some old folks who couldn't stand up to him, what couldn't he do to them?"

Spearman started. Through his mind flashed a dread vision: that of an isolated house on the headland of Saline, tenanted by a helpless old man and a defenseless girl, tyrannized by a maniac. Van Horn had spied on Jack and Lolita; might he not also have spied, yesterday, on Lawrence and Céleste? Crouching unseen somewhere near by, he could have watched the careless stroller over the divide; could have followed, lain hidden until the visitor returned, then gone down there. . . .

The inevitable conclusion made the thinker flinch. The resultant excitement would kill old Pierre. And Céleste, captive in the power of a madman. . . .

Behind him his companions were arguing. The room was fast growing dark. With unobtrusive speed he picked from a near shelf his electric torch and stepped out. Making the best of the faint light remaining, he hurried up the hill. Montez had vanished. Along the eastward cross path he loped, almost reaching the top of the pass before it became necessary to switch on his torch. By that time the rapidly thickening dusk had become dense darkness: the gloom preceding moonrise. He clambered onward by the aid of his battery, never pausing until he found himself out of the brush and beside the edged boulder. There he stopped, hot, breathless, but relieved. Down on the headland all was well—silent.

At least, all looked peaceful from his eyrie. In the obscurity below him, the little square of window and the rectangle of open door showed a light burning serenely within the house. Yet, as the observer relaxed and recovered breath, his nerves tensed again. On the breeze came a disquieting sound: a loud laugh in the tones of a man.

Pierre Blanchard, unable to walk without losing breath, manifestly could not laugh with that vigor. Lawrence scowled, peered narrowly, listened intently, and heard the noise again.

Mouth tight, he descended the rough path, shading his light with his free hand. Reaching level ground, he extinguished the telltale illumination and advanced stealthily to a spot where he could look in at the window. There he almost grunted aloud in self-derision.

A strange man was there; two of them, in fact; but neither was a madman. They were merely a couple of Barths countrymen making a Saturday night call.

Father and son, they seemed; a grizzled, squatty old-ster, sallow faced, and a loutish young fellow of similar physique and features. The father talked, in droning monotone, to Blanchard père, somewhere out of sight. It was the son who laughed, in fitful, jarring outbursts seemingly arising from self-consciousness, or perhaps from desire to appear jovial; for the banal converse of the elder held little humor and no wit. If his intention was to simulate ingenuous amiability, however, his inane mirth served only to betray him; for at each repetition an innate harshness was more noticeable. After vainly seeking sight of Céleste, whose clear voice sounded once in a brief reply, the man outside gave critical attention to the laugher.

Bristling black hair, low brow, restless dark eyes, hard mouth, mulish jaw, ox-like shoulders; physical strength, mental obstinacy, mediocre intelligence, coarse sensibilities; such was the instinctive verdict of the unseen judge. Another moment of observation, and to the man in the dark came a conviction which caused his brows to draw down. This bumpkin, despite old Blanchard's violently expressed opposition to the coming of any man a-wooing, was here for that very purpose. His eyes, though shifting often, were continually darting to the same spot, to linger there as long as they dared; and on his flat lips, between laughs, rested a simpering smile. Manifestly these dumb devoirs were not being paid to unlovely Pierre.

Silently Lawrence moved, seeking a line of view approximating that of the tongue-tied youth. After a bit of maneuvering he caught sight of Céleste. She was sitting far down the room, with hands folded in her lap; looking aside now and then, apparently at her father, who still was not visible; at other times gazing with no particular interest at the loquacious caller, or meditatively contemplating the floor. So far as the would-be gallant was concerned, she gave no indication that she even knew of his existence.

There came a pause. Céleste looked again at the older man, then let her gaze rove out the window, to rest on the blank blackness where lurked the watcher. For an instant he experienced a shamed sense of guilt, as if caught in the act of eavesdropping; and, for the first time, realized that he actually was playing the rôle of spy. And, although the unbroken serenity of the girl proved that she had not discovered him out there, he began a noiseless movement of withdrawal. But then came something that halted him.

As abruptly as he had laughed, the hitherto wordless caller blurted:

"I sold some goats today! I made two hundred francs!"

His tone was loudly braggart. Automatically Lawrence calculated, then smiled. With francs at twenty-five to the dollar, the paltry profit amounted to eight dollars American. His smile widened as Pierre dryly asked:

"Cash?"

"Non," reluctantly admitted the financier. "I took store goods. I made more that way."

"Umph!" was Blanchard's sarcastic rejoinder.

At once the older visitor took up the conversation; so quickly, indeed, and so tactlessly, that the sequence seemed prearranged, for Pierre's reception of the boast was hardly the cue to the following speech.

"Josué is a very shrewd dealer, a very sharp money-maker, Pierre, ami. A very fine husband he will make for some lucky girl. And a girl with no *dot*, she will be most lucky to catch him. Such a girl as yours, now, who can bring nothing to her man, she would be the envy of all the women of this island if she could marry such an industrious and thrifty young man as Josué Thibaut."

Amazed by the baldness of it, Lawrence blinked. That old coot in there was trying to match his sappy son with Céleste! The thing was downright indecent! Céleste herself thought so, too, if her flaming cheeks told her feelings. From his present position the listener could not see the amorous Josué, but he could picture the silly smile which now must be on his mouth. Well, Pierre would soon knock it off.

But the expected outburst did not come. Instead, Blanchard spoke in a weary tone.

"We have spoken of that matter before now, Ruben. My mind is not changed."

"Well, it is time you changed it, sick as you are——"

"I will not change it until I am dead. No, nor after that. We shall say no more about it, Ruben."

His voice still was indifferent, though conclusive. Again Lawrence marveled. Pierre had seemed so irascible on the subject of advances to his daughter that his present calmness was momentarily inexplicable. But then, thinking further, the American sensed the situation.

These old fellows were Frenchmen of the old school. And in their code this matter of arranging the marriages of their children, this talk of dowries, this fencing for position—although the thrust of the elder Thibaut savored more of the cutlass than of the rapier—all this was according to custom. The barefaced broaching of the matter in the presence of the young couple themselves might be in poor taste, but was perfectly permissible. The visit of a young man accompanied by his father also was good form, particularly when that father had made known his object to the girl's parent. But for that same young man, or any other, to come as a free lance and seek to make love independently—that would be an insult to parental authority, and, perhaps, to the girl herself. That would make of him a "love-sick mooncalf," or worse, in the eyes of the elders. Quite so.

And Céleste was not saying a word. Since she had not been addressed, it was not her place to speak. It was evident, however, that the courtship of Josué Thibaut was not to her taste; her indignant color and her straight look in his direction made that plain. The finality of her father's tone made it equally manifest that the suggested alliance would not have his consent. Old Thibaut was silenced. Young Thibaut found no food for mirth now, either. In the ensuing silence Lawrence recommenced his retreat; and this time he made it good.

The moon now was peeping over the eastern horizon. By the time he had climbed back up the path the clear orb of night was above the edge of the ocean and flooding all his little world with radiance. He paused beside the stone on which he had first found Céleste; then sat down on it and gazed at the solid bulk of the headland and the shimmering sea beyond. Now that he knew all to be well down there, he would sit here in solitude and ponder over the disappearance of Van Horn.

But he did nothing of the sort. His mind refused to grapple again with that problem. Instead, it played about the girl whose imaginary peril had brought him across the divide in hot haste, only to withdraw unseen. The useless exertion of the dash did not matter. The knowledge that she was safe justified the effort.

Yet how long would she be safe from men? That young Thibaut, for instance, had a distinct element of cruelty in his ensemble. When old Pierre should die, as he might at any moment, Josué might be back here, unaccompanied and unrestrained. Or, if he stayed away, there might be others, even less welcome, even more ready to take advantage of an unprotected girl. Over at the harbor, Blanchard had said, were men not even white: West Indian negroes. What was to prevent them. . . .

He shook himself, trying to throw off these forebodings. What ailed him, that he was becoming so worrisome? What was Céleste to him? Just another casual acquaintance, like many others who had passed and gone—— But no, not like those others. She was in a class by herself, sincere and genuine, unversed in the wiles and artifices and hypocrisies which had engendered in him a wariness against the whole feminine sex. Yet she was of no particular consequence to him.

Voices floated up from below. The Thibauts were leaving. A brief babble at the door; then their squatty shapes, gnome-like from this high angle, trudged across the open space, heading for the beach path which ran eastward to the valley of the salt pond. In their gait was something glum and grumpy. At least, it seemed so to the man on the rock; and he chuckled. Near the water they faded from sight behind a bump of earth. His gaze came back to the house.

In the doorway stood a small figure, dark against the lamplit interior. For a moment or two it remained there as if gazing pensively out and up. Then it moved back, and the door closed. Beyond the open window the light burned a few minutes longer, then vanished.

Once more he sought the Thibauts, and found them: small dark dots, well along the white sands of the bay, which presently moved inland and were gone. Now remained only lifeless land, vacant ocean, stars and moon and little clouds. But he did not arise and depart. He contemplated the far reaches of the rippling waters, across which he and his mates had come and again must go: the trackless road to all the world. That way lay escape from the hopeless sterility and futility of this lost island.

Suppose, now, Céleste should sail away to the American island of Saint Thomas. Over there was a colony of her own people, among whom she would soon feel at home, and where she would find life far more happy than here—and much more safe. The young fishermen over there made good money, too, and if she should find one whom she liked. . . .

He frowned. Somehow that thought was unpleasant.

Suppose, instead, she should journey even farther, all the way to the States. The cyclopean proportions of the cities and the roaring maelstrom of their activities would daze her at first, fresh from the rustic simplicity of her isle. But she would soon adapt herself to the new conditions. Although she might be of peasant stock, her mentality was not obtuse. Given opportunity to observe the modes of American life, how swiftly she would absorb and adopt them!

He visioned her stylishly gowned in something blue, something that really fitted her, with silken stockings and dainty shoes, and a jaunty little hat instead of that enormous straw or that hooded capote, and her hair tastefully coiffured (he would never let her murder that wonderful hair with a "bob") and her face alight with vivacious enjoyment of living. . . .

His breath came faster, and his pulses pounded with a strange exhilaration. As he continued to gaze out over the sea his eyes held a steady glow. Through his rumpled hair, tossed by the ceaseless trade wind, the moonlight struck evanescent glints. He was hatless. And, as every West Indian islander knows, odd things may come to the man who sits under the tropic moon without a hat.

Chapter XIX

AN OLD MAN'S PROPHECY

MacLeod, rising from the breakfast table, filled his pipe, looked at his watch, and squinted out at the eastern hills. It was Sunday, and, although no revelry had taken place last night—for, with the shadow of Van Horn's disappearance hourly darkening, none had been in festive mood—all had slept late this morning. The hour now was nine-thirty.

"The time has come," he announced, "when I'm goin' to do a little ramblin'."

"Where?" asked Mallory.

"Oh, hither and yon. Far enough to make sure that Van's not lyin' busted up somewhere where we ought to find him. Maybe over those hills yonder to eastward——"

"I'm going over there myself today," interrupted Spearman. "Thought of it last night."

Jack's eyes rested speculatively on him a moment. His sudden departure and long absence last night were still unexplained.

"Well, all right. You know the ground over there better than I do, I guess. I'll go the other way, towards the harbor. And what about you birds, Daniel and William?"

"I'm staying right here," asserted Devlin. "I've had enough sun this week. If you find anything, sing out. Until then I'm taking my ease."

"Me too," agreed Mallory. "Somebody ought to be here, anyway, in case anything breaks. For all we know, Van might come back here any minute. Or if some gendarme or some other snooper should come nosing around, we don't want him walking off with whatever he can pick up."

"There's nothing worth stealing, unless it's the grub," said Spearman, "and that's running pretty low."

The others looked ruefully at the depleted shelves.

"All the more reason to watch it," opined Dan.

"Not to mention the bottles, of course," grinned Jack. "Well, all right, you tipplin' topplin' topers, stick around. If any ladies come yearnin' for me before I get back, entertain 'em with charades. And if you, Larry, find anything you can't handle, let us all know. So long."

With another quizzical look at Spearman, he donned his helmet and stepped out. Then he halted abruptly, looking at the doorstep on which he had just trodden. His descending foot had squashed something.

"Well, well, see what's here!" he murmured, stooping and rising. "Apples! Juicy golden apples! That's right thoughtful of a certain little lady, I'll inform the cock-eyed world. Four of 'em. Just one apiece. She's playin' no favorites. But I planted my hoof on one of 'em, thereby reducin' my share to an unappetizin' wreck. You lazybugs draw the prizes. Catch 'em!"

He tossed them to Mallory, nearest to the door, who

caught them with the ease of a former baseball player, then examined them with interest not shared by the others. They were luscious looking pomes, resembling apples from the temperate zone, and more tempting than any of the dull-hued tropic fruits hitherto seen. But Devlin gave them only a cursory gaze, and Spearman hardly glanced at them. All were full fed.

"Tell her to put them on the table the next time," yawned Dan. "I want my fruit as the first entry, not as an also-ran. The service in this hotel is getting worse every day."

"You're an ungrateful cuss," Jack grinned. "Well, here goes nothing."

He departed, to climb the western slope by almost the same route taken previously by Van Horn. Spearman, after fingering his bristly jaw, got out his shaving kit and put it to use. Devlin took another drink, and Mallory somnolently smoked.

"Say, Bill," suggested Dan, in a loud stage whisper, "let's split that last can of crabmeat between us while these energetic detectives are out. It's the only thing left that I could relish, and they won't know about it till they get back."

"I'm with you," rejoined Bill, in similar tone. "I think they've both got dates somewhere, anyway."

"Go to it, bully boys," laughed Spearman. "I'm off crabmeat for life. Haven't touched it for years. The last time I did, it nearly killed me."

"Bad?" asked Devlin, rather unnecessarily.

"Oh, it looked all right, but it laid me out for three days, and if the doc hadn't known his business my retirement would have been permanent, complete and final."

He stepped over to the lone tin under discussion and inspected it. So far as he could discern, it was absolutely tight.

"Good enough, I guess," he judged, setting it back. "But don't let it stand in the can one minute after you open it. Well, I'm off. Have a hot time while I'm gone."

"No chance of anything else," responded Bill, wiping his forehead. "So long. Behave yourself."

Spearman left, with a casual wave of one hand. For the next hour he worked systematically on and around the northern hill; that hill over which he had made more than one circuitous approach to the Blanchard home. Tardily had come the thought that perhaps Van Horn, lured by inquisitiveness, had ascended this height and stumbled to his death. There was more than one hazardous place where a man falling headlong could break neck or skull. The searcher left no such trap unexamined; and, now that he was looking for them, he found them unexpectedly numerous. When the possibilities were exhausted he followed the familiar route across the divide and down to the headland.

His coming was unobserved, except by a few goats. Céleste probably was busy with preparations for dinner. So, without making known his arrival, he reconnoitered the eastern side of the hill range, then followed the shore line, scanning the water's edge, until he had completed the entire loop of the headland and reached the junction of the bluffs and the sand. The emptiness of the beach was self-evident. He walked to the house.

Céleste met him with frank welcome, which he acknowledged with his usual outward nonchalance. Nevertheless his gaze lingered on her with an undisguised approval which caused her color to deepen. Very winsome she looked in her Sunday gown and white apron, combining in spotless ensemble the dress of both hostess and housewife, and, despite her activities of the forenoon and the heat of midday, giving an impression of refreshing coolness. The thought of arraying her in more modish style, which had been with him last night, did not now recur to him; but other thoughts sequent upon that one arose again, and as he turned to greet her father he felt an odd diffidence.

Somewhat to his surprise, he found Pierre out of bed; sitting close beside his narrow couch, but in a chair, and dressed. Moreover, the invalid looked remarkably well; and his cheerful salutation proved that he was in good spirits.

"Bon jour, docteur! I am glad you come on time. I have the appetite of a horse."

"Bon jour, mon père," smiled the visitor. The form of address brought a quizzical look to the old eyes and swift glance from those of the girl. "I am sorry that I have brought no leaves."

"Eh? Ah! Ho ho ho! this old horse does not eat leaves, nor grass either. You shall see! Céleste, fetch our fodder, tout de suite!"

The table, Lawrence now noticed, had been moved, to stand beside Blanchard's chair; and it was set for service. The host's thumb indicated his seat, and he sank into it. At once Céleste served the meal, which Pierre attacked with a speed and vigor corroborating his claim to an appetite. With more deliberation, but with no less enjoyment, the guest did justice to a repast far more varied than he had expected: flowl, tiny potatoes, rice, cooked cucumbers, and small flat cakes, followed by sapodillas, fresh pineapple, and a drink new to the American—a warm decoction, heavy with goat milk, which seemed a weak but odd-flavored tea. This he drank without comment, but with a puzzled look at the emptied cup as he sought to identify its taste. Céleste, watching him mischievously, asked:

"You have not drunk that before?"

"No," he admitted. "What is it?"

"Creole tea, made from the leaves of the soursop. It is very good to make one feel restful after being in the sun, and at night it gives sweet sleep. A doctor of leaves ought to know of it, Laurent."

Blanchard chuckled, shrewdly observing the effect of the playful thrust. Lawrence laughed, but studied the elder in a little uncertainty, wondering whether Céleste had disclosed his recent quasi-confession of his real business here. If such was the case, his host did not betray the fact. After a few seconds of consideration, however, the guest decided to have done with false pretensions.

"I am learning new things all the time," he returned. "Now I am wondering whether this island grows leaves that make men vanish."

Pierre looked blank. Céleste smiled vaguely, thinking his question a joke, but unable to see its point.

"Eh?" puzzled the former. "Do you want a magic leaf that will remove you from sight?"

"No, oh no. But one of my companions went out two days ago and disappeared. We cannot understand it."

"Companions! Ah, you have companions!" Blanchard's pounce on the word proved that this was a revelation.

"Yes. I haven't told you of them before now because —well, perhaps because it is a habit to keep my tongue quiet. For the same reason, I haven't told them of you. They are all good fellows, but—I thought you might not care to have many visitors."

His glance moved involuntarily to Céleste. From her father came a quick grunt of approval.

"We have been carrying on work which we thought it best to keep secret," Lawrence explained further. "But now the time has come when I should like the help of an older and wiser head than any of ours."

The grizzled mustache lifted in a pleased smile. The only oral response, however, was: "Bien. I am listening. Pipe, Céleste."

The girl arose and brought the veteran clay, then began clearing the table. The guest tendered tobacco and matches, leisurely loaded his own pipe, and blew smoke to mingle with that of the oldster, meanwhile marshaling requisite facts in his mind. When he had them in order he sketched, as concisely as possible, the sequence of events since the landing of his expedition.

Candidly he disclosed the object of their coming, though without detailed reference to the lost chart; outlined their methods of search, and told of the finding of the overthrown marker and the refilled pit; touched lightly on the acquaintance of his party with Lolita and

Montez, and briefly portrayed the characteristics of Van Horn. Then, more fully, he described the disappearance of the latter, the investigatory visit to the home of Lolita, and his own recent tour in the vicinity of the Blanchard domicile.

Throughout his recital Pierre listened with a thoughtful frown. At the conclusion he relit his pipe in an absent way. When at length he pronounced verdict, it came short and blunt.

"The man is dead."

So positive was his tone that Lawrence asked: "You have heard?"

"No. Nothing. But he has not left the island. He is not at large on the island. No man can move far on this island without being seen. No man can lie two days on this island, too badly hurt to call or move, and live. Your friend is dead. And it is not to be wondered at."

"No?" Lawrence eyed him keenly.

"No! And you had best take care, or more of you will be dead! Monsieur, there is a curse on that gold, and on the place where it was hidden! It was got by blood and buried with torture, and the man taking it from that cursed earth will never profit by it."

So solemn was his tone that for the moment his auditor was impressed. Then he smiled.

"Perhaps," he granted, indulgently. "But none of us has taken it from the earth, so——"

"You have been in that earth!" A gnarled finger leveled itself at him. "You dug by turns, you tell me. You all have dug into that place of the curse. Now one of you is dead. Was he, by chance, the first to dig?"

"By Jove, he was!" exclaimed Spearman, startled.

"Aha! And he is the first to go. And the rest of you will——"

"Oh, mon père, do not say such things!" Céleste broke in, with a shudder. "Why should a curse strike men who have done no harm?"

"Why did the pestilence sweep Chaurette?" he struck back. "The people there were good people who did no harm. But they lived in that Boîte du Mort, the place of the curse——"

"They lived there for years without hurt, father——"

"But they all died horribly at the end. Be still, girl! And you, doct—monsieur—take care that you and your companions do not die in the same way or worse!"

"Well, we can't die from smallpox, because we can't catch it. But you believe, then, that the hole we found was where the treasure once lay?"

"It would seem so." Pierre frowned at his pipe bowl. "But who could have dug there? Eh bien, it will do him no good! If he found anything it will bring him only misery. And my counsel to you, mon ami, is to quit your search and look to your safety. Even if you should find a treasure and even if it did you no harm, what could you do with it? Only bury it again! Not one gold piece, no, not one silver piece, could you take away from this island, unless your own ship lay at the shore. The swine of officials would seize every franc, every sou."

"No doubt. Still, our schooner may come in, even now."

"You think so?"

"Well, I hope so. It would be a more convenient way to leave than through the office of the gendarmes."

"Oui, truly."

Pierre grinned, as if feeling himself a conspirator in stealthy movements and enjoying the sensation. He puffed a minute, his eyes assuming a far away look. Then they swerved to Céleste.

Lawrence's gaze followed his, to dwell again on the fair face which had been much in his mind during recent hours. When he looked back at his senior he was no longer thinking of Van Horn or of cached gold.

"In that connection, I've been thinking of—of what you told me at another time," he ventured, a queer hesitation hampering his tongue. "About the hard life here and— You remember all that. And I've wondered if— er—if the schooner should come back—if you and Céleste would like to go with me to Saint Thomas. You have friends there, you said, and——"

He stumbled to an inconclusive stop, feeling uncomfortably hot. Glancing at Céleste, he found her face alight with joyous surprise. Her expression quickly sobered, however, as she looked at her infirm parent.

"I should like it much," directly answered the latter. "But you come too late. It is a journey of fifty leagues, and I could not live to see its end. On Barths I was born and on Barths I must die."

It was grim truth, not to be gainsaid. And the uncompromising set of the square jaw made plain the fact that Céleste too must remain on Barths until he was dead.

"That may be true," conceded Lawrence. "But when

you are gone, would you like Céleste to live at Saint Thomas?"

"Oui." The affirmation was immediate and positive.

"That is good. But how would you like to have her live in the great United States, instead of on one of its small islands?"

At that both father and daughter looked dubious. Otherwise their expressions differed. Pierre's gaze became increasingly sharp, and its doubt seemed mingled with uncertain suspicion. Céleste, after a straight look at the inquirer, stood half smiling, while hesitant little blushes dawned and faded in her cheeks. Did this man from far away realize that in speaking thus to her father he was virtually intimating an intention to ask for her in marriage? Or were customs different in his land? As if in answer, Lawrence said, after a pause:

"I am only asking what you would like to have her do when she is alone, if she could."

"Well," temporized the untraveled islander, "I know about S'n Thomas, and about what she would find there. But of your United States we do not hear so much. Is it much larger than S'n Thomas?"

"Rather." The American repressed a smile. "Saint Thomas is about thirty square miles in size; the States, more than three millions. Saint Thomas has about ten thousand people; the States, more than a hundred millions."

"Sapristi! That is a world, no less!"

"It is a world," agreed the Northerner.

Blanchard blinked, vainly striving to visualize so vast a country. Presently he shook his head.

"Tell me more about it," he requested. "I mean about your people and their way of living—and their officials. And is it not very expensive to travel so far?"

"The expense could be met. And about the country and its ways——"

He talked on; and, as the theme grew, on and on. And he talked honestly, making no attempt to idealize either his country or his countrymen, but touching on the bad as well as the good, particularly in governmental matters. That corrupt officials existed there, that oppression and injustice could be found, he freely admitted; but, he added, such officials were put into office by the people, who, on finding themselves victimized, put them out again. He made plain the fact, too, that it was a country of white men, a land bounteously blessed by Nature, a place of opportunities and comforts and conveniences unknown on Barths; a world where one might live, rather than merely exist.

His hearers followed his talk with unflagging interest; Céleste looking amused or serious by turns; Pierre, from time to time, prompting further disclosures by some pertinent query; both imperceptibly appraising his statements and, as well, the man himself. When at last Lawrence took note of the time, he discovered with surprise that the afternoon was nearly gone. With an apologetic laugh he stood up.

"I have robbed you of your afternoon nap, mon père," he said.

"I shall sleep all the better tonight—mon fils," rejoined the invalid, with a grin. "It is not every day that I can travel so far."

"True. Well, now do you think you would like Céleste to make that journey?"

"Perhaps yes, perhaps no," evaded the old man.

"Well, Céleste, would you like to live in America?" He turned directly to her.

"Perhaps." Her little smile was as noncommittal as her father's reply.

"Well, think it over, both of you." He walked toward the peg on which hung his helmet. "I shall see you another time."

"Oui, I shall think," promised Blanchard. "There is nothing to do but think." Then, his mind reverting to earlier topics: "I am glad that you have spoken out the truth today. When your dead friend is found I shall hear of it—if he is found, and is not in the sea. And then I shall tell you what I hear—if you still live to hear it."

"Mon père!" reproached Céleste.

"As long as you stay in that Boîte du Mort," solemnly concluded the elder, "take care."

"Very well. I shall take care." Lawrence smiled. "And now au revoir."

He moved outward. Céleste, sober faced, followed. At the door he paused a minute to look down at her. And he said:

"The dinner was most excellent. And it tasted twice as good because you ate it with me."

Her quick color rose again, and she laughed in mingled pleasure and shyness. With a wave to Pierre and another glance into the bright blue eyes, he walked away.

Up over the hills and down into the Box he ambled, accompanied by pleasant thoughts. But for the recurrent gloom cast by the Van Horn mystery, it had been the most enjoyable day since landing. As he swung down the cross path and looked over the lifeless expanse of debris he smiled again at Pierre's forebodings.

The old man was superstitious; that was all. The fact that Van Horn had been first to dig into that hole was mere coincidence. If there were any such potent curse as the native had declared, and if it were to follow the indicated sequence, it would fall next on Dan Devlin and Bill Mallory, the second and third excavators of that worthless shaft. But the rough old box of rocks was powerless to hurt them, except, perhaps by bruising their shins and wearing out their nerves.

With another contemptuous glance at the rubble he turned his attention toward the camp and began whistling the song of the Gambolier. Had the rambling MacLeod returned yet?

MacLeod had. As the whistler neared the doorway he appeared in it. One look at his drawn face, and Spearman cut off the tune as if throttled.

"Hullo! Anything wrong?" he called.

"I'll say so!" croaked Jack. "Dan's dead and Bill's dyin'!"

CHAPTER XX

APPLES OF HELL

Under the merciless sun of midforenoon two haggard
men leaned on their spades beside a new-made mound.

Ever since the first light of dawn they had been laboring. For hours they had attacked the stony soil of the
Box, which, not content to repulse all efforts of the outlanders to unearth its secret treasure, would deny them
even sepulture. Conquered at last, however, by pick
and crowbar and spade, it had yielded a biding place to
the comrades who, only yesterday, had lingered within
its inhospitable confines while their mates fared abroad.

What could be done had been done. For Devlin, at
the point of death when MacLeod returned from his
fruitless search, no help had been possible. For Mallory,
speechless and virtually senseless, yet stubbornly retain-
ing a feeble hold on life until long after nightfall, heroic
remedial measures had been attempted, but to no avail.
Since the government doctor at the town had deserted
his post, no skilled aid could be summoned. So in the
end Bill had gone to rejoin Dan somewhere beyond the
horizon; and upon the two left behind had devolved the
prompt burial necessary in the tropics.

Yet there still remained one duty: to determine the

cause of the deaths. For the time, though, the survivors said nothing. Physically exhausted and mentally fagged from strain, sleeplessness, toil and heat, they dragged their leaden feet to the house, only a few yards distant. There waited their cots, mutely bidding them recline and relax in long deferred rest. Instead, they drank deep of brandy and dropped into chairs, to sit loosely while the shade and the circling breeze cooled their super-heated bodies and the stimulant revived their flagging faculties. At length both straightened up and looked at each other, hollow eyed and drawn, but temporarily reinvigorated.

"You said it wasn't the crabmeat," reminded Jack, harking back to words spoken hours ago. "Then what was it?"

The other looked out of the door at the malign Boîte du Mort, on which, old Pierre had asserted, rested a lethal curse. After a silent interval he spoke with judicial deliberation.

"I don't insist that it wasn't, but I don't believe it was. It worked too fast. I've been poisoned once that way. Of course I had a doctor then, and these lads didn't. And Dan, to put it bluntly, had rotted himself out with booze; and both of them had lost stamina by exposure to the sun. So their resistance was none too good, and the poison could take hold sooner and harder than it might at home—especially on Dan. But still I don't feel that that poison was ptomaine. And what's more——" his voice hardened "I believe the poison-ing was intentional! And I believe that when we find the poisoner we'll find the party who did away with

227

Van Horn! I believe all those fellows were murdered, and unless we watch our steps we'll go out by the same route!"

"Right!" Jack thumped a big fist on the table. "Somebody or somethin' is playin' snake around here! And I'm out for that damned reptile's hide! But who is it? And why?"

"That's what we've got to find out." The gray eyes held an ominous glitter, but the steady tone again became cool. "And we've got nothing to work on but deductions. We know just this much: Bill and Dan ate that crabmeat, those apples, and some hardtack, and drank a quart of wine. If they ate or drank anything else we don't know what it was or how they got it. If they didn't, they were killed by the crab, the fruit, or the wine. The hardtack couldn't hurt them."

"And the wine was sealed."

"Yes. And the crab can looked all right. So that leaves only the fruit."

MacLeod eyed him narrowly, weighing both the statement and its implication. That fruit presumably had been left there by Lolita. If it had been poisonous she must have known it.

"The fact that it was left so mysteriously looks bad to me," Spearman pursued. "So does the fact that there was just one apiece. The supposition evidently was that we'd find them before breakfast and each eat one. And the intention obviously was—if they were poisonous— to kill every man jack of us. And they were left by somebody who knew there were just four of us—not five. And the only people who knew Van had——"

"Just a minute," coolly interposed Jack. "Your reasonin' is logical, but your conclusion won't hold water. Lolita doesn't want to kill *me*. I'm the last man in the world she does want killed. And what would it get her to kill any of us? Nothin'. Worse than nothin'. We've got nothin' she'd want, except possibly some knowledge, and damn' little of that; and we couldn't even tell that little if we croaked. No, it don't make sense. And what's more, Larry, you're not comin' clean with me. You've got somethin' of your own hid over there behind those hills to the east. I haven't been keepin' cases on you, but I'm wise. Who's *your* friend?"

A touch of sternness was in his tone, a cold glint in his eyes. Lawrence flushed, scowled, but answered equably:

"I don't quite fancy your way of putting that question, Jack. But the question itself is fair enough. I was coming to that point, anyway. Over there are two people, father and daughter, named Blanchard. The father has heart disease so badly that he can't leave the house. The daughter is afraid of this place—the smallpox, you know—and she wouldn't come here on a bet. Besides which, she's absolutely on the level."

"Sure about that?"

"So sure," asserted Lawrence, with sudden heat, "that I'm thinking of marrying her—if I can!"

MacLeod's momentary bleakness thawed. His lips puckered in a low whistle. Then they widened again in a slow smile.

"The higher they sit the harder they fall," he mused aloud. "You, the critical crochety old bach, divin' into the whirlpool of matrimony—if you can! You, the blasé metropolitan, marryin' a girl from a godforsaken island—if you can! Humph! Well, with all due respect to the lady, take a good long look before you leap, m' lad, a look both serious and searchin'."

"I have," came the brittle retort. "And that's enough said on that point. And nobody else lives over there; so there's nobody else to come here, except Lolita and Montez. The Saline people don't know we exist. Both Pierre and Céleste—that is, the Blanchards—promised to keep mum about us, and they're the kind who keep their word. Therefore, unless Montez has been talking in town, only four people know we're here; and two of them are above suspicion."

Jack reached to his cot for his pipe, which he mechanically loaded and lit. For a brief interval he puffed. Then he quietly declared:

"Usin' the process of elimination, Larry, we get exactly nowhere. There are four possibilities, and we can count them all out. This old man Blanchard, you say, can't leave the house. The girl, accordin' to you, wouldn't come here anyway and wouldn't do anybody any harm. Lolita's got nothin' against any of us, especially me. That leaves Montez. He might possibly want to rub me out if he knew some things. But he doesn't know 'em. Even if he did, he'd have nothin' on Bill or Dan or you. So what would be his object in plantin' poisonous fruit on all four of us? There's no sense in that. So that lets everybody out, and nobody did it. On the other hand, we might think up circumstantial evidence enough to convict all of 'em."

"Not the Blanchards!" contradicted Spearman. Yet, even as he spoke, into his mind flashed the memory of Céleste's advice to eat fresh food, including fruit; the fact that she had twice shown knowledge of local leaves; the additional fact that Pierre, although disclaiming knowledge of Van Horn, had flatly asserted that he was dead; the still more damaging circumstance that the old man had predicted the deaths of all the others. From such innocent irrelevancies, could not a web of evidence be woven by a prosecutor determined to make out a case? And was there any more tangible proof against the less reputable pair at the west? Not even so much. Suspicion, prejudice, sophomoric logic could construct a network about them, but it might be merely a tissue of false premises and conclusions.

"Maybe no, maybe yes," persisted MacLeod. "But, as I was sayin', the boys are dead. And, as you were sayin', it might be the fruit. And before goin' any further, how could that fruit be poisoned? Up home somebody might squirt it in with a hypodermic needle, but down here nobody but a doctor would know there was such a thing."

"Down here some fruits are poisonous by nature. Particularly——"

He stopped short, eyes widening, then narrowing. Suddenly he arose.

"Jack, do you remember what you did with the remains of that apple you smashed yesterday?"

"Why—ah—I gave it a kick to the right, I think."

Spearman strode out. MacLeod got up quickly and followed. Together they searched the ground near the

231

door. Then Jack stooped and straightened, holding the crushed fruit, which had been lying under the shelter of a lopsided stone. Thus protected from the sun, it had remained fairly fresh despite the ground heat. Moreover, nearly half of it was still intact, having escaped the heel which had crushed the rest.

"What is it?" quizzed Jack.

"I'm not quite sure." Lawrence studied the remnant narrowly. "I've heard of one fruit in particular that ought to be dodged down here, and this looks to me as if it might be that one. But I've never seen it, though I know the tree it grows on. Naturally, the natives never gather things they know to be deadly. So nobody ever served one to me—until yesterday morning."

He looked up suddenly.

"Jack, how much do you care about Lolita?" he asked.

Jack stared, then laughed shortly.

"Why, she's nothin' to me but a good pal when I want her. None of 'em are. At the same time I like the kid, and I want her to get a square deal."

"Very well. Yesterday morning you credited this contribution to her. Whether you were right or wrong, she ought to know what this is. I'm going to find out if she does."

"All right," shortly answered Jack. "Let's go!"

They went, with no further words. As quietly as on their previous visit, they passed through the sun-scorched Montez yard and stepped into the house. This time, however, Lolita received them with composure.

Perhaps, more alert than before, she had heard the swish of their feet in the short grass. At any rate, she met them just beyond the threshold and greeted them with insouciant jest.

"Hah-lo, Jack! Good day, Monsieur—ah—Ministre! I been thinking maybe you come today, Jack, but I not thinking you bring the minister again. You wanting marry me some more, maybe, yes?"

She laughed, glancing at each, and, with a toss of the head, shaking back the unbound mane of ebon hair. Yet her eyes were watchful; and as she studied their faces her laughter waned and her intentness waxed.

"Ho-o-o!" she exclaimed, in falling tone. "You looking very fatigué, messieurs! What you doing, eh? You having hard night with bottle? Maybe you drink up the whole basket, an' now you wanting more——"

"We had a hard night, all right," grimly interrupted Jack. "Where's that brother of yours?"

"Eh? Why, he's gone to town, early, like usual." She shrugged carelessly, regarding him in a puzzled way. "You very well know he goes every Monday morn'. But I having here some wines an' a little cognac, if you mus' have it."

Spearman, hitherto watching her closely, now spoke with cool directness.

"That's not what we need. Tell us what this is."

He extended the fragment of fruit. She took it, looked casually at it a second or two, then grew rigid.

"Diable!" Wide eyed, she stared from man to man. "Where you getting this?"

"What is it?" repeated Lawrence.

She flashed another glance down at it and, with swift repulsion, cast it from her. An instant later she threw herself at MacLeod.

"Jack! Jack! You not biting that thing?" she cried. "You not—mon Dieu, you not eating it? You tell me! Quick! You not eating that?"

Her hands beat frenziedly on his chest. Her cheeks were blanched, her voice shrill, her lips quivering. The men glanced sidelong at each other.

"You tell me! Jack! You eating that?"

She seized him now by the shoulders, striving to shake him in her mad haste for an answer.

"No, girl," he responded. "But what is it?"

"Oh, merci à Dieu!" For a moment she lay limp against him. Then, looking at Spearman: "Nor you, monsieur? You not eating that apple of hell?"

"No."

"Ah! Good, very good! But where you getting it, you men? Where is the rest of it? You having only piece of it." She drew away from MacLeod, glancing at both. "What's 'come of the big piece, eh?"

"I stepped on it," explained Jack. "That's all there was left."

"Oh, good! You—you giving me terrible scare, Jack. Jus' that piece—an' you both looking so bad——" She drew a deep breath, gazing at MacLeod with terror still plain on her face. "That thing, you mus' never eat it, no, never touch it. It look so good, it smell so sweet, many many eating it 'foretime in these islan's— sailorman an' other man that don' know it—an' they

234

die, tout de suite! It is apple of the devil! It is poison! It is the mancenille!"

"M-hm. Thought so," muttered Spearman.

Her eyes flashed to him.

"Ah! So you knowing about that tree, monsieur? Then why you bring that thing here, eh? An' where you finding it? In this valley is no mancenille. Where you getting it?"

Again the men looked at each other, and at her. Coolly Spearman answered:

"I've seen the tree, but not its fruit. And we found that fruit on our doorstep yesterday morning. There were three others like it. Jack and I went walking and didn't eat any. Bill and Dan stayed there and ate all three. We have just buried them."

Blank horror overspread her face. Open-mouthed, she stood motionless. When at length her lips moved, they gave forth only a whisper.

"Buried? Dead?"

"Buried and dead. Poisoned to death by those hell-apples. And there were just four of those fruits, understand? Four, not five! Four, put on our doorstep by somebody before breakfast. If Jack and I had eaten ours we'd be dead too."

"Four," she repeated in a dazed manner. "Four. On doorstep. 'Fore breakfas'. Yes'day morn'—— Sacré!"

She started, stared strangely at each of them, turned, walked away along the room. Her hands opened and shut with the stress of some violent emotion—fear, anger, hatred, or, possibly, nerve shock. At the far end she stood a moment battling with unspoken thoughts.

Then she rapidly returned, head high and eyes stormy.

"So! You thinking I put those poison apples at your door, eh?" she challenged. "You thinking 'cause I giving you fruits 'foretime I doing this thing too? That what you thinking 'bout me, Jack? That why you coming here now? You are the damn fool, an' you go to hell! You—you——"

"Whoa!" broke in MacLeod. "That'll be enough. Cool off. Nobody's accusing you of anything."

"No? Well, you better not! An' you better get out an' stay out! I don' know nothing 'bout this thing, an' you can both go to——"

"Shut up!" snapped Jack. "My temper's short today. I've told you we're not chargin' this up to you. That's enough."

Her eyes blazed more furiously, but her lips pressed tight. Not until Spearman asked another question did she open them. Then her response was cold.

"Where was your brother yesterday morning early?" he probed.

"Asleep in this house, monsieur. Sleeping until mid morning. Every Sunday he sleeps so, after working all week."

Her gaze clashed with his, unflinching. Slowly he nodded.

"All right. Excuse our intrusion," he formally apologized. "And thanks for telling us what the apple was. Now we'll go. Bon jour."

He walked out. MacLeod, after a long look into the hot eyes confronting his, shrugged and followed his partner.

"So long, kid," he said. "I need some sleep. When I'm rested I'll see you again. Meanwhile, don't worry."

"Don' come back!" she flared. "I never wanting see you again!"

"Oh, all right."

Jack swung away, tread lifeless, shoulders drooping, body and mind too tired to care whether he ever saw anyone again. Before he had gone ten yards she was running after him, contrite and anxious.

"I not meaning that, Jack, I am upset, me. You come back soon! An' you be very careful, you watch, don' let anything bad get you! Something—something is very wrong in this place!"

"Believe me, we know it! And believe me, girl, we're goin' to get that thing!"

He plodded onward. She stood watching until he passed from sight. Then, wheeling, she returned within. And now, no longer under surveillance, she flamed with rage and gave way to violent impulse. The sudden fury which had swept through her a few minutes ago, but which she had masked by simulating the righteous anger of injured innocence, broke forth in futile but ominous action.

From its place beside the door she snatched her long knife. With it she stabbed fiercely into the fragment of mancenille lying on the floor; stabbed repeatedly, as if that bit of poisonous pulp were a living man, driving the point into the boards so far that it came away only after hard tugging.

"When you come back, you devil!" she panted. "When you come back——"

237

Out in the Box, staggering with sheer weariness under the bludgeoning sun, the two tall men retreated to their barrack. The temporary strength of cognac was gone, leaving them even more exhausted. Passing the grave without a pause, they entered the house, dropped helmets, and eyed the cots. Spearman drew keys from a pocket and opened his locker trunk.

"Well, you were right," vouchsafed Jack. " 'Twas the fruit. But what d'you think now about how it got there?"

"I've stopped thinking until I've rested."

Jack nodded; then moved to his own trunk. When the locks snapped shut again each man held a heavy police revolver. Thereafter, leaving all openings wide for the sake of the breeze, but armed for action against any stealthy creature which might come, they dropped on their beds and slept.

Chapter XXI

PIERRE PASSES

"Laurent! Laurent! Wake up, please wake up!"

Spearman, though sleeping heavily, heard and heeded the call. Starting up, he stared into the frightened face of Céleste; Céleste, hatless, pale, panting from haste and trembling with agitation.

"What's wrong?" he asked.

"Mon père, Laurent! He—he is dead!"

"No!"

"Yes, dead! And he—he is lying out in the field and —I can not carry him into the house—he is too heavy. I— Oh, you will help me?"

"Why, of course!"

He tightened his belt and pulled on his canvas shoes, while she, nervously intertwining her fingers, looked in a dazed way at the hills over which she had just come. Their crests were tipped by the last rays of sunset.

"How did this come about?" he asked, as he hurriedly tied shoe laces.

"He went out of the house—I cannot comprehend why—while I was away. I had to go to Saline—it was necessary to get fresh food. He was quiet and contented when I left. But I had to stay longer than usual, and

239

he must have become worried—I cannot understand why else he should do such a thing—and come out to look for me. When I came back he was on the ground —on his face——"

She broke off, pressing her lips tight together, while tears flooded her eyes.

"There, now, don't grieve," he urged, though his own expression was solemn. "Remember that it had to come, and his pains and worries are all over. We shall go to him at once."

She nodded quickly, striving for control, and lifted her apron to dry her eyes. He cast a glance at Mac-Leod, and found him awake and silently watching. Now Jack drawled:

"If you don't mind, you might tell a fellow what's doin'. I don't compreeny frog, you know."

"Pierre Blanchard's dead, Jack. This is Céleste. She needs help to get him into the house, so I'm going over."

"The devil you say! Another man dead! Things are comin' thicker all the time." Jack sat up. "Wait a minute and I'll go along with you."

"No, never mind, you're not needed. I can handle him, and there's nothing you can do. And it's no mystery this time. His heart just quit on him. It's been due any minute."

Jack nodded and relaxed, peering at the girl, who, after one quick survey, looked away. Tousle-haired, bristle-jawed, heavy-faced from insufficient sleep, he was not at the moment prepossessing. She stepped to the door, Lawrence following.

"Got your gun?" reminded Jack. "No, you haven't. Here, catch it."

Reaching to his partner's cot, he flipped the forgotten weapon through the air. Spearman instinctively caught it, gave him a glance of rebuke for such careless handling of a loaded weapon, but wasted no words. Céleste already was gone, running away up the hill in useless but natural anxiety to reach again the father who had long been her habitual charge. With rapid strides he pressed after her.

Not until they reached the fallen man did either pause. By that time the sun was gone and gloaming had come. But the air still was transparent, and, with the moon already brightening in a clear sky, all was plainly visible.

Pierre lay on his back, face peaceful, one arm lying across his torso, the other on the ground, as if he were merely relaxed in slumber. For an instant the newcomer thought the girl might be mistaken, that possibly the old man still lived; for she had said he lay on his face, and, obviously, no dead man could turn over. A steady pressure over the heart, however, confirmed her declaration. It was stilled for all time. The change in position, he now realized, had been caused by her efforts to move the body to the house.

He looked toward that house, estimating the distance; and, in so doing, became aware of a fact not easily explained. Blanchard's course had not been toward the sands of Saline bay, as would be the case if he had been seeking his daughter, but away from them. He lay several rods from the small domicile, and the

241

line marked by his body and the house led toward the hills.

"You found him just here?" he questioned.

"Yes, just here. He—he is truly gone?" Even now she was reluctant to accept the inescapable truth.

"Yes."

He scanned the ground beyond the supine man, seeing only a bulky stone or two. Then he braced himself and lifted Pierre.

The Frenchman was more weighty than he looked; thick bone and heavy thewed; evidently powerful in his prime, and even now too ponderous a burden for the girl, herself no weakling. Spearman's own muscles, stiffened by recent arduous toil, cracked as he rose. But he was stronger than his lean build would indicate; and, once under way, he plodded unfalteringly to the house and inside.

Beyond the doorway he stopped, peering through the inner darkness and listening. The place was soundless.

"Light the lamp," he prompted.

When the yellow flame banished the gloom he moved to Pierre's bed and laid down its dead master; then examined him closely, and scanned the meagerly furnished room. At one side of the wrinkled forehead was a small abrasion, evidently caused by impact on hard earth. Otherwise Blanchard was unmarked. Within the house was not the least indication of any unusual occurrence. On the table lay the old clay pipe, carefully set down before its owner essayed his inexplicable walk out under the sun. All else was in order. With a puzzled headshake Lawrence looked down at the girl, standing now

close beside him and gazing mournfully at the blank
face against the pillow.

"Where did you leave him?" he asked. "In bed, or in
his chair?"

"In the chair, smoking. He was feeling well——"

Her voice faltered, her lips quivering again. All at
once she turned to him, blindly, instinctively, as she
had gone over the hills to him in her first need of aid;
and, as if he were one of those lost brothers on whose
strength she had once relied, she dropped her head on
his shoulder and wept. He drew her close, and, for a
time, stood silent. At length he said:

"You must be brave, chérie. What is to be must be;
and you knew this must come."

"Yes," she sobbed. "But to have it come so—to have
him die alone—I ought never to have left him——"

"It was necessary. And it must have been all for the
best. And now you must look to the future."

Trite consolation, but effective. Outwardly, at least,
her grief lessened. Her head lifted, and then, as realization of her position dawned, she drew back, shame-
faced. His arms opened, releasing her without resistance.
She turned to her father, and he, after a moment, toward the door. Quietly he walked out, leaving her alone
with her dead.

In the thin moonlight he drifted again to the spot
where Pierre had lain. What on earth, he wondered,
had incited the invalid to make this short but fatal expedition? Had someone come and angered him—young
Thibaut, perhaps,—so that he strove to chase the intruder away? There was no indication of anything of

243

the sort. No other person was there now, certainly, nor any sign of one, save the dropped and forgotten basket of Céleste and her big shade hat, lying on the ground a few paces away; mute witnesses to her startled discovery and swift rush to the side of the prone man. Passing on to the boulders toward which Blanchard apparently had been heading, he looked in vain for evidence that anyone had lurked there to spy, or done any other thing likely to arouse the choler of the owner. Beyond them were only the silent hills and the empty night.

Retracing his steps, he retrieved hat and basket and reentered the house. Céleste, now mistress of her emotions, came composedly to meet him.

"Thank you, Laurent, for—for everything," she said. "Now I must go to Saline."

"To Saline? Why? I can do what needs to be done."

"No. There are things you cannot do, mon ami; and I shall not ask more of you. One of the good fathers must be called from Gustavia, and men must dig, and —and all must be done speedily. So I shall go now to friends who will attend to those things for me. Perhaps I should have done so at first, instead of disturbing you, but——"

"Don't say that!" he broke in. "You know I wanted you to come to me at need, and I'd be much hurt if you hadn't done so. And I can dig— You intend to have the burial here?"

"No. The cemetery is at Saline. My mother is there." Her lips quivered again; but she continued in the same controlled tone. "So there is nothing more you can do."

"I see. Well, then I shall go with you to Saline, and be sure that you are safe."

"Why, nothing will harm me."

"No. I'll see that nothing does," he asserted. "Come!"

With a last look at the calm figure on the bed, she followed him out. They walked away under the moon.

"Who are your friends at Saline?" he asked.

"The Maréchals. They are good friends, very good. Why? Do you know them? But no——"

"No." He was glad to know that she was not seeking friendly offices from the Thibauts. "I was thinking. Do you intend to stay with them after the services?"

"I—I do not know," she hesitated. "I have not thought. But no, I must stay here a little time. Perhaps then— But I shall decide later."

"All right. I shall want to talk to you soon, Céleste, when your mind is more at ease, about several things. In another day or two, perhaps."

She glanced at him, then away, making no reply. Soberly they walked on until they were out on the long white sands.

There both halted, looking quickly back. From behind them had broken a blunt, abrupt sound, not loud, but arresting in the quiet; a dull thump, seemingly distant, striking once through the soft susurrus of the breeze and the ceaseless murmur of the sea, gone as soon as heard. No repetition came. They listened a minute or two, then resumed motion, their minds once more reaching into the future.

They had covered half the distance to the cliff opening behind which nestled the salt pond valley, when the man, looking down into the sweetly solemn face beside him, spoke impulsively.

"Céleste! 1 ought not to say this just now—it is not a fitting time—but it must be said. Your father wished you to leave this island—whenever he should leave you —and go to live at Saint Thomas, you remember. At Saint Thomas or, perhaps, in the United States. He wanted you to live in a better place than this. And so do I. And when I go I want you to go with me, to Saint Thomas first, and afterwards to the States. I shall say no more about it now, and you needn't give me any answer now. But I shall say more in a few days, and I want you to think about it. And— Well, that's all. Just remember what I am saying."

She looked straight ahead, seemingly watching her path. But one hand rose and lightly touched his arm, then fell away.

"I shall remember," she quietly responded. And they walked on, saying no more.

So they came to the gap between the stony hills, through which led the way to the peaceful homes of the salt pond people. There she stopped.

"There is no use in going farther, Laurent," she said. "You had better turn back here. And thank you, thank you for what you have done!"

"I've done nothing. And I'm going with you——"

"No. I would rather go on alone."

He frowned ahead, loath to leave, but aware that his presence might hamper rather than help her; for her arrival escorted by a stranger would undoubtedly arouse avid curiosity as to his identity. For her sake, therefore

—and, incidentally, for his own, if the virtually abandoned hunt for treasure was ever to be resumed—it
would be best to efface himself now. Yet, so wary had
he become as the result of the rapid succession of mysterious deaths, he looked for menace lurking beside the
path she must tread. But the way lay open and plain,
patently harmless, and beyond shone cheery lights in
the humble but hospitable homes of her friends.

"Very well," he conceded. "Au revoir."

"Au revoir," she echoed.

He watched her pass on, sure and unafraid, to the
first house; heard a dog bark and a feminine voice call
greeting. Then he swung away and strode fast back
along the strand.

Twice on the return journey he looked behind, finding no figures in sight. Surmounting the sharp slope
where the beach terminated and the headland began, he
surveyed the homestead anew. That bumping noise lingered in his memory. It might possibly, though not very
probably, have been caused by the slamming of the
heavy plank door.

On reaching the portal, however, he found it as he
had left it. All was very quiet. Stepping to the window,
he looked within. No living thing was there. Nobody
had been there. The lamp burned steadily, and on his
bed Pierre lay in the untroubled rest from which there
could be no awaking.

For a little time the American stood gazing at the
worn-out Frenchman who had known so much of work
and sorrow and pain and so little of pleasure and ease.
How jealously protective of his girl child he had been,

even when the sole defensive strength left him had been that of mind and tongue! And now where was that sturdy soul of his? Was it still here, disembodied but still watching over Céleste, still troubled by anxiety for her future fate? Perhaps. Despite all clerical dogmas, who really knew the ultimate haven of the soul or whether it kept cognizance of mortals after passing from human ken?

"Don't worry, old-timer," he said quietly. "I'm going to take good care of your girl. Of *our* girl!"

In a flicker of lamplight the still face seemed to smile. And, with that farewell promise, the Northerner left him forever.

Across the flat he walked, and up the hill path to the tall stone whence he could view all below and far away. From that coign he perceived life moving on the long stretch of sand. A small group of people had emerged from the cliff gap and were steadily trudging toward the headland. The friends whom Pierre had called negligent in life now were coming to do their devoirs to death.

So he withdrew to his own valley, thinking deeply as he went. Nearing the barrack, he noted perfunctorily that it was dark, and told himself that Jack had gone to sleep again. All at once he realized that he too was tired, and exceedingly hungry as well. He would fix up a meal and then return to bed. There was nothing else to do now.

But there was more to do; much more.

Entering the darksome house, he groped for the matchbox, struck a light, and, glancing casually toward

Jack's cot, took a step toward the lamp. Then he halted, holding the match higher and peering. An instant of rigidity was succeeded by a jerky movement and a quick exclamation.

MacLeod was gone. And Lawrence now recognized the nature of that unexplained thump on the night air. Muffled by intervening hills and contrary wind, it had been a gunshot.

CHAPTER XXII

A FLAME DIES

MacLeod, looking at the empty doorway through which Céleste and Lawrence had disappeared, rubbed a hand reflectively along his jaw. For several minutes he sat pondering. Then he arose, sleepily opened a can of salmon, and made a meal from fish and hardtack; drank some wine, lit his pipe, and thought again. As he smoked, grim lines deepened in his face. Abruptly he laid down his pipe, returned to his cot, and put on his shoes, his movements now quick and decisive.

It was time, he told himself, for a complete show-down with Lolita; time to abandon his careless attitude toward her equivocative, half incriminative allusions to the treasure box, and force her either to reveal any knowledge she possessed or to confess the emptiness of her pretensions; time, also, for straight talk on several other matters, chief of which was the stealthy assassination of two, and probably of all three, of the men now gone. For all his outward acceptance of her noncomplicity in those murders, he was not entirely convinced that she might not be withholding some salient point connected with them.

Darkness now lay thick within the house, but the slanting moonshine at door and windows enabled him to discern all essentials. Shod, he drew from under his thin pillow his revolver; opened it, inspected the cartridges, tested the action, and pocketed it. Although there seemed to be little likelihood that the weapon would be needed, he was no longer inclined to be heedless in this ominous Boîte du Mort.

Soft footed, he trod the familiar way to the hidden house. Rounding the corner, he found the door ajar. Light was shining through a foot-wide interval between it and the jamb. Through that space now came a sound which stopped him dead: the voice of a man.

Low, curt, indistinct, the words meant nothing to the surprised newcomer. But the loud, angry reply in Lolita's tones was comprehensible at once. She spoke now in Spanish; and with that language MacLeod was quite familiar, thanks to his bygone adventuring in Mexico.

"Fool? You call me fool?" she blazed. "You misborn son of a goat, you are the fool! Idiot! Blundering ass! Slime—scum—spittle that you are! When have you done a thing that was right? Where is the ship you were to get? What good is the money to us? When am I ever to leave this hole of hell? I rot here for months in this desolate place and keep guard, and you fumble about and get nowhere! And now you do this villainous thing, you brainless snake——"

"Silencio!" hissed the man. "Hold your tongue or speak more quietly. The night has ears——"

"Bah! You miserable coward, those men sleep! They are dead with weariness. And if they were not I should not care! No, not if they stood here this moment!"

MacLeod moved forward, stealthy as a stalking puma, to stop just outside the portal. As he saw the disputants he barely repressed a grunt. Halfway down the room they fronted each other, Lolita standing over the man, who sat morosely in a chair. That man was Montez; Montez, who ought to be at the town. Either he had returned unexpectedly tonight from his work or he had not gone to work at all today, hiding himself somewhere, perhaps to spy. Now he peered fixedly at the furious woman, and in the wavering lamplight his pocked visage was an evil thing.

"You have reason to care, woman!" he countered. "You have more reason than I. I am only carrying on what you began. Be still! These many weeks I have endured your vicious tongue and your vile temper, and I am sick of them. Fool? Yes, I am a fool, perhaps. I was a fool that I ever brought you here. Your chart was not good, and it was only by chance that I found what I found. I could have done as well or better without you. And you, for all your conceit and vanity, have not been able to get the true chart from those Americans or to learn from them what is on it——"

"They do not know where the box lies! They have been hunting blindly. That one—that white-headed pig —he told me they did not know——"

"He lied. They know. They have not worked for days. They have found it, and now they wait for their ship. And because you have been simple they know we have something else, and they want that too. Blunders? It is you who have blundered, not I. As for our ship, you know well that I posted the letter to Jaime Lopez, and that since then I have sent two others secretly by sloops that came in, so that the postal official could not lose them as perhaps he lost the first. I could do no more——"

"Oh, shut your mouth! Excuses and blunders— You are good for nothing! And this last thing you have done—por Dios, it is too much! You are a snake, a spitting stinging snake striking in the dark! And you crawl away then and leave me to meet the suspicion and the blame and save your filthy skin for you!"

Her voice rose high, vibrant with wrath and scorn. The man's ugly countenance contracted, and he tensed as if to rise and silence her. But he remained in his chair, glowering.

"What of that?" he growled. "You saved it—and your own too—and you could not have done so if I had let you know. You would have betrayed yourself and me by the same panic that was upon you after you killed that first one. You do not control yourself well. So when I found last night that two of them had not eaten the fruit I knew it was wisest to keep you in ignorance and to go to my work today as usual. And it was not my plan that any of them should live to disturb you. If all had eaten as they should, all now would be out of the way. But it does not matter. Those two who are left can be disposed of tonight, while they sleep so heavily. One quick stab to each, and then——"

"What? Madre de Dios! You are a snake in truth! You would do that?"

"Most certainly. It is necessary. So we shall save our own lives and our riches, and win also all they have.

But I will not do the trick alone, woman. I have no mind to let one of them leap on me while I am attending to the other. You shall help. You killed the first man of the five. Now you can kill the last!"

His lips stretched away from his teeth in sinister grimace. Upon the mouth of the man outside came a similar grin, no less cold and menacing; and his right hand stole back to loosen the weapon in his pocket. He knew Montez now for what he was; he had met the same type ih Mexico: a creature, outwardly stolid and stupid, inwardly sly, and venomous and merciless as any snake; a reptile in the body of a man. As for Lolita, her guilt in the disappearance of Van Horn was manifest. He lifted his left hand to shove back the door, swayed forward to stride in and confront them both. Then he caught himself and stood motionless.

Lolita, stricken silent an instant, now spoke in an altered tone, poignant with alarm and revolt.

"I will not! I killed that Van 'Orn one because I must. But I will not do this thing! You are insane, Miguel! You are——"

She caught her breath, staring into the slitted eyes watching her. Then her voice rose once more, and her words came rapidly.

"You shall not do this either! You shall not strike again, snake! Por Dios, I will warn those men myself to be on their guard! I will—yes, I will go to them and tell them what you have done! If you interfere I will put the knife to you, you lump of filth! I am done with you—now—this moment!"

"Ssssi?" Montez leaned farther forward, his interrogation a serpentine hiss. "And you will say I killed all three, and thus clear yourself, yes? And having done this, what will you do then? Who will be your man and take you from this place? Who will——"

A derisive laugh cut him short; a laugh edged with contemptuous malice.

"Do not worry over that matter, Miguel mío," she jeered. "I shall be well cared for by one far more handsome than you, turtle face!"

The pocked visage darkened and bloated. With sudden swiftness he arose. Yet, having risen, he made no further move. His hands, half shut, hung loose at his sides. Only face, eyes, and voice showed the rage burning within him.

"Yes?" he snarled. "It is as I suspected. While I worked at the town to play the part of poverty and blind the officials you have played another game with a man here! Yes, with all of them, no doubt!"

"Perhaps I did," she flung back at him, hatefully. "Perhaps I did, with all of them! And if I did, what of it?"

For a few seconds her hot gaze met his in withering defiance. Then his thick lips twisted in a malevolent smile.

"Nothing, señorita, nothing. It is of no consequence. I myself have a sweetheart at the town, Lolita mía, who is younger and more loving than you, yes, and more beautiful, although she is a negress——"

"What!" she screamed. "You beast!"

"But yes. It surprises you? Ha! Most strange! What man would not find for himself another girl after knowing your temper? What man would not soon tire of you? And now that I know your mind I will tell you more than that. I tell you that for weeks you have been to me nothing but an animal to keep my house and guard my gold. I tell you that now I shall remove that gold and spend it on another woman. I tell you that you can starve, or go to your men and tell them you come as the cast-off of Miguel Montez, a faded, worn-out hag who———"

With a hoarse cry of anger she sprang at him, her right hand darting aloft and down. In that hand, hitherto concealed by her intervening body from the sight of MacLeod, flashed steel. But Montez, for all his former bovine slowness, could move with speed greater than her own. A sidewise twist, a pounce, and he held her wrist motionless in air, the slender blade a foot from his throat.

"Old and slow, woman!" he jeered, grinning mirthlessly as she fought vainly to drive the knife home. "Tell this also to your men, that you tried to stab me and failed. Yes, tell them all, everything you know!" His voice sharpened with reckless rancor. "Tell them I killed that first one, if you will! It does not matter how much you lie! And tell them also this which is the truth: that I killed all the people of that Boîte du Mort when I came, and will kill all in it before I go! Yes, woman, I, Miguel Montez! You thought the plague was a lucky piece of fortune for us, clearing our way to work unseen, yes? Yes, so it was. But I brought that plague in a sealed bottle from Domingo, querida mía! I got it from a caco doctor on the Haiti side, and I

256

used it here when I was ready. Go and tell that to your men! And tell them I will see to it that they never repeat it! Ha! Go now and yelp to them!"

Stricken dumb by this last revelation, staring incredulously at him as he gave her carte blanche to reveal his crimes, Lolita stood motionless. Outside MacLeod stood equally astounded, awaiting any further disclosures. Now, with a sudden movement, Montez turned her to face the door, simultaneously twisting her wrist. Her knife fell—but did not reach the floor. He seized it as it dropped.

"And," he grated, "take this with you!"

Too late, Jack crashed the door inward. Too late Lolita tried to spring forward. Montez had sunk her own knife into her back.

A sharp moan, and she fell. Montez, petrified by the instantaneous appearance of Nemesis from the empty night, gaped at the tall man striding at him. MacLeod, eyes glittering, fists clenched, advanced with implacable ferocity.

Lolita, attempting to rise, blocked his path. He slowed an instant, looking down. She fell back, her eyes on him, her blanched lips moving.

"Jack!" she gasped. "Kill him!"

"I will!" he promised, his voice harsh as sliding stone.

Montez moved. He still held the knife. Here was one of his intended victims, unarmed. A venomous grin formed on his lips, and he took one step. Then he recoiled, flinching in fear. MacLeod's hand had darted back, swung forward. Now it gripped a gun.

Montez cowered, shrank away, fumbling voiceless for words. They never came. With the cold precision of an executioner, MacLeod shot him through the head.

The heavy report blasted the stillness. The body toppled and fell. The avenger stood rigid an instant, watching the motionless form; then, with a stiff-muscled movement, jabbed the weapon back into its pocket. His hard eyes switched to the stricken woman, to find on her pallid face a vengeful smile. Unspeaking, he stooped and drew her over on her breast to examine her wound. As he did so she coughed, then fought for breath.

Montez had known where to strike. The short, slender slit just below the left shoulder blade now was virtually closed; but the internal damage was deadly. Lolita herself, after that strangling cough, recognized her doom. The look she found in Jack's eyes as he lifted her from the floor confirmed her own intuition. There could be no hope.

Her arms closed tight around his neck as he bore her to the bed. When he laid her down she clung all the more closely, holding to him with desperate strength.

"Jack—Jack—don' let me go!" she breathed. "Hol' me—keep me!"

"I can't help it, Lolita. There's no chance."

Gently he drew her hands away and straightened up. But those hands closed hard on his own, pulling him down. He sat on the edge of the bed, regarding her gravely.

"Lolita, I heard what was said," he told her. "You killed Van Horn?"

"Oui. He was spying——"

Another sudden cough halted her. When the spasm passed she lay weak and wan, her grip now a mere handclasp. But she held to the thread of her confession.

"He was traitor to you—he would be traitor to me. He was no man—he was greedy pig. So I kill him. I stab him in neck—in cave—voilà! He is dead! You never finding him, Jack,—the sea get him—I sink him in bay where—where our ship was to come—for you an' me! But these other thing—the mancenille—I didn' know it, Jack, I didn' know——"

"I understand, Lolita. Don't talk any more."

A moment she lay silent, breathing with increasing difficulty, her hands pressing feebly upon his. Again came the cough. When it was over he had one arm around her, holding her high and close against him. Her head drooped on his shoulder. Somehow she found strength to clasp him once more about the neck.

"Jack," she whispered, "I love you! You—firs' man I ever—really love! An' Jack—you dig—you dig in cave —you know—dig in middle—an' you find—gold——"

Her voice failed. Heavily she lay against him, her arms quivering and beginning to slip down. Suddenly came one more cough, ending in a shuddering gasp. Then the arms fell away.

He lifted her head, looked at her a moment, and gently lowered her.

Lolita, the Flame, had gone out into the dark.

Chapter XXIII

PIRATE GOLD

Spearman, bounding in at the open door, stopped short.

On the floor lay Montez, obviously dead. On the edge of the bed sat MacLeod, chin in hands, eyes somber. Behind him was partly visible a still form and a face of pale gold framed in hair of jet.

At the thump of footsteps Jack straightened sharply, then relaxed.

"Hullo, Larry," he croaked.

"Hullo yourself! Are you all right?"

"Oh, sure."

Slowly Jack arose, turned, looked again at the face on the pillow. Spearman advanced, eyed him keenly, gazed long at Lolita. Then he turned to peer once more at Montez.

"How come?" he demanded.

"I plugged him. He stabbed Lolita. In the back. And there I stood at the door, like a damn' dummy, and let him do it!"

His tone was heavy with self reproach. Spearman studied him again, then laid a hand briefly on his shoulder.

"A stab in the back is always swift. You couldn't stop it," he comforted. "But what was it all about?"

"They had a showdown. She was goin' to quit him, and he couldn't stand for it, because she'd give him away. He's the skunk that's been doin' all the killin' around here."

With that he walked to the doorway and stood there, staring gloomily outward. His partner watched him go and thoughtfully rubbed his jaw, while his eyes went back and forth between Lolita and her slayer. Presently he, too, walked over to the portal and leaned there, looking at the silent field.

"You've done a good job, Jack," he approved. "But are you sure about that? Montez killed all hands?"

"All hands—and then some," asserted Jack, unwinking. "She knew nothin' about any of it, Larry. But she suspected. She put it up to him tonight and he spilled the whole works. He was comin' down tonight to get you and me, too, but she wouldn't let him. I'll give you the whole thing later on. Right now I'm feelin' sort of rotten."

"All right, old man. But tell me this: Do you know where Montez was this afternoon? There's something queer about the way old Blanchard passed out. He left the house, for some reason I can't fathom, and he might possibly have been trying to chase somebody away from there."

"Any wounds on him?"

"No. His heart simply stopped. But— Well, I'm puzzled."

MacLeod cogitated.

"No, I wouldn't say this snake had anything to do with that, Larry. Judgin' from what I heard, he worked in town today. Alibi stuff, you know. That would keep him there till about sundown. And what would he be doin' at the Blanchard place?"

"I don't know." Lawrence gazed outward again, meditating; then looked behind him. "Well, I suppose we'd better get the tools and dig two more graves."

"One more," morosely corrected Jack. "That snake on the floor goes into the sea."

"Think that's safe?"

"Safe enough. I've seen shark fins a couple of times lately."

"Oh. Well, all right. Let's get it over with."

They grasped the assassin by thighs and arm pits and, walking tandem, bore him out and away. A laborious journey down through the sloping valley and out along the western point, a pause for breath at the verge of a miniature precipice, a concerted swing and heave, a splash—and Montez was gone.

The waves, tonight more boisterous than usual, seized him and shoved him down to the rapacious undercurrents, which bore him away to oblivion in the outer deeps. Along the jagged shore line gurgled a hoarse chuckle of waters, and inland the myriad rocks grinned up at the moon. The Boîte du Mort had witnessed the passing of one more pirate; a prosaic pirate without ship or men or flag, but with as black a mind and as deadly a hand as any of the brutal brotherhood of centuries ago.

MacLeod, gazing hard-eyed at the spot where he had

disappeared, presently turned and mounted the steep slope dividing the neighboring bays. Spearman, though puzzled, followed without comment. At the summit Jack looked long at the inscrutable waters, the farther promontory, the blank sand where once had rested a mermaid now gone for all time. Empty of all life, the cove gave no hint of what had taken place within its confines. But after a time Jack pointed to the heaving surface.

"Van's in there," he announced.

His mate started, looked hard at the waves, harder at the speaker, but said nothing. His waiting attitude, however, was in itself a pointed question.

"Judgin' from what I heard," carefully declared Jack, "Montez caught him snoopin' up yonder and bumped him off, then sunk him in here. The reason why was because Van was keener than the rest of us and was workin' a good hunch. He wasn't playin' the game square, Van wasn't, but he had the right dope. The gold we've been rakin' hell's back yard for, Larry, was lifted before we got here, lifted by Montez and Lolita, and right now it's cached in that little cave she was so secretive about."

"Good Lord!" ejaculated the astounded listener. "Are you sure?"

"Pretty sure—judgin' by what I heard. And Lolita —she told me to dig in there. Seems the pair of 'em had a chart, somethin' like ours, and they came here to get the stuff, and after some trouble they got it. First off, Montez killed everybody in the Box by plantin' smallpox germs he'd brought from Domingo. She didn't know that, either, till tonight. Then they must have located the loot and moved it. They had a boat comin', but it never came—same as ours. So he worked down in town, playin' poor man, to fool the officials and sneak out a letter when he could; and she stayed here on guard. 'Twas a deep game. How Van got wise to it I don't know. Chances are that 'twas just a queer kink in that funny mind of his that started him off. But that's why he was spyin' and how he ended up."

Spearman stood in amazed silence. At length he said:

" 'Deep game' is right. But why should Montez try to poison the rest of us, when he already had found the gold?"

"Well, we were huntin' hard for Van and might find out somethin'. And besides that, he was afraid we'd got wise to his gold and might rob him of it. And moreover, he thought our map was for some other treasure, and we'd found said treasure, and so by knockin' us off he'd get that too. From what was said, I judge the gold he'd found wasn't as much as he expected; so he figured there must be another deposit somewhere."

Lawrence nodded, and they stared out across the cove, seeing things similar, yet not the same. Spearman reviewed the efforts of Lolita to glean from MacLeod and Mallory, and, once, from the useless chart in camp, knowledge of their quest. Jack recalled her bold hints —amazingly bold, they now seemed—of the knowledge she really possessed; realizing at last that, bored to revolt by loneliness and repugnance for Montez, she had wished to give not only herself but her fortune into

his own keeping, yet had not quite dared to risk all
with a man who refused mutual confidence.

Silently they turned away from the restless harbor
of Van Horn to construct a more peaceful haven for
the woman who had put him there. Somehow the corol-
lary fact that they were about to unearth the long
sought pirate hoard aroused scant interest.

Taking picks, spades, and electric torches from the
camp, they plodded back to the clearing and its cavern.
After clearing the earth floor of its jars and provisions,
they dug.

Two feet down, in the center of the place, the pick
in MacLeod's hands struck something hard; something
resistant, faintly resonant, giving neither the grating
protest nor the jarring nerve shock of smitten stone.
Spade work uncovered a box, its top deeply dented
by the blow of the pick.

On the tired faces bending above it dawned quick
light, which as quickly faded. This was no chest of
treasure; or, at best, a small and very crude one, made
not long ago from sections of weathered boards. When
Jack essayed to lift it, however, its weight evoked from
him a surprised grunt. Tumbled out on the floor, it gave
rth a metallic clink.

Two short swings of the pick and a pry with a spade
rced up the end of a board. A wrench by MacLeod's
rong fingers tore it away. Spearman turned down the
rilliant ray of a torch.

"Well," said Jack, flat toned, "this is it."

Gold coins gleamed in the light; gold interspersed
with blackened discs, evidently of ancient, long tar-

nished silver. Lawrence squatted, and both, with momentary eagerness, picked coins from the top and studied them.

"Spanish," nodded Lawrence, examining a gold piece. "Date 1630. A doubloon, or maybe an onza. And this old silver is pieces-of-eight."

"What's it worth, d'you suppose?"

"That's hard to say. Depends on how much is gold and how much is silver. A doubloon was worth twelve and a half dollars, an onza twenty-five, a piece-of-eight one. What they're worth today I don't know. At a rough guess I'd say we might have ten thousand dollars here, but that may be away off. Humph! It just goes to show how big these buried treasures grow in stories. Old Pierre knew the story of this box, and it was supposed to be so big that a Spaniard was crucified on its lid. This isn't the original chest, of course, but it's large enough to hold what was in the old one. And it's no longer than my arm."

"It's big enough to have cost five lives," moodily answered Jack. "Five that we know of—and all the people that got the smallpox, and God only knows how many others before that. And I'd give the whole bloody layout for one minute of time."

His partner looked curiously at him, then nodded in comprehension. If Jack had sprung into the house one minute sooner——

"Look here, Jack," he remonstrated. "For a fellow as hard boiled about women as you are, you're taking this pretty hard. And only this morning you were saying she was nothing but a pal——"

266

"I know. But she was the first pal I ever had—girl
pal, I mean—that would stick up for me in danger. It
takes a regular pal to do that. And I, standin' there at
the door and doin' nothin'—and with a gun on, too—
I was a hell of a fine pal, wasn't I?"

"Cut it out, Jack. What's the use?" rejoined Spearman, evenly. " 'The moving finger writes, and, having
writ——' You know the rest. Come on, let's finish up
here."

They dropped the coins back into the box and arose.
As they resumed work Spearman suggested another
trend of thought.

"That box is new, comparatively. Maybe there are
others like it in here; several small ones to hold what
was in the big one."

But there were no more. Further digging disclosed
only solid rock. When all the soil had been lifted, there
remained a concavity, a natural fold in the stone, which
would serve another purpose than that to which Montez had devoted it.

Spearman looked significantly at his companion. The
other nodded and walked to the house. After an interval he returned, bearing in his arms a sheeted form.
Together they lowered it. Then said Spearman, after a
glance at his partner's face:

"You carry out that box, Jack. And stay out."

"Thanks," gulped Jack. And he went forth.

When the floor was once more level, save for a long
mound in the middle, Spearman shouldered the tools,
took the torches, and departed. Outside he found the
moon high and bright, the house closed and dark, and

Jack and the treasure box side by side on the step; that step where, on a hot morning not so long ago, the rambling gambler had first seen the flame of the life of Lolita, and where tonight he had witnessed the striking of that flame into darkness. Now he arose and hoisted the box to a shoulder. The footsteps of the two men receded, and the moon alone watched over the deserted house, the whispering trees, and the sinister cavern which had sheltered food, drink, gold, and death.

In the barrack Jack let his burden down, lit the lamp, and loaded his pipe. Lawrence wolfed food. From time to time each glanced at the box of coins, but with listless eyes. At length Jack grumbled:

"We'll have to bury it again before we strike for the harbor."

"Uh-huh. Plant it where you can locate it when you come back."

"When *I* come back? How about you? Half of it's yours."

"No."

"Huh? What d'you mean?"

"It's plain enough, I should think. We came for what was on the chart. This moved off the chart. None of us had a right to it then; nobody but the owners. The last owner gave it to you, not me. That lets me out."

"I don't see it. Don't be a fool."

"Well, I see it. And if I want to be a fool that's my privilege."

"Humph!" Jack scowled at the box, puffing fast. "You're superstitious, afraid of bad luck or something."

"Not I. But that was Lolita's legacy to you. She'd never leave it to me, and you know it. And you've no right to give it or I to take it. And I won't. That's flat."

His voice was calm, but conclusive. Now he arose, undressed, and dropped on his cot. MacLeod finished his smoke, got into pajamas, and blew out the light. A moment he loomed at the window, brooding out at the mound beneath which lay Devlin and Mallory. Then his cot creaked, and thereafter the house was still.

Doors and windows stood wide, unbarred. Revolvers lay in dropped clothing, unready. Pirate gold rested on the floor, unguarded, virtually unwanted. It had cost too much.

CHAPTER XXIV

PLANS

To look with jaundiced eye on a treasure in time of darkness, when body and soul sag and life holds no zest, is one thing. To spurn it in the resurgence of sunlight and strength is quite another. So, when the brilliance of another day routed the shadow enshrouding the sleepers, the golden gleam of the doubloons exerted its lure.

Until after breakfast the box lay untouched, but not ignored. MacLeod, sluggish after lying long wakeful, eyed it now and then with heavy lidded somberness, yet with undeniable pleasure of possession. Spearman, refreshed by sounder sleep, accorded it occasional glances of lively interest. Upon both of them the ancient coins, won by wild sea battle and buried by men long since vanished into the mists of time, acted with magnetic power. Yet Spearman, though sensible of their spell, coveted them not at all. To him a renunciation once made was final, as Jack presently learned.

Enlivened and cheered by food, coffee, and tobacco, they emptied the box upon one of the cots and examined various pieces. As MacLeod noted that most of the coins were of gold his eyes began to glow. He lifted handfuls of them and let them slide between his fingers, listening with a half smile to the rich ring of the doubloons and the sharper clink of the pieces-of-eight, ancestors of the American dollar. After a time he slyly eyed his partner, absorbed in inspection of a clear-cut gold piece.

"Changed your mind yet?" he suggested, craftily dropping several coins with a mellow clang.

"No," was the prompt rejection. "What I said goes." And Lawrence arose, tossing aside the doubloon as if it were a mere disc of tin. "What's more," he added, "I don't want to know where you put it. Stow it somewhere out of sight, and the sooner the better, but don't tell me where."

"You're a queer cuss," grumbled Jack.

"Always was," cheerfully agreed the other. With that he donned his helmet and walked out.

MacLeod sat awhile pondering; then nodded and began refilling the box, roughly calculating values as he worked; reached for a hatchet, nailed down the dislocated lid, and set the crude chest on end beside the door. Outside Spearman was carrying stones from the wall of the goat corral to erect a cairn above the mound of Bill and Dan. Jack moved to join him.

"I can handle this alone, Jack," refused the builder. "Maybe you'd rather wall up the little cave."

"I was meanin' to," acquiesced the other. "But that's a two-man job you're tacklin', and——"

"I can swing it. You go ahead."

MacLeod went, taking his box with him. Up to the brushy entrance of the deserted clearing he carried it, and there he turned sharp aside, forcing his way to an odd-shaped stone which he had noticed more than once as he came and went: a knob-topped thing which, through the brush, somewhat resembled an ambushed man lurking on watch. Behind it he set down his burden. A few minutes of work in selecting and transporting small slabs lying near, and he had housed the treasure in a cage of rocks; a simple hiding place, easy to loot, if the looter knew exactly where to seek it; yet less likely to be sought, or accidentally found, than if buried and marked by a telltale patch of newly turned earth. Moreover, the treasure would remain there only until its master could return—by schooner, by sloop, by anything that would travel the sea lanes—and retrieve it in the shadowy hours of night.

Now, emerging from the screen of verdure, he proceeded to the goat corral, the inmates of which were vociferously demanding their usual release, and opened the plank gate. As the sturdy little beasts crowded out he eyed them calculatingly. Food was scant, meat non-existent; and these animals embodied both. But he let them go their way unharmed. The thought of killing was repulsive this morning. They would come back, anyway, for a night or two, to their customary dormitory; and by that time some decision must be reached as to the procedure to be followed in the ensuing days. So, lifting a stone from the top of the wall, he carried it to the cavern and began sealing the tomb.

Steadily he toiled until the work was done. When the darksome orifice had become a solid wall he stood a minute gazing at the barrier, his mind reaching through it as if it were but air. Then he lifted hand to helmet in silent salute; turned, and marched away, sober faced but dry eyed. What had been had been, and now it was ended.

At the camp he found the cairn complete and its builder gone. A survey of the beach revealed a lone towel swaying on a branch, and he knew that somewhere beyond the intervening trees his comrade bathed. By the time he reached the sands Spearman was lying in shade and meditatively smoking.

"Through?" laconically asked Lawrence, glancing up.

"Finished." Jack undressed and waded in.

While he took a leisurely swim a few yards out from shore, floating more than stroking, the man under the trees kept watch. In the course of his own bath he had twice descried a sinister triangular fin cleaving the surface not far beyond the promontories. Hitherto free from sharks, the water laving the edge of the Boîte du Mort now was harboring at least one of the destroyers, as if some malevolent spirit ruling the place had summoned from the deep a ruthless ally to annihilate the surviving invaders. The telltale fin now had vanished, but its very absence bothered the watcher, even though his companion remained in water only neck deep. No ordinary shark, wary of the shallows, would attack him there; but this creature might be more bold and ferocious.

When MacLeod came ashore unharmed, the self-appointed sentinel became aware of the futility of his concern; moreover, of the fact that his nerves, until recently almost imperturbable, had become unduly apprehensive. The rapid recurrence of tragedies, with their attendant and consequent stress on mind and body, had worn him down when sun and labor and monotony had failed; and now, though the mystery was cleared and the menace was removed, the strain persisted. Jack, too, showed plain effects of the bygone hours: his face was seamed, his body thinned to corded muscles and angular bones, his movements jerky. It was high time for both of them to quit the island.

Jack's first words proved his realization of the same fact. Toweled and trousered, he squatted and lit the cigarette extended by his comrade; then remarked:

"Exceptin' a shave, which we're both considerably in need of, and some laundry work, which our clothes sure are pinin' for, we're cleaned up. And exceptin' a little matter you've got on your mind, everything else is finished and done with. And it behooves us to get goin' somewhere in the near or immediate future. Havin' said which, I pass the buck to you."

"Accepted and understood," smiled Lawrence. "I've been casting about for the most plausible way of making our début and departure at Gustavia, and I figure that the shipwrecked sailor yarn's as good as any. We're both burned to leather by the sun, we're exceedingly unkempt as to haircuts, our hands are all calloused and knocked up by hard work—half my nails are broken—and our clothes, some of them anyway, are about worn out. A few days' growth of whiskers would help, too, but I'm shaving today just the same. Anyway, we're sailors off a tramp schooner, say, which sunk or burned or had a mutiny or something off to the eastward, and we got here in an open boat that hit a rock and sunk under us a bit offshore, so we had to swim to land. You can't speak French and I know only a few words, just enough to make ourselves understood but not enough to answer questions we don't want to understand——"

"Maybe the officials can speak English," interjected the listener.

"Um, that's so, they might. But we can be pretty dumb, even so. Maybe we're Danes or Norwegians or something like that. The ship was an American boat, though, because our money is American. We've got just a few dollars between us, and we'll pay it all to the fellow who carries us to some steamship port. There must be a sloop or two down at the harbor. As I figure it, the officials will get rid of us as quick as they can, to prevent our becoming public charges. How does the general idea sound to you?"

"Slick as frogs' hair," chuckled Jack. Then, with a quizzical glance: "But you were makin' threats awhile ago about gettin' married. Where does that fit in?"

"Well, that—that's not settled yet," hesitated Lawrence. A pause, while he traced random figures on the sand. "They're burying the father today at Saline, and of course everything else must wait." Another interval. "I don't see any way to marry on this island without starting an inquiry as to who I am and how I got here, and that would explode the shipwrecked sailor yarn and raise the devil generally. But there are plenty of other islands, and——"

"And we've just got to go together and come back

together, and while I lift the gold you grab the girl," finished the other. "Regular pirate stuff."

"That's about it, except the grabbing part. If she doesn't want to go——"

"Humph! I wouldn't worry about that little detail. She'll go."

"Meaning what?" Spearman's eyes narrowed.

"Meanin' that when a girl comes straight to you when trouble breaks, you're the fellow she relies on."

"Oh. Well, maybe. But it doesn't necessarily follow——"

"When a girl trusts a man everything follows, brother, everything follows. So sayin', I now pull on my shirt and hie me hence."

And so he did. Lawrence, smiling, followed. And both, as they went, felt more light hearted. The groundwork of the plan of exit was laid. Their return, hope whispered, would be only a matter of days. And then —away, with the gold and the girl!

Perhaps the Fates, looking to left and right of the walls of the Boîte du Mort, smiled as they spun the twisted threads of life of these two men. And perhaps Lachesis, whose duty was to see into the future, laughed aloud. Blind mortals, these, groping for their way as they had fumbled about for treasure; meaning to leave behind the precious things they had found and come back another day. The Fates had ordered it otherwise. They knew that, once the comrades left this isle, the day of their return would be—never.

Chapter XXV

A MAN AND A MAID

Sunset once more gilded the hilltops, and low in the darkening east the ghostly moon awaited its time to brighten into radiance, when Spearman crossed the divide.

An afternoon of welcome leisure had ended; an afternoon devoted mainly to a long siesta, preceded by semi-somnolent converse regarding the details of the plan for departure, followed by shaving and shifting to clothes never used in work, and terminated by a good meal from the supplies remaining. Now, walking with springy step, Lawrence traversed the pass toward the headland, half hoping, yet hardly expecting to find Céleste at home; for it would be but natural for her to spend this night among friends. Back at the barrack door MacLeod, who had stood smoking and watching him until he passed from sight, turned with a sigh and stepped to the table; lit the lamp, though the house was not yet dark, and shuffled cards for a dull game of solitaire.

At the top of the Saline path Lawrence paused in doubt. Down below, the little house seemed tenantless, looking forlorn in the gray light now lying over the lower levels. Yet both door and window stood open. Had they been left thus through heedlessness in departure, or was Céleste there, alone and sad?

As if in answer, beyond the threshold dawned the sheen of lamp light. She was there.

Unnecessarily fast he descended the track and approached the house; then slowed and began a cheery whistling. The response was immediate: a patter of shod feet and a swift-appearing form in the doorway. Céleste, in Sunday dress, greeted him with eager welcome.

"I thought you would come, Laurent! And I am so glad!" Impulsively she extended a hand toward him, but as quickly withdrew it. "It is a little lonely."

"This is the lonely hour," he said. "The end of day is always so if one is alone. But the new day will be brighter."

"I hope so." She looked a little doubtful of his meaning. "This one has been gloomy to me."

"Naturally. But all went well?"

"Yes."

She moved back, but he did not enter. Stopping at the door, he said:

"It is to be a beautiful evening. Let's stay here, where it is cooler. You sit on the step."

"Bien," she acquiesced.

Sinking on the threshold, she unconsciously arranged her long skirt, then looked pensively at the hills. He leaned against the jamb, contemplating the sunny hair glowing in the lamplight. And then for a time there was a silence between them; a silence not of diffidence but of unexpressed pleasure in companionship, and, on his part, of protective sympathy. Beyond the heights the last afterglow vanished, and upon their steep slopes the moonlight brightened, and all around ruled luminous night.

At length she began telling of the events of the day: the services conducted by the bon père from Gustavia, the kindliness of the Maréchals and other friends at Saline, the well meant but lacrymose commiserations of certain old crones, which, far from soothing sorrow, had impelled her to return early to the tongueless quietude of her home. It was lonely here, yes, but less lugubrious than the vicinity of such doleful folk.

She spoke as if musing aloud, expressing her inner thoughts rather than seeking to create conversation. He listened without reply, but with thoughtful attention to her words, and more to her manner. Except for natural pauses, she talked without faltering; and her calm voice proved her to be complete mistress of herself, imbued with a self reliance worthy of the daughter of rugged Pierre. Upon the observant listener grew the feeling that within the past twenty-four hours the shy, hesitant girl had become a grown woman.

When she lapsed into silence he made no comment on what had passed. After a minute or two, though, he sank to a squat on one heel, bringing his face to a level with her own. Quietly he said:

"I am glad that I found you here tonight, Céleste. I wanted to tell you that I shall be leaving tomorrow morning."

She glanced up, startled. Quickly she asked:

"Your ship is coming?"

"No, I fear it will never come. But we have decided that it is best for us to go. In fact, three of us have already gone. So only one other and I are left. And we can see no use in working longer in the Boîte du Mort."

Her eyes went again to the barren hills. After a moment she said:

"Yes, I remember that only one man was there yesterday with you. Why have the others left you, Laurent?"

"Two of them grew sick and could not stay longer. And we have heard that the one who disappeared went to sea; so we are not worrying about him now. The other man and I intended to carry on the work, but now we think it best to stop." His voice was matter-of-fact. In the same casual tone he went on: "So we shall go to the harbor, and there we shall be shipwrecked sailors when the officials ask questions. That may be dishonest, but it's safest. We shall be very poor men, and leave the island as soon as we can. But we shall also come back as soon as we can. And—and then——"

He did not complete the prediction, but looked at her with an odd smile. She did not return it. While he talked she watched him intently. As she heard his promise, however, she turned her gaze away.

"You will come back?" she echoed. "But why?"

"Well, we have trunks and—and various other things that we don't want to lose. So we shall return on our new boat to get them."

"I see. And so, after all your search, you have found nothing?"

"The only thing of value I have found is you!"

A quick laugh brightened her face, dying to a demure smile. She looked down at her work-hardened hands.

"I am of very little value," she deprecated.

"I think otherwise. I think you are the most——"

The confidence died half born. She had started and glanced aside, and as he halted his words he heard a footfall at one corner of the house. Now around that corner came a squat figure which stopped short, voicing an astounded grunt.

Lawrence and Céleste looked into the gaping countenance of Josué Thibaut.

Josué, barefoot and patch-trousered, straw-hatted against the mysterious maleficences of the moon, goggled in dumfounded alarm at the long shape which straightened up at the doorway and blocked him from fulfilment of desire. Josué had not brought his father with him this time. He knew that Pierre Blanchard was buried, Céleste Blanchard was alone in her isolated home, and no other Blanchard was alive to defend her. The presence of Thibaut père was, therefore, unnecessary to his present plans. He was much stronger than she; and the sooner she learned to submit, the better. But the rising of this formidable apparition in the shadows beside her was a most disconcerting contretemps. In truth, it was downright diabolical.

One of the Blanchard boys who had gone to death in France had been tall and slim. Was this his ghost, materializing to protect his sister? He did not look the same, but he had been dead a long time, and——

"Va-t'-en!" snapped the phantom. "Get out!"

Josué gave back a step. But then his innate obstinacy rose to bolster his courage. This obstructor was no Blanchard, but a stranger. The thick Thibaut shoulders took a stubborn set; and, though his tongue was slow to find words, his attitude bespoke mulish resistance.

The ghost sprang forward. A terrific shock smote Josué on the jaw. The ground leaped up and struck him in the back. Dazed, he pushed himself up to a sit, to stare groggily at the menacing figure above him.

"Va-t'-en!" commanded the hard-fisted blaster of hopes.

This time the order was obeyed. Josué lurched to his feet and went, wobbling. A few rods away, though, he slowed and turned his head. But the demon had not vanished. It was glowering after him, and now it started in purposeful pursuit. Forthwith he resumed his retreat at double time; nor did he look back again until his feet were on the long sands. There at the edge of the bluff was the fearsome figure, grim as ever, watching him with ominous readiness. With a groan of mingled fear, anger, and despair he fled on toward home and father.

Spearman, returning toward the house, alternately chuckled and frowned, flexing the abraded fingers of his right hand. The Thibaut jaw had been hard and rough.

"Now the fat's in the fire," he muttered. "He'll squeal like a stuck pig, and by tomorrow the news of

that sock in the jaw will be all over the island, and by
the time two Americans reach the harbor they'll be
candidates for jail because one of them assaulted the
sacred person of an amorous frog. And that will precipitate an avalanche of investigation which— Umph!
The ocean's growing a bit dusty for shipwrecked
sailors!"

Then he laughed again and left the things of tomorrow to develop as they might.

Standing at the corner where Josué had appeared,
Céleste met him with a queer look of mingled approval
and rebuke.

"Why did you do that?" she asked, trying to speak
with severity.

"Because we don't like him."

"We? How do you know I don't like him?"

"Your face told me."

He grinned, and all at once she laughed merrily,
glancing at the hat left on the ground by the overthrown interloper. Crude and clumsy, it lay as gro-
tesquely as had its owner.

"No, I do not like him," she admitted. "And I am
glad you were here. But I never thought he would——"

She stopped. He became serious.

"You never thought he would bother you? Well,
I've been afraid that some man would, and I'm still
afraid that after I go—— You should not be alone at
night, Céleste, without some means of defense. Before
I go I will give you a revolver and show you how to
use it. But perhaps it would be better for you to live
at Saline until I come back; you would surely be quite

safe there, among your friends. You must tell me just where I can find you, though, when I return, because I shall be coming in at night and going before sunrise, and there will be no time to lose."

To this she gave no reply. She too was serious again, very serious, and her gaze dwelt on the moonlit ground beyond him. For a short period the place was very still.

"Have you thought about what I said to you last night?" he asked then.

"Yes," she acknowledged, low voiced. "I have thought."

"And are you ready to answer?"

The blue eyes rose to his; and, though her color deepened, they did not swerve nor drop. Squarely and steadily they met his gaze, and she spoke with frank directness.

"Laurent, just what do you want of me?"

The candid question permitted no misunderstanding or circumlocution. The grave eyes forbade evasion, or even hesitance.

"Dear girl, I want to marry you, and take you home to America, and keep you forever! What did you think?"

"You never have said, you know. You have told me only that you would take me away to S'n Thomas and, perhaps, to your own country. And I do not know much about you, Laurent!"

The eyes smiled at him, but still searched his own. He flushed, but admitted the justice of her doubt. For centuries, among these islands, men had come from the sea to win the love of women, and, having won, to loot their souls and cast them off. And Céleste knew of this man only what she had seen of him and heard from his own tongue—a tongue proven sometimes even deceptive.

Whatever her heart might urge her to do, she possessed a clear mind and a firm will. She was not the girl to give herself lightly away or, despite the barrenness of Barths, to fare forth on the seaways with a man in whom she had not full confidence.

"Quite right," he conceded. "But I think that in your heart you know I am speaking honestly; and since you know that, you know everything of importance. If you don't care enough for me to marry me, I am sorry. But I shall take you to Saint Thomas—if you will go, as your father wished you to do—and make sure that you are safely settled there before I leave you. I want you to be happy, whether you are with me or not. If you believe you would be happy as my wife, then we shall be married at Saint Thomas and go home together. And I hope that is what we shall do. I want you, Céleste!"

His hands closed on her shoulders, drawing her closer, half resistant, half yielding. Her breath quickened, and her steadfast gaze momentarily dropped.

"Why—why do you want me so much, Laurent? You know I have no *dot*, and——"

"Dear girl, you are your own *dot*," he laughed. "You are you, and I want just you! In my country it's not the custom to marry for dowries; and I'm not that sort of fortune hunter, even if I did come here looking for gold. And we shall need no dowry to live on. I have a little income from some investments I made years ago. I'm not rich, but we shall have enough, and I can make more. Come, now, look up again, and tell me all that's in your heart. You know what is in mine."

Her head lifted, and once more their eyes met and held. Suddenly impulse banished all uncertainty. The barriers of reason, logic, maidenly caution fell before the resistless sweep of intuitive trust.

"I will go with you."

The low-spoken promise held no reservation. There was no need to ask whether she would go only to Saint Thomas, or to the home in the far-away North. Her voice told it all.

His arms swept around her, and for long seconds they stood silent. Then to the little ear below his lips he murmured:

"The doctor orders a kiss."

The head against his shoulder shook refusal; but then, slowly, her face rose, laughing in the moonlight.

"One must—obey the docteur, Laurent."

Then, for the first time, Céleste learned that there were kisses more ardent than those of parents or brothers.

Breathless, she drew away. As his clasp tightened again she resisted, bracing her hands against him.

"No—no, Laurent—not now. Let me go!"

Reluctantly he released her. For a moment she stood wordless, subduing strange emotions, while her gaze went to the spot where she had found her father dead, and on toward the rocks beyond. When her eyes once more rose to those of her fiancé they held a cryptic message.

"Laurent, I have something to show you in the house," she said. "Come with me."

She led the way, moving eagerly. Within, she drew from a tiny cedar box an old, clumsy pocketbook, worn by long service. As she opened it she betrayed mounting excitement.

"This belonged to my father," she said rapidly. "He told me several times, after his heart became bad, to look into this when he should die. And once before that time, when he was a little sick, he asked me to write down a number of words for him, so that he could see how they looked. He never had learned to write; my grandfather did not believe in schools. So I wrote the words to amuse him, and then forgot about it; they did not mean anything. But today I remembered his bidding and looked into this purse, and I found a few francs and these words I wrote so long ago. And I wonder—I wonder— What do you see in them?"

He took the creased paper which she unfolded, and peered at it with knit brows. Perhaps twenty words were there, written in a clear round hand, and neatly columned. The sequence meant nothing; the first word was "chat," meaning "cat." But each alternate word was thinly underlined. And when, after puzzling over the senseless whole, he reread the column, he found the marked words forming a sentence:

Entre — deux — pierres — nord — ouest — se — trouve—ressource—au—besoin.

"Between two stones, northwest, can be found help

in case of need," he read aloud. "That's queer. I don't comprehend—let's see. Two stones, northwest——"

"Yes!" she broke in. "The two stones beyond the spot where father fell—they are to the northwest from this house! And I have looked between them, and there is another stone, a small sharp one, set in the ground. And I think something must be buried there! I wonder—I wonder if I have a *dot!*"

Chapter XXVI

THE *DOT*

Midway between those two stones toward which Pierre Blanchard had been moving when smitten by death, a much smaller stone projected from the sun-baked soil; an inconspicuous, angular fragment seemingly flung there many a year ago and gradually encompassed by sediment from the rain-sluiced slopes beyond. In his first puzzled scrutiny of the vicinity Lawrence had given it only a perfunctory glance. But now, as he strode back to that spot, with Céleste eagerly hopeful beside him and the enigmatic prophecy of the coded column limned on his mind, that hitherto despicable excrescence dwarfed in importance both the ponderous boulders flanking it.

Ressource au besoin—resource in need—that must mean money. Yet, in view of the pitiable poverty in which Pierre had lived and died, how could that be the meaning? It seemed most unlikely. Perhaps, though, in the days of his strength he had managed by rigid economy to lay aside a few occasional francs, and thus gradually to form a tiny hoard for use only as the *dernière ressource*, the last expedient in dire emergency. Yes, that probably was the explanation. When that small stone should be lifted a little bag of silver would be disclosed, and Céleste, poor girl, would find her romantically visioned *dot* a mere handful of small coins.

Rounding the first boulder, they halted beside the lowly marker—if such it was. He scanned it a moment; then, with a glance at the star-eyed girl, cautioned her:

"Don't be disappointed, chérie, if it's not what what you expect. You know it can't be large."

"Yes, I know," she nodded. "But let us see."

He stooped and gave the stone a tentative tug; braced himself, and heaved hard. It did not move. He worked around it, applying stress from every angle. Still it stood immobile.

"It's set deeper than I thought," he said. "Have you tools?"

"Yes. I will bring them——"

She darted away. He doffed his coat and rolled up his sleeves. Soon she trotted back, carrying an ancient mattock and a worn-down spade. He chose the mattock, and with it attacked the stubborn soil, at first with short strokes, then with uncompromising swings. The deceptive stone he found to be roughly pyramidal, the subterranean portion comprising two-thirds of the total mass and holding tenaciously to its hard-packed setting. It cost him a score of strong blows, and subsequent toil with the spade, to bare its base. Then, hooking his fingers under the lower edge, he heaved it up and out.

"Oh!" cried Céleste, dismayed.

In the cavity was no pouch, no box; nothing but more earth.

"Well, this seems to be the wrong place," he said,

wiping his forehead and frowning about. "And I don't
see any other signs."

Soberly she followed his gaze. Between the boulders
stretched perhaps twenty feet of surface unbroken by
any projection. The rocks themselves were at least a
dozen feet long. To dig up the entire terrain enclosed
between them would mean long, hard labor, rewarded
only by a paltry sum—if, indeed, repaid at all. And in
the past few days he had experienced overmuch of
delving.

Possibly, though, one of the larger stones would yield
a clue: a mark on its surface, an almost indiscernible
stub at its base. Moving along each in turn, he minutely
inspected it, peering, feeling with finger tips for any
invisible grooves; then, crouching, pored over the ad-
jacent ground.

"Well, dear, I'm afraid it's hopeless," he told her.
"But what does it matter? The *ressource* must have been
very small; and you will never need it. If you do need
some money to keep you till I come back, I can give
you some before I go. You are almost my wife now, you
know, so——"

"It is not that, Laurent," she interrupted. "I can live.
But——"

She turned away, tears stealing down her cheeks. The
collapse of her air castle, modest though it had been, was
not merely a disappointment but a humiliation. She had
wished so ardently that she might bring to her husband
at least the semblance of a dowry! And now the proffer
of money from him served only to accentuate her poverty. It was thoughtful of him, and generous, but——

How obtuse was the understanding of men with regard to some things!

"Laurent, there must be something!" she asserted, facing him again. "Father would never have left that message if there were not!"

"It was written long ago, you said," he reminded her. "And a number of things may have come about since then. Perhaps somebody stole what was here. But don't feel so badly. It's just possible that I haven't dug deep enough or wide enough. And rather than have you cry I'll tear up every inch of ground, and move these rocks too. Now you rest and watch your man work."

With determined strokes he widened the perimeter of the rough circle about the former seat of the rock, and with careful sifting of the loosened soil he cast it farther out, assuring himself that each small lump was only earth or pebble. Then, having cleared a four-foot space, he dug straight down. After the removal of the hardened upper crust he found the underlying dirt yielding more readily; so he used only the spade. Deeper and deeper it bit, until he was working in a pit reaching to his waist. All at once he paused.

The cutting edge had met something it could not cut: a thing offering solid opposition, but not the inflexible antagonism of stone or wood. Probing about, he learned that the obstruction filled considerable space. His pulses quickened. Rapidly he shoveled out the intervening gravel. The moon, now high, revealed a pair of cylinders of cloth.

Lying side by side, the twin rolls resembled the trousered legs of a man. But their unvarying thickness, uniform from end to end, showed them to be well filled bags. And when, squatting, he poked and pinched them with investigatory fingers, the nature of their contents became unmistakable. They were full of coins.

"Good Lord!" he muttered. "He was a miser! There are francs enough here to buy half the island!"

Grasping one of the bags, he lifted it with a jerk. Something gave way. Instantly a weight of metal poured down on his feet, and the stillness was broken by a ringing cataract of sound. One end of the bag had ripped, and before he could shift it half the contents had escaped.

"Oh!" cried Céleste, springing to the edge. "Oh, it is true!"

"Yes, it's true!" He laughed exultantly, swinging the remaining half bagful to rest on the lip of the hole. "And it's all good honest silver—— Great guns! No, it isn't! It's gold!"

His hand, diving into the container to bring forth a sample of her treasure, had brought out coins which now gleamed yellow. For a second or two both stood paralyzed. Then, with an inarticulate murmur, she sank to the ground, and together they stared at the heavy discs in his palm. All were doubloons.

Speechless, he turned them into her lap and drew forth another handful: more doubloons, and two onzas —double doubloons. From below, as he moved, sounded a subdued chink of the spilled coins around his feet; and when he looked down they laughed up at him with the same golden shine. Spanish gold! Pirate gold! It could be nothing else.

Moving in a daze, he squatted and gathered it up by the double handful, rising to lay it beside her, lowering himself again and standing again, until all had been picked up. As before, all were gold. Nowhere among them was a single silver piece. To the man who had concealed this hoard, silver had been too cheap to be worth keeping.

In gathering up the last of it, Lawrence found that the bag had lain not on earth but on another bulging cylinder of the same coarse cloth. A sudden fever swept him, banishing the stunned feeling. Speedily, though so carefully that no second shower resulted, he raised the second bag; then a third; then a fourth. And still there remained two more. Now that he had penetrated to the hidden *ressource*, it seemed inexhaustible.

With the removal of the sixth sack, however, the cache was emptied. Lower down remained nothing but earth and crowded stones. Assured of this, he vaulted out and squatted to inspect the bags.

Clumsy things, they were: double-ended cylinders, tied at each extremity, with ragged ends drooping beyond the corded puckers. His fingers, sliding along their gritty surfaces, detected patches. Suddenly their true nature became evident. They were the legs of jean trousers: overalls. A king's ransom was encased in the cheap clothing of peasants.

The incongruity of it evoked a chuckle. Then he looked at the inheritor of the wealth within those crude cloths.

The magical growth of her unbelievable riches had struck Céleste into voiceless stupefaction. Lips parted, eyes clouded with incredulity, she sat almost breathless. Twice she extended a hand toward the last bags, only to withdraw it as if fearful that all would vanish at a touch. Not until Lawrence took that hand in his own and placed it upon the lumpy cloth could she convince herself of its actuality.

"It's real," he affirmed, yanking open an end of the nearest cylinder. "Look!"

The revelation this time, however, was not quite what he expected. No doubloons came forth. The metal tumbling out was in lumps. A flash of doubt swept him. Sharp scrutiny, though, proved these lumps also to be of gold, each stamped with a cryptic mark of inspection and guaranty. They were small ingots of pure bullion, even more valuable than the antique coins, since they were unalloyed.

He dumped them out, then emptied all the other bags on the earth. Three of them he found filled with ingots; two with coins; and the sixth with a mixture of both. All was gold. Nowhere glittered a diamond, a ruby, or any other gem. But the rich gleam of the yellow heaps was in itself enough to enthrall the beholders. Side by side they sat and marveled.

Ressource au besoin! The words reiterated themselves in his brain, flickering like an intermittent light in an umbrageous labyrinth of questions. Where and how had Pierre gotten this? Why, having gotten it, had he never used it? Why had he never revealed its existence to his daughter, save by that blind will in her own handwriting? These and other riddles stood out at every turn, demanding solution. As his mind coursed along the tortuous path, however, other words arose as guides, and presently the road became clear.

"He has lifted too many stones." "There is a curse on that gold—and the man taking it from that cursed earth will never profit by it." "Misery and want, thanks to Guadeloupe and France!" "The swine of officials would seize every franc." Such sentences as these leaped out of the past with new significance, as did forgotten tones and covert looks and crafty interrogations. A subtle old fellow, Pierre Blanchard! In his sly way he had told the truth about the gold of the Boîte du Mort, yet so obscurely as to leave that truth still unseen.

This was the treasure of the long lost box; loot wrested with bullet and cutlass from Spanish ships, buried probably by command of Montbars himself, sought by generations of Barths Blanchards, unearthed at last by the sole remaining male descendant. Feigning disbelief in its existence, he had toiled secretly while all others slept. In the end he had won; won with a surprising suddenness which caught him unprepared for the immediate problem of removing his find. That problem had been solved, however, by the improvisation of sacks from his own overalls and by similar utilization of other trousers taken from his house—the abandoned clothing, perhaps, of his vanished sons. Thus, working in mad haste, he had rushed his treasure trove to the sanctuary of his own land—only to learn, when all was done, that he had earned not ease but disease, not pleasure but pain, not life but death. Probably it was the effort of transporting an overweight of gold across the divide which had given his heart its irreparable strain.

At any rate, he had doomed himself by his discovery. He had taken the gold from the ground where it lay, but never profited by it.

He could not profit from it so long as he remained on Barths. Nor could he leave Barths. To reveal his possession of even one doubloon or ingot would inevitably set the whole island to buzzing; the officials would hale him before an inquisition, and by the time they finished with him he would be in even worse case than before. He could not, without betraying himself, engage a reputable vessel to carry him and his fortune elsewhere. If he should make a stealthy departure on some craft of dubious character, he would face the probability of being murdered at sea; he was an invalid, unable to defend himself, powerless to protect a fortune and a girl against unscrupulous men inflamed by lust for both. Thus, though possessor of wealth, he was condemned by a malign fate to die in the penury to which he had been born.

It was his brooding upon this fact, no doubt, which had germinated his belief in a curse on the gold. Certainly no such belief had previously deterred him from exhuming it. Once this conviction obsessed him, however, it had become a dread shadow hovering ever above the transferred hoard, and still potent to blast the next possessor. Thus he could not permit even his daughter to make use of that wealth; for, if she unearthed it, she must incur its blight. Yet, perhaps gnawed by fear that life might hold for her some form of misery worse than any the gold could bring, he had made a way for her to find it at need. It was a cunning way, too, and a clever one for a man of his limitations—forming his message in alternate words and, after they were unsuspectingly written, marking the characters which he knew must constitute the right sequence. Yes, Pierre had done well.

It must have been a torment to him at times, that useless wealth, tantalizing him with its suggestions of what might be. Yet what a sardonic satisfaction he must have derived from the knowledge that he was cheating the grasping officials, the hated Guadeloupe, and the France which had slain his sons, out of any share in it! "We old ones have not much more to endure," he had said. And so he had endured. Grim old stoic!

But why had he come forth yesterday and sought this spot? To this there was no answer. Perhaps, alone in the house, he had become worried as to the safety of what lay here. There was reason enough to worry, too, or would have been if Montez had suspected the truth. Perhaps the Frenchman had long been suspicious of that pocked Spaniard and had made more than one surreptitious trip to this cache. Quite likely.

Queer about the find which Montez actually had made. That comparatively small treasure must have been buried by some other pirate, perhaps an under officer of Montbars, before or after the concealment of the master's chest.

There his conjectures ended. Céleste stirred, awaking from a reverie as deep as his own. Happily she said:

"Eh bien, Laurent, I have a *dot!*"

"Yes, you have a *dot,* and no other girl in the whole wide world has one just like it." He smiled at her, then looked once more at the heritage from Spanish galleons. "But now we'll have to hide it until we——"

He stopped short. Out of the surrounding stillness suddenly broke a new voice. It came from high on the hill path; a booming bass, quick and imperative.

"Hey, Larry!"

"Hullo!" answered Lawrence, springing up.

"Wind up your affairs and snap out of it! Our ship's come in!"

CHAPTER XXVII

A SHIP COMES IN

MacLeod, gloomily playing his solitary game, flung down his cards and pushed back from the table. The stark loneliness had become intolerable.

Those inanimate kings and knaves could not replace human fellowship. Rather, they recalled the nights forever gone, when around this table had grouped comrades matching wits, exchanging repartee, drinking, smoking, gambling, singing, driving dull care to the outer dark. Try as he might to hold his mind to its time-killing task, it persisted in dwelling on the past and emphasizing the emptiness of the present. In the end it routed him.

From the depleted brandy bottle he gulped a stiff drink. From his tobacco pouch he thumbed and tamped a fresh pipeful. Trailing smoke, he walked out into the night-shine, there to look wistfully at the high pass where Spearman had disappeared. 'Twas taking Larry a devil of a long time to console his girl. And this was a dismal hole to stick in, all alone.

His gaze drifted westward, toward the invisible ravine beyond which stood the desolate house of Lolita. It turned abruptly back, and fell to the cairn beneath which lay Dan and Bill. Once more it dodged, going now to the empty bay. A moment of moody contemplation, and he lounged away down the hill. Lifeless though the strand was, it held companionship of a sort —the ceaseless movement and the inarticulate voices of the waves.

Down on the sands he lay at full length, chin on folded arms, pipe smouldering, eyes absently watching the rush and retreat of the water. Life was like that, he mused; a constant surge of effort and an unending rebuff by unfeeling obstacles to achievement, breaking the strength of those who strove; a senseless, useless expenditure of energy, ending in nothing. Look at Dan and Bill and Van Horn, for instance. Yes, and at Lolita and Miguel. What had all their planning and striving gotten them? Nothing. And look at this man MacLeod, too. He had won, in a blind gamble, a store of pirate gold; but what good would it do him in the end? It would go the way of all other moneys he had ever held: squandered on another gamble or another woman——

No! Not this time! No woman should get that legacy of Lolita. He would invest it in something up home; some good bonds, maybe. Larry could give him sound advice on that point. Larry had a level head, and he knew a thing or two about investments; and it was high time for this rambling, gambling son of a gambolier of a MacLeod to show some sense and play safe. Yes, Larry would steer him right. However, it was still a bit early to consider the ultimate use of the treasure. It had a long road to travel, and as yet there was not even a ship to carry it.

He started up. There *was* a ship!

She was offshore, beating up into the wind. Hope shouted that she was bound for this bay; hope backed for reason, since no fishing vessel would be out at this time of night. Even as he looked, she put about and steered for him.

No further doubt could exist. Out of the west she had come—out of the west, where lay distant Saint Thomas—and she was heading into L'Anse Gouverneur! Thurston, at last!

No maroon on a desert isle ever beheld the approach of deliverance with greater joy than that now stimulating MacLeod. For a minute or two his exuberance swept away all control. He sprang into the air, he pranced about the sand, he waved arms and voiced incoherent yells. Then the outburst checked as suddenly as it had begun.

This rapidly approaching craft was not the one on which Thurston would travel. It was smaller. It was not even a schooner, but a sloop. From the heights of joy he dropped to the depths of doubt. Another moment of watching, and his mouth tightened and a hand went back to the gun on his hip. He remembered that Montez had sent letters to one Jaime Lopez.

The dingy single-sticker swept in, caught anchorage, dropped sail. Two men on her deck squinted warily at the lone figure on the sand. Neither of them called or spoke.

"Hullo there!" challenged MacLeod. "Who are you?"

A pause. Then a retaliating question:

"Who speaking?"

The voice sounded familiar. Jack peered hard, but could not distinguish features.

"MacLeod," he enunciated clearly. "Are you bringin' Mister Thurston?"

"Non, monsieur," came immediate response, in tones of recognition. "Monsieur Thurston being dead. Me, I am Louis. I bringing ship to you. We cyome ashore, yes?"

"You bet! Come on!"

Jack's voice rang heartily, and his hand sank. At once the pair lowered a small boat. One sat and one sculled hurriedly. At the edge of the sand the sculler dropped oar, sprang out, and, grinning, loped to meet the tall American. The other lingered to beach the boat securely.

"Bon soir, monsieur," chuckled Louis, bowman of the ghost ship which had landed the treasure hunters here. "I thinking maybe you like to see me again, so I cyome."

"You guessed right, man!" Jack extended his hand, giving the faithful fellow a grasp that made him wince. "Never was so glad to see anybody in my life! But who's this with you?"

"Dis being Gaspard Leblanc, from S'n Martin, sir. He owning de sloop. I being on S'n Martin all de time since de schyooner burn, an'——"

"What? The schooner burned?"

"But yas, sir, she burn de very night we leaving you. I go sleeping on deck, an' Jean holding de wheel, an' Monsieur Thurston sitting on de gas tank. An' I waking up quick, an' de ship all fire—*pouf! wheessssh!*"

With waving arms and explosive hiss he dramatically pictured the catastrophe.

"De gas tank she blow up—everyt'ing going to hell! I see notting but fire—it burning me—I jump in sea. If Monsieur Thurston an' Jean burning or drowning I don' know—I never seeing dem no more. De schyooner burning long time, but I not finding dem. Me, I swimming mos' all de night, I cyoming ashore on S'n Martin like dead man. I am sick long time—I getting damn bad burn, sir! Den I saying myself, maybe les messieurs wanting go 'way now, I cyome an' see. Dis Gaspard, I know him long 'foretime; he living one time on Barths, now on S'n Martin. So he saying if you like pay him good price he be taking you all way to S'n Thomas, asking no questions. You wanting go, sir?"

MacLeod took one swift survey of the sturdy, open-faced Gaspard, now standing quietly near, and nodded.

"Right! We'll pay him well. And because you lost your pay on the other trip we'll pay you double, and give you a present besides. And we'll leave at once."

Chuckling joyously, Louis rattled a mouthful of French at Gaspard, who smiled at MacLeod but said nothing. As Jack strode away they plodded after him. At the camp he paused, saw that Spearman still was absent, told the oncoming Frenchmen to wait there, and rapidly followed the route by which his sole remaining comrade had gone over the hills.

Emerging within view of the lamplit house, he loosed his questing hail. The reply from the field revealed to him the two figures standing as one between the rocks. As he threw back his startling news he grinned. If Larry had wasted all this time sitting out in the moonlight and working up to the point of proposal, he'd have to do some fast work now: either abduct the girl in true pirate style or jump out and leave her.

Lawrence did neither. For a few seconds he stood almost incredulous of this second stroke of good fortune. Then he quickly translated the announcement for Céleste and raised his voice in answering command:

"Jack! Come down here!"

"All right."

The acquiescence was a trifle tardy, for MacLeod was turning away with mind now intent on his treasure, and unnecessary delay irked him. However, a few minutes more or less would make little difference. So, watching the unfamiliar and rather vague path, he swung downward. Meanwhile Lawrence advanced, leaving Céleste struggling with conflicting emotions—joy that a way of escape had opened, anxiety lest evil befall her marvelous *dot* at the hands of the unknown men on shipboard, doubt as to what to do.

At the foot of the hill the two comrades met. And Lawrence demanded:

"How come?"

"Well, now, 'twas like this, young fellah me lad," jested Jack. "After you basely deserted me I went to the seaside and practiced some occult rites known only to such sons of Belial as me, myself, sayin' over and over: 'Rise ye from the vasty deep to waft us from hither to thither,' and similar abracadabra. And at last she rose from said deep, a snoopy sloop, bearin' our old friend Louis, who has been to hell and back, and no

305

kiddin'. And she waits without. And since life is short and time is fleetin'——"

"Boil it down, Jack. How come?"

"Well, if you insist on unadorned truth and nothing but the truth——"

Then, seriously and concisely, Jack narrated the facts revealed by Louis, concluding with the accurate surmise:

"Thirsty must have hit the bottle again and got careless with matches. Now that's the whole story. And if there's nothin' more I can do for you—"

"Maybe there is. Come over here a minute."

As they walked toward the boulders Lawrence added:

"I've been practicing some black art myself, and——"

"Hypnotized the fair damsel into your diabolical clutches," guessed Jack, "and now you want my blessin' on your nefarious work. Well, you've got it."

Lawrence, smiling mysteriously, left his announcement unfinished. Jack, with vision intent on the girlish figure of his partner's bride-to-be, was almost upon the gold before he discovered it. Then he stopped, dumbfounded.

"The real thing, Jack," quietly said Lawrence. "The treasure that was on the chart. Old man Blanchard found it years ago and reburied it here. Now it all belongs to this young lady."

Wordless, Jack stooped and for minutes pored over the strewn masses of metal. Céleste watched him apprehensively, with occasional anxious glances at Lawrence. Her first impression of this man had not been favorable;

306

and now she saw the revolver butt protruding at his hip. Had it been wise to summon him here?

Slowly MacLeod arose, his face alight with heartfelt pleasure. He smote his partner on a shoulder, he gripped his hand hard, and his hearty tones banished all the girl's doubt.

"You're lucky, man! And I'm damn' glad!"

"Thanks, old chap."

Then Jack did an odd thing. He stepped to Céleste and stood looking steadily into her eyes. Surprised, she drew back a little, but thereafter returned his searching gaze, unafraid. In the brown eyes was a critical question, and in the clear blue ones they found their answer. As the tall cynic stepped back he bowed slightly in involuntary tribute.

"Yes, you're more than lucky," he amended. "You've found somethin' worth more than this whole layout, if you ask me; somethin' I'll never find."

"Keep looking, Jack," encouraged Lawrence, strangely moved, "and maybe some day——"

"No. There's nothin' like that in the world for me; nothin' but imitations and damaged goods." Then, with swift assumption of levity: "Well, shipwrecked sailor, blessin's on thee and thy progeny! And now, passin' on to the next cage, we see before us, fixin' us with evil eye and lickin' its chops, the problem of transferrin' our filthy lucre to the hold of our sea-goin' barouche. And the sooner the quicker."

"Quite so." Lawrence looked back at the long sands of Saline Bay, finding them vacant. "Well, for obvious reasons I've got to stay here. You do this, if you don't mind: Go to the camp, empty the locker trunks, and have the men fetch them over the hill and leave them at the foot of the path. Then strip the camp clean of our stuff and load everything aboard; don't leave a solitary thing to show who we are or where we came from. Get your box, of course. Then go aboard. Bring the sloop around to this beach yonder. By that time we'll be ready for you."

"Ay, ay, sir!" Jack snapped a smiling salute. "I'm off."

He went. Lawrence turned to Céleste and explained the arrangements, concluding:

"You go in now and make a bundle of the things you want to take with you. I'll pack up your *dot*. And in a little while we shall be gone from this place forever and on our way to a happier world."

With a smile at him and a lingering look at her dowry, she moved away. Before she reached the house the golden heaps behind her had vanished again—covered from sight by the moldy bags which had held them, and which the guardian now had thrown over them as precaution against the telltale yellow gleams. This done, he walked again toward the hill path.

Back at the barrack, MacLeod found the seamen waiting solemnly; and, though they said nothing, he realized that in his absence they had looked about and found the mound topped by its cairn. They eyed him a little queerly, and Gaspard seemed ill at ease. Wherefore he took the bull by the horns at once.

"There will be only three to sail," he told Louis, with level gaze. "We have had misfortune. One fell into the sea. Two ate the mancenille." He nodded toward the cairn. "Mister Spearman and his fiancée and I are the three to go."

As Louis relayed this, Gaspard's face cleared. The deaths here were accidental, then. And there was a romance. He chuckled, as did Louis. And when the American gave them their orders they fell willingly to work.

Jack himself carried one of the hastily emptied trunks across the divide, guiding the following pair. At the foot of the hill waited Spearman. A brief talk with the grinning Louis, a few words in French to the observant Gaspard, and he sent them back. When they were out of sight he dragged the fiber boxes to the pit and busied himself stacking the gold.

Directed by MacLeod, the sailors labored steadily at stripping the camp and carrying loads. Soon the last burden was under way; the last the Frenchmen were to transport from this valley, but not the last to go. As they plodded down the hill their commander quietly swung away upward, journeying alone to the brushy notch where his treasure waited—and a little way beyond it.

In the little field he stood looking a moment at the forlorn house, longer at the rock wall guarding its secret. From the hidden homestead all life was gone. Even the corral now stood empty; already its former tenants, finding no shepherd at even-tide, had deserted it for freedom or for some new home.

"Adios!" he muttered.

No answer came, save the sigh of leaves swept by the

breeze. He turned, walked back to the ravine, and uncovered his box. Without another backward look he trudged away.

Once more he halted, and only once. Near the barrack he stepped aside to the cairn, to stand with box on shoulder, head bowed, somber gaze fixed on the mound. Presently, with no word, he moved on; on past the blank-faced house, on down the winding track, on to the waiting boat. Into the bow he put his burden, and on it he sat. Louis shoved out. The boat bobbed over the waves to the sloop.

The box rose. The boat rose. The anchor rose. The mainsail squeaked aloft. Helm hard down, the craft of deliverance leaned and slid across the pulsing waters, heading out around the eastern point beyond which lay the headland and the beach of Saline. The sea widened, the sand shrank, the stony valley narrowed and receded, its harsh details blurring into a mass of blended moonlight and shadow. Then the eastern promontory crawled out toward the curving wake and shouldered itself across the vision of the watcher.

The Boîte du Mort, holding its dead but looted of the gold it had so long gripped in avaricious clutch, folded up and was nothing.

CHAPTER XXVIII

WEST

Hard, harsh, hostile, the dwarfed mountains dividing the bays of Gouverneur and Saline scowled down with savage satisfaction on land and sea whence all human life had fled.

The little houses of the Boîte du Mort, the solitary cottage on the eastern headland, all were closed and forsaken. The gleaming scythes of sand were blank. The ever-undulating waters bore on their breasts only evanescent glimmers of moonlight. No ship lay at the shore, no wake lay athwart the long rollers to betoken the passage of a cleaving keel. A while ago a small vessel had bobbed at anchor within each of the bays in turn, then, in the arms of the robust trade, danced away into the open ocean; but the waves long since had erased the narrow track left behind. Now the only proofs of the recent presence of man—and woman—were footprints on the strand, newly turned earth between two boulders on the headland, and an open-gated pen wherein still slept abandoned goats, which were soon to find new quarters and companions in the valley of the salt pond.

Away at the west, lost in the tenuous night haze to all view of shore dwellers, a sloop drove steadily into the obscure distance where sea and sky were one. A drab, weatherworn craft she was, with dingy patched sail bellying from warped mast and rough-hewn sprit; a battered gypsy, poor as her owner, yet as sturdily strong. Heeled to port, with every rag of canvas set, she footed her way through the night, surging dauntlessly over the landless deeps, holding a true course for the invisible American Virgins two-score leagues below the dim horizon. Humble she might be, but she was faithful; and, for all her shabbiness, an argosy freighted with treasure, before which many a haughtier sea mistress might well bow down. Within her jumbled hold traveled golden mintage of Spain and ingots of Incaland; upon her sloping deck a wealth of love—the love of man and woman, and the love of man and man.

Of the five who journeyed in her care, one slept and four dreamed. Curled at the foot of the mast, Louis slumbered peacefully, awaiting his turn to take charge of the ship. Lounging with familiar ease on the wheel, Gaspard looked now and again alow and aloft, visioning the new dress of paint and canvas—yes, perhaps even a proud straight stick—with which he could rejuvenate his faded old servant when the Americans rewarded him at Saint Thomas. Of those two Americans, one, with eyes on the stars and arm about a fair-haired girl, sent his thoughts winging far across the surges to shape the things that were to be. The other, though facing forward, lived in retrospect, occasionally turning his head to look behind.

Céleste, too, had looked back for a time; looked back soberly, with a hint of tears, at the receding isle where life was so stern, yet where lay the only life she had ever known and the loved ones who had lived it with her. But now the brief pang was over and forgotten; the old existence was dead, the new slowly unfolding, as yet unseen, only half guessed, but filled with shining visions. If at times a momentary misgiving assailed her, it was only an awe of the great, wonderful world of which she knew so little. With Lawrence to go at her side, she had no fear of it, nor of anything it might hold.

They were lying forward, these two, on the only couches possible to this diminutive cruiser: light blankets, padded with spare clothing to ease the hardness of the planks. The steady heave and roll, the ceaseless swash of the seas, the serene watch of moon and stars gradually weighted their lids with somnolence. At length, in a sleepy little voice, she said:

"Good night, Laurent."

"This is the way to say good night," he smiled, drawing her closer.

She lifted her lips to his, then, with a happy laugh, pillowed her head on his shoulder and closed her eyes. He lay awhile gazing down at her sweetly trustful face, drew a long sigh of content, and drifted away into slumber.

Aft, MacLeod lay as before he had sighted this craft from the lonely beach: prone, with chin on arms and gaze ranging along the deck and out into the emptiness beyond, vague and formless as his own future. As Céleste moved, his eyes centered on her. He saw the caress, heard the murmur of voices, watched her snuggle down to rest in the guarding embrace of her man;

contemplated the pair lying quiet, wrapped in untroubled sleep. At length his gaze lifted, to dwell again on the pathless vacancy. Low toned, so low that none heard, he droned:

"I've taken my fun where I've found it,
An' now I must pay for my fun,
For the more you 'ave known o' the others
The less will you settle to one;
An' the end of it's sittin' an' thinkin'
An' dreamin' hell-fires to see——"

There his voice died. For some time he peered far into the mysterious night, as if seeking there something never yet found, something typified by the dreaming couple beyond him. Then he shrugged, laid his head down on one arm, closed his eyes, and was still.

The moon sailed on—west. The sloop sailed on—west. Little by little the sea mist drew its blue-gray veil across the diminishing black bump of Barths, now far behind. Slowly a fleecy cloud drifted along the high blue, presently to enfold the bright-faced lady of the night in lingering embrace. And then there was nothing but a little dream ship on a starlit ocean, bearing dreaming hearts onward, ever onward—west.

THE END

www.ingramcontent.com/pod-product-compliance
Lightning Source LLC
Chambersburg PA
CBHW021949010726
47494CB00003B/663